Mack Bolan swung his sights along the hillside and froze

In the middle of his cross hairs it looked as if the muzzle of a small cannon was pointed directly at him. The Executioner squeezed the Dragunov's trigger, then rolled abruptly to the left. The lip of the trench fountained up a spray of dirt as the .50-caliber bullet struck his former position.

Bolan brought the scope to his eye and fired off a quick round. Dust flew up in front of his target and spoiled the sniper's next shot. The soldier heard the supersonic crack of the heavy bullet as it flew overhead, and he steadied his sights on his enemy.

Every muscle in the Executioner's body tensed as he looked into the face of his opponent, and he knew with absolute certainty that the talk in Sarajevo of a giant killer was true. Bolan had seen the butcher before, in the Sonoran desert of Arizona. His name was Captain Igor Baibakov and he was utterly insane.

MACK BOLAN ®

The Executioner

DON PENDLETON'S
THE EXECUTIONER®
BLOOD CIRCLE

A GOLD EAGLE BOOK FROM
WORLDWIDE®

TORONTO • NEW YORK • LONDON
AMSTERDAM • PARIS • SYDNEY • HAMBURG
STOCKHOLM • ATHENS • TOKYO • MILAN
MADRID • WARSAW • BUDAPEST • AUCKLAND

First edition November 1997
ISBN 0-373-64227-X

Special thanks and acknowledgment to
Chuck Rogers for his contribution to this work.

BLOOD CIRCLE

Printed in U.S.A.

Revenge proves its own executioner.

—John Ford
1586-1639

…revenge is always the delight of a mean spirit, of a weak and petty mind.

—Juvenal
c.50-c.130

A man bent on revenge is ruled by his emotions. If he comes at me without a clear head, I'll take him down. Count on it.

—Mack Bolan

THE
MACK BOLAN®
LEGEND

Nothing less than a war could have fashioned the destiny of the man called Mack Bolan. Bolan earned the Executioner title in the jungle hell of Vietnam.

But this soldier also wore another name—Sergeant Mercy. He was so tagged because of the compassion he showed to wounded comrades-in-arms and Vietnamese civilians.

Mack Bolan's second tour of duty ended prematurely when he was given emergency leave to return home and bury his family, victims of the Mob. Then he declared a one-man war against the Mafia.

He confronted the Families head-on from coast to coast, and soon a hope of victory began to appear. But Bolan had broken society's every rule. That same society started gunning for this elusive warrior—to no avail.

So Bolan was offered amnesty to work within the system against terrorism. This time, as an employee of Uncle Sam, Bolan became Colonel John Phoenix. With a command center at Stony Man Farm in Virginia, he and his new allies—Able Team and Phoenix Force—waged relentless war on a new adversary: the KGB.

But when his one true love, April Rose, died at the hands of the Soviet terror machine, Bolan severed all ties with Establishment authority.

Now, after a lengthy lone-wolf struggle and much soul-searching, the Executioner has agreed to enter an "arm's-length" alliance with his government once more, reserving the right to pursue personal missions in his Everlasting War.

PROLOGUE

Bosnia

The killer watched the Lincoln Continental wind through the streets of Sarajevo. Through the ten-power magnification of his weapon's optical sight, he could see the shadows of his targets through the car's tinted windows. He waited patiently, as the car was well within range. He had no doubt he could hit the vehicle at 1,800 meters if it was required. However, he would wait until the vehicle was well within the jaws of the trap. The Lincoln was in a convoy with two other vehicles. A four-wheel-drive Ford Explorer led the way, and another just like it followed behind as a rear guard. Each of the escort vehicles carried four armed Marine Corps embassy guards. The Lincoln carried the target, the Marine commander and three more armed Marines, as well.

The assassin watched the convoy approach—three vehicles, with a full squad of United States Marines. It was an intriguing target. He had heard much in his career about United States Marines, but he had never had the opportunity to actually engage them in combat. He was well pleased with the opportunity. It would also give him a chance to test his confederates' mettle against something more substantial than unarmed men and unsuspecting women and children.

The killer spoke softly into his headset. "Do you have the targets in sight?"

His two flanking teams reported back. "Confirmed, target in sight."

The assassin nodded to himself as he watched the convoy approach down the street. From his fourth-floor vantage his targets wouldn't see him, even after he struck, and by then they would be too busy with the flanking teams. He smiled unpleasantly and spoke into the microphone again. "Wait for my signal."

"Confirmed."

The Lincoln Continental was the main target. Once it stopped, so would its escorts. The Lincoln's tires were self-sealing and bullet resistant. Its windows and body were guaranteed by the manufacturer to stop shell fragments and full-metal-jacket rifle bullets of up to NATO .308 caliber at point-blank range. The killer flicked off his weapon's safety lever with his thumb.

Unfortunately the car's designer had never envisioned the vehicle facing an opponent armed with a precision .50-caliber rifle.

The killer focused the cross hairs of his scope on the center of the Lincoln's hood and fired.

The Barrett .50-caliber semiautomatic rifle recoiled brutally against the man's shoulder. The 750-grain full-metal-jacket projectile tore through the Lincoln's hood and into its engine at over 2,900 feet per second. The engine screamed and came apart as it absorbed more than ten thousand foot-pounds of energy. The armored car fishtailed as the driver tried to retain control and take evasive action, but the engine was already dying as the second bullet hit it.

The assassin raised his sights to the tinted windshield as the car halted. His cross hairs focused on a spot half a foot above the left windshield wiper. He squeezed the trigger, and the windshield shattered under the blow. The driver slumped forward over the wheel as the immense bullet went through him and tore through the floorboards behind his seat.

The two other Marine vehicles screeched to a halt, and soldiers armed with M-16 rifles deployed rapidly. The killer chose one and smashed him to the ground with a .50-caliber bullet through the chest. He spoke calmly into his headset.

"Now."

Automatic rifles opened up from windows facing both sides of the street. The killer smiled again. The Marines were living up to their reputations. They had swerved their cars diagonally and were using the car doors for cover as they covered a pair of their comrades who raced fearlessly for the Lincoln. The flanking teams poured fire into the escort vehicles, with more intent to disable them than to kill their crews. Still, four of the Marines were down already.

The doors of the Lincoln burst open, and Marines poured out. They linked up with the others and surrounded a tall man in an expensively tailored gray suit. The killer's eyes flared slightly as he examined the primary target. He could shoot him now, but that wasn't the plan. First they had to divest him of his Marine escort, and if he shot again he would betray his position.

The assassin nodded his approval as the Marines raced toward the shot-out building. The building's main doors had been shattered off their hinges and offered the security of darkness and solid cover. The plan was going perfectly.

They were racing straight toward him.

More of the Marines fell to the withering automatic fire of the flanking teams. The Marine commander, three of his men and the target reached the shelter of the building, then they were out of the killer's sight.

They were directly beneath him.

The killer rose from his firing position and folded his weapon's bipod. The Barrett .50-caliber rifle was more than five feet long and weighed nearly thirty pounds loaded, but he handled it with the ease of a man carrying an infantry rifle. He pressed in a fresh 10-round magazine and moved to the stairs.

Below him he could hear the Marines returning fire out of the first-floor windows and one of them yelling desperately into a radio in English. The killer rounded the bottom of the stairwell and paused for a moment as he examined the scene. The three Marines had set themselves in a three-point triangle in the main lobby to give themselves interlocking lanes of fire across the entire front of the building and the street beyond. Their commander was back near the stairwell by the reception desk. He held a map in his hand and was busily giving co-ordinates over his radio. The target stood beside him.

The assassin brought the heavy rifle to his shoulder and came out of the stairwell firing.

The thundering report of the .50-caliber weapon in the enclosed lobby was deafening. The first two Marines died before they knew what hit them as the immense projectiles tore them apart like rag dolls. The third Marine whirled to return fire, and the killer smashed him to the ground with a round through the chest. The Marines' armored vests were ineffective against the brutal power of the gigantic Barrett rifle.

The commander had dropped his map and radio. His rifle was propped by his knee against the reception desk, but he didn't bother to try to bring it to bear. He instinctively slapped leather for the .45 Colt automatic on his belt.

The killer's eyes flared as the .45 pistol barked at him, and he felt a punch against his armored vest. The massive .50-caliber rifle roared in return. The Marine commander hurtled back against the desk, then fell forward to the floor in a shattered heap.

The target's hand darted toward the Marine commander's rifle, then froze. His eyes nearly bugged out of his head as he took in his assassin. The target was a tall man, at least six foot one or two, but his head tilted back as he stared up in horror at his adversary's face.

The killer unslung the Barrett and moved toward his quarry, who suddenly broke for the door. The assassin reached behind his back to a wooden handle that protruded from behind his immense right shoulder. An entrenching tool came out of its nylon sheath with a rasp. The tool's short blackened shovel blade glinted in the gloom from where its edges had been honed to razor sharpness.

The entrenching tool was slightly over twenty inches long, and its blade formed a shallow wedge point. Its edges had been sharpened all around its circumference. The tool was extremely versatile and had proved itself in combat on several continents. Blows with the flat of the blade were paralyzing in riot situations. In close battle it was used as a deadly battle-ax capable of severing limbs. It was balanced for throwing, and a well-trained man could sink the blade into a car door up to twenty feet away. It was a standard joke that in an emergency the tool could even be used to dig a hole.

As the target scrambled for the door, the killer squinted one eye as he aimed and let the shovel fly in an overhand throw. It whistled through the air end over end and buried itself in the middle of the target's back. The target screamed and fell to the floor a few feet short of the door.

The assassin strode forward and yanked the weapon out of the target's back and rolled him over with the toe of his boot. The man looked up at him in agony. The members of the flanking teams began to enter the building and nodded appreciatively at what they saw. The killer wiped the shovel blade and replaced it in its sheath and surveyed the battle ground. The Marines were all dead. They had fought well, but they had never really stood a chance. He glanced down at the target.

This man was a different matter. He was still alive, and he was to be made an example of. Two members of the flanking teams strode forward in camouflage and olive drab ski masks. They drew their knives, and the target moaned in terror. The killer grimaced. The Marine commander had gotten on the radio, and United Nations peacekeeping forces would be arriving quickly. There would be little time to enjoy the work or make the target suffer, but they would certainly leave something interesting for the would-be rescuers to find.

The killer drew his combat knife and bent to his grisly task.

1

Washington, D.C.

Hal Brognola's face tightened as he looked at the photograph on the table before him. He steeled himself as he picked it up and examined it more closely. He had been with the Stony Man team for a long time and had worked for the organized-crime unit of the Justice Department for even longer. In the course of his long career, Brognola had seen human depredation in its worst forms.

The state of the human body in the photograph chilled him to the bone.

The President of the United States regarded Hal Brognola from across his desk. The big Fed had never seen the Man like this. His face was locked in a glare of stone-cold rage. Brognola swallowed and put the photograph back on the desk. "Who is it?"

The assistant secretary of state spoke icily from the chair at Brognola's left. The man was a study in controlled anger. "Those are the remains of Special Envoy Kyle Albrecht."

Brognola blinked. Albrecht had been a key negotiator for the State Department in the crisis in Bosnia and an integral part of the administration's peace plan. The remains in the photo rivaled anything the big Fed had seen done to informants by the Mafia or the Colombian drug cartels. Albrecht had been butchered alive.

"Has anyone claimed responsibility?"

The director of Central Intelligence shook his head slowly. "No."

"Do we have any theories?"

The CIA director grimaced. "As I am sure you are aware, Mr. Brognola, no faction in the crisis in former Yugoslavia has a patent on terrorism or war crimes. Europe hasn't seen these kind of wholesale atrocities since the Nazis, and all sides have participated. Take your pick—Serbs, Muslims, Croats, the streets are running red whichever way you look."

Brognola nodded. War was an ugly thing, and civil war uglier still. Civil war based on religion and ethnic hatred was as ugly as it came. "Yes, but as far as I'm aware, this is the first deliberate—" Brognola searched for a word as he took in the photograph again "—assassination of an American diplomat in Bosnia."

The President's voice was as cold as the grave. "It's going to be the last."

The State Department man cleared his throat. "The President has suggested sending in Delta Force. I prevailed upon him to wait until you could be summoned."

Brognola raised a curious eyebrow. The State Department had little knowledge of his actual function, and what they suspected they highly disliked. For them to suggest his involvement to the President spoke to the gravity of the situation. "What happened?"

"Mr. Albrecht was being transported to a meeting. He had a full squad of Marines from the reinforced embassy guard as an escort. All three of the vehicles in the convoy were disabled. All twelve of the Marines were killed, including the commander. Apparently survivors of the initial attack made it to a shot-up building. It seems they were flanked, and the rest of the Marines were killed. Then what you saw was done to Mr. Albrecht. The Marines managed to get out a distress call on radio and reported their position in the building. French troops were scrambled and arrived on the scene within fifteen minutes. They found the convoy wiped out. Their attackers had disappeared."

Brognola frowned. "I gather the radio message never described the attackers."

The CIA man shook his head. "No. Just that they were under heavy attack. The French found some evidence, but not much. There were lots of shell casings lying around. A lot of them were from U.S.-issue M-16s, as you would expect. The attack came from both sides of the convoy, and lots of shell casings from AK-47 rifles were found on both flanks. That doesn't tell us much, either. Everyone in the conflict over there is using loads of ex–Communist bloc weapons. What is interesting is that five of the Marines were shot with a weapon firing .50-caliber heavy machine gun bullets. The armored limousine was disabled with .50-caliber bullets, as well."

Brognola shrugged. "So they had a Browning heavy machine gun. They're used all over the world."

The CIA man shook his head again. "No. Each Marine took one hit in the chest. The limousine took three, two in the engine block and one through the windshield to kill the driver. It was precision shooting on the street. Ballistics indicate the same weapon was used to kill the Marines in the lobby. A Browning .50-caliber heavy machine gun is a crew-served weapon. Whoever did the killing in the lobby was using the weapon like a semiautomatic assault rifle."

The big Fed blinked. "A Barrett .50."

The CIA director nodded coolly. "Indeed."

Brognola mulled that over. The Stony Man teams had used the Barrett .50 in a number of actions. But it was a thirty-pound sniping rifle. Using one to clear a room in close-quarters battle was insane. But apparently the user had taken out four armed Marines in just such a fashion. "It would take one hell of a large individual to do something like that."

"Yes, it would." The CIA man grimaced. "You can't really tell it through all the rest of the trauma, but according to the autopsy, Mr. Albrecht's cause of death was a broken neck. The vertebrae and the spinal column were severed. Bruising patterns of the throat indicate it was done by hand. A pair of very large hands. Mr. Albrecht's assailants butchered him with knives while he was still alive, then snapped his neck to finish it quickly and evacuate. Probably when they heard the French armored vehicles approaching. That's our best guess.''

The man sighed and turned to the President. "Sir?"

The chief executive steepled his hands on the desktop.

"Gentlemen, I would like a moment alone with Mr. Brognola if you please."

The men filed out of the room. As the door closed, the President almost seemed to be looking through Brognola without seeing him. He spoke almost as if he were talking to himself. "Kyle Albrecht was a good friend of mine. I'm the one who appointed him as a special envoy and sent him to his death. It has been repeatedly pointed out to me today that I can't allow my personal feelings to color my judgment in this matter." The President locked eyes with Brognola. "I realize I can't just send in Delta Force and kill everything that moves. The United Nations would have a fit, and many of our allies wouldn't stand for it. For that matter we can't be sure yet who did it. But even if my personal feelings were not involved, an American peace envoy has been brutally assassinated. He was used as a sadistic example. For what, we aren't sure yet, but I'm sure it has to do with United States policy in the region. I want those responsible found, and I want them terminated. Quickly, and with extreme prejudice."

Brognola met the President's stare. "You want to send in Striker."

The President nodded slowly. "I want Mack Bolan in Sarajevo within the next forty-eight hours."

2

Mack Bolan stood in the misting rain in Sarajevo. The streets were dirty and gray, and broken glass crunched under his boots. Somewhere off in the distance he heard the crack of a rifle shot. His "guide" stood before him. The Bosnian was a short wiry man with a Chinese-manufactured AKM assault rifle crooked in his arms, and an Egyptian Tokarev automatic clone was holstered at his hip. Bolan smothered his irony. The United Nations arms embargo didn't seem to be having much of an effect. On his belt the man also carried a pair of Russian-made offensive hand grenades and a horn-handled hunting knife that appeared to be locally made.

The man was obviously a veteran. His short black hair was peppered with gray in a military crew cut that had started to grow out. His face was heavily lined, and his gray eyes glared out of a sunken, and seemingly permanent, piercing squint. He had the look of a man who had been in-country for a very long time. Bolan had seen the look many times before. In the United States military it was called the thousand-yard stare. There were no short-timers in a civil war. For this man, in-country was his backyard.

Bolan would have preferred to have been better armed himself, but the cover of free-lance war correspondent limited his armament options. Beneath his quilted black leather jacket he carried a snub-nosed 9 mm Smith & Wesson Centennial revolver, and a skeleton-handled stiletto rode on his ankle under his khaki pants. In his camera bag he carried a Canon F-1 35 mm camera and his Leica laser range-finding binoculars, and beneath the false bottom of the bag rested his .44 Magnum Desert Eagle pistol and five spare magazines.

The soldier smiled in a friendly fashion, and the little man peered up at him narrowly. He scrutinized Bolan's photo-ID press card again and spoke in heavily accented English.

"Canadian, huh?"

Bolan nodded.

The man's face brightened slightly. "Canada, good skiing, huh?"

Bolan grinned. "The best." He jerked his thumb toward the snowcapped peaks just south of Sarajevo. The Jahorina Mountains had been the site of the 1984 Olympic Winter Games. "Though I haven't skied Jahorina yet. I hear it's some of the best in Europe."

The man grinned up at Bolan crookedly. "Yes, Jahorina is very good skiing." He sighed heavily. "I have not skied in a very long time." He dismissed the subject with a shrug. "You work for CNN?"

"If I can give them a story they want, they'll pay me." Bolan shrugged in return. "If not, then maybe I'll work for Reuters."

The man grunted. "Very well. My name is Vlado Sarcev, lieutenant, Muslim Militia of Sarajevo. You wish to accompany me and my men on a patrol. I will allow this, but you must follow orders at all times. I warn you now I will accept no responsibility for your being wounded or killed."

Bolan nodded. It was fair enough. "I understand."

"Good. Let us go." He jerked his head at the other thirteen men in combat fatigues who were lounging around smoking cigarettes under an awning. Sarcev's oversize squad was heavily reinforced with special weapons. The largest man in the group was leaning on an RPK light machine gun, with belts of ammunition slung all around his body. The man next to him carried an RPG-7 rocket-propelled grenade launcher over his shoulder, and an Uzi submachine gun was slung across his chest. One man who appeared to be sleeping crouched on his heels cradling a Russian Dragunov semiautomatic sniper rifle. Nearly every man in the squad carried a personal hodgepodge of handguns, knives and grenades, as well as his rifle. Bolan smiled slightly. Despite the supposed cease-fire of the week, things were still deadly serious in Sarajevo.

The driver gunned the engine of the olive drab Mercedes utility truck, and Bolan climbed into the back behind Sarcev as the rest of the men clambered in. The vehicle ground into gear and with a lurch pulled out into the street. The Executioner scanned the shelled high rises as they drove along and turned to his companion as they headed out into the suburbs. "What's our objective?"

Sarcev grimaced and shook his head unhappily. "We lost contact with one of our observation posts in the foothills during the night. We are to investigate this."

Bolan raised an eyebrow. "You seem to know what you're going to find already."

"It is not the first time we have lost a listening post recently. Yes, I believe I know what we will find." He looked hard at Bolan. "I suspect you will get some very interesting pictures. CNN will probably pay you well."

"Atrocities?"

"Yes. Atrocities. Killing your enemy in battle, it is ugly, but it is war." The Bosnian spit on the floorboards of the truck. "What he does…"

"Who is 'he'?"

Sarcev's eyes went cold. "The Giant."

Bolan's eyes narrowed to slits. "A giant?"

"Yes. The Giant. No one knows who he is, but he kills for the Chetniks, the Serbs. He comes into Sarajevo and kills with impunity—men, women, children. And how he kills them, with his knife, with his hands, these things would give even the strongest man nightmares."

Sarcev locked gazes with Bolan. "I will tell you something. I have been in this war for four years now, and I have seen many things in that time. When I come upon something the Giant has done, my blood boils, and I pray to God that I may find him." He gestured outside to the gray and misting rain. "But in the cold of morning, going into the hills, sometimes in my heart I almost hope that I do not find him."

Bolan nodded. He knew the feeling all too well. "You have no idea who this giant is?"

Sarcev shrugged. "Few who have seen him have lived. He is special forces, of that I am sure. He is too good to be a simple militiaman or a Serbian soldier. Perhaps he was part of the old Thirty-sixth Parachute Brigade from before the partition of the country, or perhaps he was part of the Mountain Brigade. They specialized in guerrilla warfare, and Serbs always filled most of their ranks." Vlado spit again. "Chetniks."

Bolan knew the word. The Chetniks had been the Serb resistance fighters who had fought the Nazi occupation forces. Now the term was slang for Bosnian Serb militiamen and the Nazilike tactics they were accused of using in the current war.

The truck ground to a halt in the foothills. Sarajevo lay behind them, and the mountains loomed ahead. Sarcev unslung his rifle. "From here we go on foot. The truck would attract snipers and mortar fire on the road."

The militiamen hopped out of the truck and unslung their weapons as they formed into a loose, diamond-shaped combat patrol and moved into the trees. Sarcev whispered over his shoulder at Bolan. "Stay close to me. Make no sound. Our objective is two thousand meters southeast. I do not expect resistance, but snipers are everywhere."

Bolan followed behind Sarcev and scanned through the trees. He was impressed with how quietly the squad moved. Experience was an excellent teacher. They were moving slowly and steadily uphill, and the forest was getting denser. At about one thousand meters from the truck the squad leader raised his fist, and the squad halted. He beckoned his sniper forward with a jerk of his head. Sarcev pulled out a pair of Russian field glasses, and the sniper peered through the telescopic sight of his rifle.

The Executioner pulled out his laser range-finding binoculars and took a look at the objective for himself. Through the trees he could see a semiconcealed listening post. A covered trench had been dug among a jumble of boulders, and several hardened foxholes were spaced at intervals from the main bunker.

No one was visible, and nothing appeared to move. The forest was very quiet.

Sarcev grunted and lowered his field glasses. Bolan held out his own binoculars. "Try these."

The militiaman took them and peered forward. A small smile split his face. "Ah!" His own binoculars were standard Russian six-power infantry glasses. The Leica was eight power, and its optics were nothing short of magnificent. With the press of a button the built-in laser range finder bounced a beam invisible to the human eye off of the object, and then gave the precise range in meters on a readout in the bottom of the reticle's view. He nodded grudgingly as he examined the objective. "You have very excellent glasses."

Bolan waved his hand away as Sarcev handed them back. "You didn't have to bring me along today. Why don't you keep them?"

The lieutenant's head jerked up, and he regarded Bolan shrewdly. Both men realized the gift was a blatant bribe, but for a man fighting a sniper war in the streets and a guerrilla war in the hills, such a piece of high-power optics was simply far too good to pass up. Bolan doubted the man would give up any state secrets over a pair of binoculars, but he would take brownie points with the locals wherever he could earn them. He smiled at Sarcev guilelessly. The Bosnian sighed as if he were compromising his principles but slung the binoculars around his neck and nodded at Bolan.

"Thank you. You are very generous."

Bolan shrugged. "Think nothing of it."

Sarcev waved his men forward, and they slowly crept toward the listening post in a wide skirmish line. They reached the first foxhole, and one of the men shook his head and shrugged as he peered into it. Across the skirmish line another man peered into the opposite hole and made the same gesture. The militia leader frowned and moved to the covered trench.

The trench was reinforced with sandbags and carefully covered with turf. From the front it would appear to be little more than a rise in the ground with some bushes in front of it. The bushes skillfully covered the firing-observation ports. From the rear it was more recognizable as a field fortification.

Sarcev slung his rifle and took a small flashlight from his belt. He drew his Tokarev automatic and knelt by the narrow entrance to the covered trench. He cocked the pistol and played the flashlight into the dim interior. Then he froze, his face draining of color.

Bolan stepped forward and crouched beside him, knowing what he would see. He had seen the photographs at Stony Man Farm before he left, but they didn't prepare him for the carnage inside the trench. The Executioner's blood went cold. He had seen more violence than most living men. Grenades, high explosives and bullets did terrible things to human bodies. He had also seen the results of specific acts of mutilation and torture more times than he cared to think about.

The carnage in the trench was beyond anything he had ever encountered. It was butchery for the sheer love of it. Before the job was finished, whoever had done it would have been hip deep in human gore.

Bolan swallowed hard as he was forced to count severed heads to make a body count. "There were four?"

Sarcev stared ahead woodenly, and his voice was faraway when he finally spoke. "Yes. There were four."

The Executioner grimaced as he examined the scene a second time. The men's weapons were gone. The post had been stripped of communications and optical equipment, as well as maps and personal effects. The trench was a grave. Bolan ran a critical eye at the blood-mired floor of the trench, then around the immediate area.

There were no spent shell casings littering the ground, and no lingering smell of burned gun powder or high explosive. There were no torn divots from bullet strikes to the ground, and no shrapnel scarring in the bark of the nearby trees. It was as if someone had just walked in and slaughtered the Bosnian observation team with utter ferocity and total impunity.

Bolan gestured into the trench. "You said you've lost other observation posts recently. Were they like this?"

"Yes. Not as bad as this, but the same." He turned to his radioman. "Serge, inform headquarters that—"

Serge flew backward as if he had been swatted by a giant invisible hand. A split second later an immense cracking noise boomed through the trees. Bolan shoved Sarcev into the trench opening and dived down behind him. He recognized the weapon's thundering report. It was the sound of a rifle chambered for .50-caliber machine-gun ammunition.

The militia team hurled itself behind cover. The team sniper crouched behind a tree and shouldered his rifle. Up on the hillside the massive .50-caliber rifle roared like a thunderbolt. Even a large tree was no cover from the 700-grain steel-jacketed bullet. The tree shuddered as the huge bullet tore through its trunk and smashed the man behind it into a red ruin. Automatic weapons began to open up from the hillside and rain down on the besieged militia team. One of Sarcev's riflemen crouched behind a fallen log as small-arms fire tore into it.

The .50-caliber rifle roared from on high, and the log exploded into splinters. The militiaman jerked as if he had been stepped on by a massive boot and lay still. Bolan grimaced. Only solid stone or three feet of dirt or packed sand would smother the .50-caliber rifle's massive energy. More small-arms fire struck the trench, and the massive sniper weapon killed the loader of the RPG-7 team as he crawled for heavier cover.

Bolan smiled coldly. The problem with the Barrett was that it was a rifle firing a heavy machine-gun bullet. Its muzzle-flash was immense. Every time you fired, you announced your location to the world at large. As the RPG loader went down, the soldier saw the yellow flame and the dust thrown up by the big .50's muzzle brake through the trees approximately 350 yards up the hill.

The Executioner yanked open the false bottom of his camera bag. Sarcev had risen angrily from the bloody floor of the trench, and he glared at Bolan. "Forget pictures now! We are…" His voice trailed off as he looked at the massive Desert Eagle pistol that suddenly filled Bolan's hand.

The Executioner crouched at the opening of the trench.

"When I start shooting, get the sniper rifle."

Sarcev glanced backward at his fallen man's Dragunov rifle. He nodded. "Yes."

Bolan rose over the lip of the trench. The .50-caliber roared from above. The sniper had moved his firing position fifteen yards to the right. The yellow flame lit the trees up on the hillside, and dust plumed up out of the foliage.

The .44 Magnum Desert Eagle pistol boomed in Bolan's hands.

Three hundred and fifty yards was at the extreme range of the massive handgun, but .44 Magnums were flat shooters to begin with. Bolan's pistol had been custom tuned to his specifications at Stony Man Farm, and he had put so many thousands of rounds through it in practice and in battle that the weapon was an extension of his will.

Bolan methodically fired round after round into the rifleman's position. Behind him he heard Sarcev's boots on the soft turf as the Desert Eagle clacked open on an empty chamber. Both men dived into the trench. The Executioner dropped behind cover and slipped a fresh magazine into the big pistol. Sarcev panted and handed him the 7.62 mm Dragunov sniper rifle. "You are familiar with this weapon."

"A little," he replied, retrieving a holster from the bag and leathering the .44.

Sarcev grunted. "I suspected so."

The big .50 boomed again, and sand erupted out of one of the burst bags above their heads. Bolan had driven the sniper under cover, but he hadn't killed him. He chambered a round in the Dragunov. "Is your RPG man still alive?"

Sarcev peered backward. The loader was lying dead in the open with his spare rockets. The RPG gunner was crouched behind a boulder barely large enough to cover his huddled frame. He nodded. "Jup lives, but he is pinned down."

Bolan jerked his head up toward the hillside. "I need Jup to put a rocket into the sniper's position."

"I need the radio. We have a platoon that followed us ten minutes after we left for reinforcement. We must contact them and counterattack."

Bolan stared at Sarcev, and the little man shrugged. "I did not tell you the disposition of my troops because I did not know if you were who you claimed to be." He looked Bolan up and down and grinned ferociously. "I do not believe that you are."

The soldier shrugged in return. "Get to the radio. I'll try to attract our friend's fire. Have your man Jup ready to fire at his muzzle-flash."

The militia leader shouted toward his men. Jup nodded grimly from his tenuous position behind his rock as he clutched his rocket launcher. Sarcev turned to Bolan and took a deep breath. "I am ready."

Bolan snapped up over the lip of the trench. "Go!"

Sarcev burst from the trench at a dead run, and his men began to fire their rifles en masse to cover him. By Bolan's estimate, the next-best firing position for the sniper on the hill would be a clump of rocks ten yards down from his last shot. Bolan fired three quick rounds into the position from the Dragunov and jerked himself down. The air over the hillside split with the big .50's crack, and a sandbag exploded where Bolan's head had just been.

Jup stood and shouldered his RPG-7. He took a quick aim through the optical sight at the rocks and fired. The rocket-propelled grenade sizzled out of the launch tube and hissed up the hill. The five-pound warhead detonated in a ball of orange fire, and black smoke obscured the rocks. Bolan rose from the trench and put the Dragunov's cross hairs on the rocks and swept the smoke for movement.

Something flashed through his sight picture, a large shape moving fast. Bolan tracked it in his sights. It was a man, but something was wrong. At 350 yards the man wouldn't fill the entire scope. It was as if something were wrong with the perspective.

Bolan led the target and fired a round from the Dragunov. A split second later the figure suddenly dropped out of sight behind some low rocks as the Executioner fired a second shot. He wasn't sure of a hit. Small-arms fire chattered into the sandbags around him, and Bolan dropped behind cover. He moved into the gore-covered trench and peered out one of the firing slits. Orange fire strobed two hundred yards up on the hill. He sighted and found the head and shoulders of a man firing an AK-47 over a tree stump. The Executioner put his cross hairs on the man and fired.

The rifleman shuddered and slumped over the stump.

The right wall of the firing slit exploded in a burst of sand, and flying grit stung the Executioner's face. The big .50's report reverberated down the hill. The soldier grimaced; the sniper just wouldn't stay down.

Bolan froze at the sound of hollow thumping behind him, then a grim smile split his face. It was the sound of mortars— Russian-made 82 mm mortars, by the sound of them, and the sound was coming from downhill.

The Bosnian reinforcements were counterattacking. Bolan moved to the trench entrance and peered over the lip quickly. An orange blast of fire lit up the gray hillside, and another followed as the high-explosive mortar shells looped up into the enemy positions with startling accuracy.

Bolan suspected that Sarcev had reached the radio, and that the laser range-finding binoculars were already proving themselves useful.

The Executioner scanned with the Dragunov's scope. The Serbs were retreating; they had no desire to slug it out. They had left the wiped-out listening post as bait and hoped for a quick slaughter. Now that they were getting their noses bloodied, they were retreating back into the hills. Bolan swung his sights along the hillside and froze.

In the middle of his cross hairs it looked as if the muzzle of a small cannon was pointing directly at him. Bolan squeezed the Dragunov's trigger, then rolled abruptly to the left. The lip of the trench fountained up a spray of dirt as the huge .50-caliber bullet struck his former position. The Executioner brought his scope to his eye and fired off a quick shot. Dust flew up in front of his target and spoiled the sniper's shot. Bolan heard the supersonic crack of the heavy .50-caliber bullet as it flew overhead, and he steadied his sights on his target.

The figure in his scope rolled as Bolan squeezed off his shot, and dirt flew up again. The Executioner steadied his aim and fired his last round. Sparks flew in yellow streaks as his bullet slammed off the sniper's massive rifle. For a split second Bolan kept his scope on the target.

Every muscle in the Executioner's body tensed as he looked into the face of his opponent, and he knew with absolute certainty that the talk in Sarajevo of a giant killer was true. Bolan had seen this man before in the Sonoran Desert of Arizona, and his name was Igor Baibakov. He was formerly a captain in Spetsnaz, the Russian special-forces troops. In the brutal guerrilla war in Afghanistan he had built a reputation for savagery and ruthlessness unparalleled in modern Russian military history. He was nearly seven feet tall, and he was utterly insane.

Bolan dropped the spent Dragunov and pulled his Desert Eagle pistol. He took half a second to adjust for the range and began to fire the pistol as fast as it would cycle. He saw a glitter of light up on the hill as the morning sun hit the hillside. The Executioner knew the big Barrett's scope was pointed at him. He dropped behind cover as the .44 Magnum clacked open on an empty chamber. There was no bullet strike and no .50-caliber report. The big rifle had either been disabled, or he had hit his target.

Mortar rounds continued to fall, and well over a dozen automatic weapons had joined in firing with Sarcev's squad. To the left and right, men had jumped into the foxholes and were pouring fire up the hill as more men advanced.

Sarcev dropped into the trench beside Bolan and fired several rounds from his rifle up at the hillside as more mortar rounds descended. He turned and grinned at Bolan. "We have routed them!"

Bolan nodded grimly as he slid a fresh magazine into the Desert Eagle. "Yes, you have."

The militia leader stared at Bolan curiously. "You came here for something, but I do not see you taking pictures. Did you find it?"

Bolan reloaded and holstered the big .44 Magnum pistol. "It wasn't what I was expecting, but I did."

Sarcev frowned. "Is it permitted to ask what that is?"

Bolan shrugged. "Your giant."

"You saw him?"

"We traded shots."

"And so?"

The Executioner rose and watched the fresh militia platoon sweep up the hill after the fleeing Scrbs. "Your giant is an old acquaintance of mine."

3

Mack Bolan sat in his room at the Sarajevo Holiday Inn. It was the hotel most used by foreign journalists, and with good reason. It had been built in 1983 for the Winter Olympics, it was totally modern, its two restaurants, three bars and its modern plumbing all functioned and it had managed to remain relatively intact.

He sat on the queen-size bed and cleaned his Desert Eagle. The Beretta 93-R pistol lay on the bed next to him locked and loaded. He had swept the room for bugs and found nothing out of the ordinary. Bolan slid the Desert Eagle's slide into battery as Aaron Kurtzman spoke in his earpiece. The clarity of the satellite link was amazing. It had sounded as if the computer expert had strangled on his coffee, but he had swiftly regained his composure. His voice was incredulous.

"Igor Baibakov?"

Bolan pushed a loaded magazine into the big .44. "The same."

"I was under the impression that he was dead."

Bolan shrugged. "So was I."

The Executioner thought back to the Crucible operation. What had started out as an investigation into the death of one of Hal Brognola's friends had uncovered a conspiracy to dig underground smuggling corridors under the border between Mexico and Arizona, a conspiracy led by Russian sleepers in the government and strong-armed by ex-Spetsnaz soldiers. Jack Grimaldi had been the last man to see Igor Baibakov alive. The giant Russian had been standing on top of a disabled truck with a spent SAM-7 shoulder-fired missile. Grimaldi had been behind the controls of an AH-64 Apache gunship and had sent more than a dozen 2.75-inch Hydra rockets back at the Russian in response.

Baibakov had gone up in a ball of high-explosive fire. His body hadn't been found, but in the furious fighting of that battle there were more blown-up and dismembered bodies than Bolan liked to think about. Somehow, some way Baibakov was alive and leading terrorist operations out of the mountains surrounding Sarajevo.

Kurtzman spoke quietly, almost as if he were embarrassed by his question. "Mack, are you absolutely sure?"

Bolan thought about the question for a moment. It was incredible, but he didn't doubt his eyes, and the countenance of Igor Baibakov was something one was never likely to forget or mistake. "Bear, I'm positive."

"All right. Can you link him to the murders of Kyle Albrecht and the Marines?"

The soldier mentally reviewed the remains of the bodies at the listening posts and the ambush. "It's the exact same method of operation. A Barrett .50 rifle was used to initiate the ambush, and flanking fire by riflemen was used to pin down the squad while the .50 killed them behind their cover."

Bolan could hear Kurtzman's finger tapping on the desk. "That's a reasonable clue, but there could be more than one group in the Sarajevo area using the same tactics."

The Executioner's voice was as cold as the grave. "You saw the pictures of what was done to Albrecht."

"Yes, I did."

"What was done to the men at the listening post was worse. The same MO, but a lot worse. He had all night to do the job the way he wanted."

Kurtzman swallowed hard. "All right, assuming Baibakov survived and escaped into Mexico, it's not all that farfetched. All three sides in the conflict in former Yugoslavia are receiving aid and support from the outside. The Croatians are getting a lot of ex–East German matériel from Germany. A number of Muslim states are sending in small arms and volunteers to support the Bosnian Muslims, and it's no secret the Russians support the Bosnian Serbs and have been supplying them with arms and possibly advisers. It's also no secret that all three sides are employing mercenaries. I'm sure there are Bosnian Serb groups operating in the hills outside of Sarajevo that would just love to have an 'active adviser' like Baibakov to help them.'' Kurtzman paused. ''My main concern at the moment is for you. Do you think he saw you and recognized you?''

Bolan recalled the flash of light off the scope on the hill. He had been firing the Desert Eagle at Baibakov as fast as he could. The flash could have been from the man dropping to cover, or being hit. Or he could have taken a moment to examine his attacker if he was cool enough. The Executioner frowned. ''I can't be sure.''

''Well, if he did, do you think he'll come after you?''

Bolan let out a slow breath as he remembered the giant's relentless pursuit across the Sonoran Desert. ''I don't think anything on earth will stop him.'' Bolan smiled with grim irony. ''I think that's our one advantage in this situation. He'll come to me.''

''That has to be one hell of a cold advantage, Striker, knowing that freak of nature is coming for you.''

''I have one other one.''

''Oh?''

''He's a psychopath. When it comes to dealing with me, he probably won't act rationally.''

Kurtzman was silent for a moment. ''Oh, well, you're holding all the cards, then.''

Bolan grinned. ''I've got him right where I want him. But one thing is bothering me.''

''What's that?''

''Why kill Kyle Albrecht? It doesn't make a whole lot of sense to kill an American envoy. It's likely to get the United States riled with the Serbs, and the administration isn't fond of them to begin with.''

"Hmm. That's a good question. I'll have to give that one some thought."

"What other news have you got?"

"Not much. I'll contact military intelligence and have them dig up anything they can on our boy. I'll try the State Department, too. Maybe they can convince the Russians to give us something. I'll send what you've found through channels. I suspect the President will be happy. You dug up a hell of a lot for your first twenty-four hours in town."

"I'm faxing the pictures I took at the listening post to you through Hal at the Justice Department. I'm going to have a meeting in the bar with the leader of the militia platoon I went out with this morning in a few minutes. Maybe he can give me something to work with. Barring any startling developments, I'll contact you again same time tomorrow. Out."

Bolan replaced the earpiece in the satellite link's storage briefcase and snapped it shut. He tucked the Beretta 93-R into its shoulder holster and put three spare magazines into the holster slots under his other arm. He checked the loads in the snub-nosed 9 mm Centennial revolver and slid it snugly into his ankle holster. He tucked his stiletto into the back of his waistband and checked his watch. Sarcev ought to be in the bar by now.

The soldier locked the door behind him and walked toward the elevators. At the end of the hall an old woman in a kerchief pushed a cleaning cart. Loud music and laughter came from behind the door of one of the rooms on his left. Bolan pushed the Down button, and the elevator pinged almost immediately. The cleaning cart made a sudden rattle as it stopped. Bolan's combat senses flared. A woman had been cleaning the rooms when he had left in the morning to join the militia patrol, and the rooms wouldn't be cleaned twice in the same day.

The Executioner whirled as he ripped the Beretta from its holster. The woman dropped behind her cart as the elevator door opened and a voice like breaking granite boomed out of the elevator car.

"Die!"

As Bolan turned to face his attacker, a heavy black blade whipped down in a terrible arc, its razor-honed edge glittering. He yanked his blocking arm out of the way to keep it from being lopped off and took the blow in the chest. The entrenching tool sheered through the outer layers of the woven Kevlar of his armored vest and came to a violent stop on the ceramic trauma plate. Bolan felt the plate crack as the blow slammed him backward against the opposite wall.

The soldier saw stars as the back of his head bounced off the wall, but he raised the Beretta 93-R on instinct and fired a 3-round burst at the looming shape before him. The man attacked without pause, and Bolan's hand went numb with shock as the flat of the iron shovel blade swatted the pistol from his hand. The Executioner dropped on his haunches as the blade whipped around and whistled past his head. The blade sank into the wall, and he coiled his body to strike. As the giant yanked at his weapon, the Executioner planted his palm on the floor and kicked both feet upward between his attacker's massive legs.

The giant raised his knee to block the blow to his groin, and Bolan drove both boot heels into the upraised leg. For a second his adversary was standing on one leg, and the blow sent him tottering off balance into the elevator doorway. The soldier rolled backward on the floor and drew his right knee to his chest as his hand reached for his ankle holster.

The giant ducked around the steel frame of the elevator door as the 9 mm Centennial revolver bucked in Bolan's hands. Someone in a nearby room screamed at the sound of the gunshot. The elevator doors slid shut with a ping, and the lights on the wall showed the elevator car descending. There was no time to worry about the giant Russian.

The Executioner rolled prone and swept the muzzle of the revolver down the hallway.

The cleaning woman had risen from behind her cart. No longer bending over, she was nearly six feet tall. An AK-47 rifle with its stock folded had appeared in her hands.

Bolan put the front sight of the Centennial on her chest and fired.

The assassin staggered, and Bolan triggered a second round. The automatic rifle ripped into life and sent a long burst stitching high and wide into the wall over Bolan's head. The Executioner's third shot snapped the assassin's head back, and the AK-47 rifle fell from nerveless hands. The killer swayed, then fell to the floor in a motionless heap.

Bolan snapped around toward the elevator. The lights over the door indicated it had descended without stopping and had reached the lobby. He rose with a single round left in the revolver. He reholstered the little gun and scooped up the Beretta in his left hand. He grimaced as he flexed his right. Pain shot down his arm, and purple swelling was already thickening the fingers of his mashed hand. With an effort he made a fist and grunted to himself satisfactorily. It hurt like hell, but nothing appeared to be broken.

He approached the cleaning woman, who turned out to be a man. Bolan could hear whispering behind the doors, and somewhere a woman was crying. The Executioner decided he didn't want to stick around to explain any of this. He reached his room in ten long strides and slid his door open, shutting it behind him silently. Moments later he heard the pounding of feet and shouting in the hallway. Bolan stuck his throbbing hand in the complimentary bucket of ice by the minibar and waited. Two minutes later there was a quiet but insistent knock on his door. Bolan kept the 93-R at his side and slightly behind him as he spoke softly.

"Who is it?"

Bolan recognized the Bosnian militia leader's voice. "Praise to God, you are alive. It is me, Vlado."

The soldier flicked the Beretta's safety back on. "It's not locked."

The door opened slowly, and a moment later Sarcev cautiously stuck his head in. "You are all right?"

Bolan took his hand out of the ice bucket and shook off the water. "I'll live. Come in and close the door."

The little man entered. He had shaved and combed his hair, and wore a worn but presentable wool jacket and pants. He held his Tokarev pistol close to his leg, and he holstered the weapon as he came in. He looked at the Beretta thoughtfully as Bolan replaced the partially spent magazine. "You have many large and impressive guns."

The Executioner holstered the Beretta. "Thank you."

"You are welcome."

Bolan drew the Centennial and replaced the four spent rounds from a pocket in his camera bag. "You got here fast."

Sarcev nodded. "I heard there had been shooting on the fourth floor. You had told me your room number when you told me to meet you here. So I make a guess that perhaps you were involved. I came as fast as I could while avoiding security." He peered around at the room admiringly. "You have a nice room."

Bolan shrugged. "It's a Holiday Inn."

"Yes. Holiday Inn is nice. Very expensive for locals, but nice. Good restaurants. My children and I enjoy the pancake breakfast very much."

The soldier suppressed a smile. "Yes, it's very good."

Sarcev pointed at Bolan's purpling hand. "May I ask what happened?"

Bolan stripped off his shirt and examined the massive rent in his vest. "Our friend paid me a visit."

"The Giant?"

Bolan nodded as the cracked trauma plate flexed under his probing fingers. Sarcev shook his head wonderingly. "He would have had to circle back around my men's counterattack and have followed us down from the hills almost immediately."

The Executioner nodded thoughtfully. That was true. Despite the falling mortar shells and more than a platoon of Muslim militiamen sweeping the battlefield, Igor Baibakov had stuck to him and followed him to his hotel and set an ambush. Sarcev jerked his head toward the hall. "And the dead woman?"

Bolan grunted as he shrugged out of the ruined armor. "The dead woman was a man. He was Baibakov's lookout and backup in the ambush. I suspect he was a plant who was already in town."

The militia leader nodded. "Yes. That makes sense." He took a deep breath and looked Bolan in the eye. "My giant, and your giant—you call him Baibakov—they are the same, yes?"

Bolan grimaced. "We have a common problem."

The lieutenant's brow furrowed. "Baibakov. That is a Russian name."

The soldier put on a fresh undershirt and restrapped his shoulder rig to his frame. "It is. Igor Baibakov is former Russian special forces, Spetsnaz."

"I have heard of them. How do you know of this Baibakov?"

"That's classified," Bolan said with a smile.

"Ah." Seeing that nothing more was forthcoming, he changed the subject. "Now what shall you do?"

Bolan shrugged. "He knows I'm here. I can let him try again."

The little Bosnian snorted. "I would not recommend that."

"Neither would I." He turned to Sarcev and looked at him seriously. "I need your help. If I wished to contact Serbian irregulars, as a journalist, where would I go?"

"Sonia's."

Bolan raised a curious eyebrow.

Sarcev smiled and elaborated. "Sonia's Kon-Tiki Restaurant. It is approximately thirteen kilometers outside of Sarajevo to the northeast in Serbian territory. You would find Serbian militiamen and guerrilla fighters there. It is a popular meeting place with the Chetniks." Sarcev's face went hard. "There is much drinking, and there are many women. Many of them are Muslim girls kidnapped out of Sarajevo. Some are kidnapped Croatian women, or so I am told. I have never been there, of course, but you might find the information you seek in this place."

Bolan flexed his hand again and then stuck it back in the ice. He remembered hearing something about Sonia's on CNN. He might indeed find out something useful there, and it beat waiting for Baibakov's next move. His fourth-story window could be reached with a good rifle from the roof of a number of buildings, and Baibakov had a rifle that would kill an elephant at a thousand yards.

"I think I'll visit Sonia's tomorrow."

Sarcev frowned. "I understand, but I cannot go with you, or send any of my men to accompany you. It is over twelve kilometers behind the Chetnik lines and crawling with their soldiers."

"I know, but do you think you can get me to the outskirts of the city without being followed?"

"That I can do. It will be a pleasure."

The Executioner pulled his hand out of the ice and wiped it on a towel. He held the injured hand out to Vlado. The little man's face grew serious as they shook hands.

Bolan bowed his head slightly. "I'm in your debt."

Sarcev shook his head dismissingly and intoned an ancient credo. "The enemy of my enemy is my friend." He grinned suddenly. "Besides, I enjoy the field glasses you gave me very much. They are very excellent for directing mortar fire."

Bolan couldn't help grinning back. "Why don't we go downstairs and see if the kitchen can rustle up some late-night pancakes? I'm on an expense account."

The little man beamed. "Ah!"

4

"They deserve whatever happens to them!" The big man brought his fist down on the table, rattling the empty bottles of slivovitz. He leaned forward and exposed a missing front tooth through his scowl. His voice dropped. "They betrayed us."

Mack Bolan leaned forward with interest. "When?"

The man's scowl deepened, and he took another pull from the bottle Bolan had bought. "In 1459!"

The other men at the table nodded grimly and drank.

"Did you say 1459?"

The man wiped his mouth, his eyes blazing. "Yes! They betrayed us to the Ottoman Turks! You understand? They abandoned their God to become the lapdogs of the heathens!" The big man peered into the empty bottle and slammed it back down on the table. His eyes grew glassy as he repeated himself. "They deserve whatever happens to them. Goddamned Turks."

Bolan motioned the waitress for another bottle. People in the Balkans certainly knew how to hold on to their hatreds. In the 1400s the Ottoman Turks had invaded the Kingdom of Serbia and conquered the province of Bosnia-Herzegovina. The majority of the Serbs in the region had converted to Islam under their four-hundred-year rule. The rest of the Orthodox Christian Serbs had never forgiven them for it. The name "Turk" was a racial insult used to describe any Bosnian Muslim, man or woman.

The Executioner glanced around. Sonia's Kon-Tiki Restaurant was full of armed, hard-looking men. Most of them were Bosnian Serb militiamen or irregulars or volunteer soldiers from Greater Serbia. Most of them were drunk. He could hear snatches of a conversation two tables behind him, and he spoke enough Russian to know that at least one of the men was a Russian military adviser.

The big American decided to change the subject. He was surprised at how easy it had been to get into Sonia's and how easy it was to get the Serbs to talk. They were aware of the fact that in the West they were mostly vilified by the press, and they were eager to give their point of view to a journalist who listened sympathetically. Bolan leaned forward again. "I hear the Bosnian Muslims are using foreign mercenaries."

The big man blearily gave the waitress the eye and took the new bottle from her. He unscrewed the cap and nodded sagely. "This is true. Iranians, Pakistanis and pagan zealots from God knows where come to fight by the side of the Turks. They wish to make this a holy war. I say kill them all. Let them all be martyrs in hell together."

"What about the Croatians?"

The man frowned. "I do not know. I have not heard of them using any mercenaries." He shrugged dismissingly. "But I would not put it past them. The Nazi-loving bastards."

Bolan suppressed a grimace. At least the man hated his countrymen equally. "And what of yourselves?"

The man's eyes became slits as he regarded Bolan. "What do you mean?"

The Executioner shrugged. "It is widely rumored that soldiers from Greater Serbia serve in the Bosnian Serb ranks."

The other three men at the table gave Bolan hard looks, then turned to their leader. The big man suddenly smiled. "You are a foreigner, so I will explain something to you. There is no such thing as 'Bosnian Serbs,' as you journalists like to call us. Serbians are Serbians. You attack one of us, you attack us all. You understand?"

The men around the table grunted and nodded vigorously in solidarity.

Bolan nodded. "I understand. But what of reports of Russian advisers in your ranks?"

The table grew quiet again. The big man looked at Bolan suspiciously. "You ask many questions."

"I'm a journalist, and I want to hear your side of the story."

The big man blinked. "Hmm, well, yes." He finally shrugged and took another pull from the bottle. "Well, I would not know of these things. Perhaps you should talk to some of the others."

The Executioner decided to press it home. "What about the rumors of a Russian giant committing atrocities around Sarajevo?"

The man's eyes flared wide, and he choked on his drink. He coughed and glared at Bolan as he tried to recompose himself. "I have no idea what you are talking about. Now, I have much to do. Good night." He stood up unsteadily and jerked his head at the other three men around the table. "Come!"

The Executioner poured himself a finger of slivovitz and watched the men leave. His gaze slid to the mirror on the wall. One of the men had split from the group and gone over to the table where Bolan had heard people speaking in Russian. The big American drained his glass as heads at the other table turned toward him. He grimaced as the liquor blossomed into warmth in his stomach. Plum brandy wasn't his first choice in a drink, but the men in Sonia's drank it like water. He poured himself another and considered his options.

He had asked questions, rattled a cage and gotten himself noticed. The only real option was to see what they would do about it. Bolan decided to go out to get a breath of fresh air. He smiled at the waitress, put money for the brandy on the table, then headed to the men's room to wash his hands and to give some time to whatever reception committee that was being organized. He unsnapped the strap that secured the 93-R in its shoulder holster, then went out into the lobby. Bolan casually glanced about. His drinking companions had disappeared. So had the men at the other table.

The Executioner stepped outside into the night. The air was clean and cold after the rain, and it was a welcome relief after the stink of sweat, brandy and cigarette smoke inside. He glanced up at the moon through the parting clouds. Boots crunched in the gravel behind him, and he turned.

The big man came toward him, holding one hand low and close to his side. Bolan gave him a big friendly smile and waved his hand obviously. "Hi!"

As the man's eyes went to the Executioner's waving hand, Bolan drove the heel of his boot into the man's solar plexus. The Serb grunted explosively and doubled over in pain. A Russian Makarov pistol fell from his hand and clattered to the wet gravel. Bolan grabbed him by the hair and yanked him back upright. The Beretta cleared leather, and Bolan screwed the muzzle into the man's temple as he put his back to the wall. The Executioner peered over the shoulder of his human shield. A voice shouted from behind a truck.

"Freeze! Let him go!"

Bolan waited.

The voice shouted again. "Let him go!"

The Executioner smiled and spoke calmly. "Come out where I can see you."

There was hushed whispering, then a command in Serbian. Three men came out from behind the truck, and two men appeared from around each corner of the building. All were armed. A tall thin man spoke with the unmistakable tone of command. "Let him go."

Bolan shook his head. "Not yet." The big man wheezed as he tried to bring breath into his lungs. "What do you want?"

The tall man folded his arms across his chest. "We want some answers."

The big American nodded. "So do I."

Beside the tall man stood a stockier, more powerfully built individual. He had short blond hair and a deep scar on his chin. His fatigues and wool cap were of local manufacture and nondescript. His physique and his bearing screamed special forces. He peered at Bolan inquisitively. "Why do you ask about a giant?" he asked, speaking with a Russian accent.

Bolan shrugged. "I want to find him."

Both men frowned. The Russian changed his tone and looked at Bolan condescendingly. "Why are you chasing rumors? Is there not enough real bloodshed for you?"

The Executioner came to a decision. It was time for the honest approach. He locked gazes with the Russian. "Igor Baibakov isn't a rumor. He's an old friend of mine."

The Russian gaped openly, and the tall man blanched. "Perhaps it's time we were honest with each other."

The tall man recovered his composure. "Why do you seek the giant?"

"I'm going to kill him."

The tall man lost his composure again. "You are American Special Forces, yes?"

Bolan considered that. Technically he operated under the auspices of the Justice Department, except that they didn't know it. Bolan countered without answering. He looked the Russian up and down. "Spetsnaz?"

"At one time."

"Baibakov isn't under your command." It was a statement, not a question.

"Captain Baibakov is under no one's command."

The men flanking Bolan fingered their AK-47s and looked back and forth between Bolan and their commanders. The tall thin man shook his head at them, and they lowered the muzzles of their rifles. The leader drew himself to his full height. "I am Captain Milan Grohar. My associate is Mr. Constantine Markov." He gestured toward Bolan's captive. "Please release Sergeant Simic. I promise we shall take no offensive action. I do not wish war with American forces. I believe we have matters to discuss."

Bolan released Simic and lowered the Beretta. "Let me guess. Igor Baibakov is a mutual problem."

The men's stony faces revealed the answer.

The big American holstered the 93-R. "Why don't we step back inside? I'm buying."

CAPTAIN GROHAR SIGHED over his drink. "Baibakov is everybody's problem."

Bolan raised an eyebrow. "How so?"

Markov grimaced. "I take it you are aware of some of his recent activities?"

"I've seen some of his handiwork."

Markov spit. "Then you know that he is a butcher, a disgrace to Spetsnaz, a disgrace to Russia."

Grohar nodded. "It is worse than that. I will tell you something. Not all Serbians fight for the same goals. Some fight to save Serbians in Bosnia-Herzegovina. Others fight to see a united, sovereign Serbia ruling all the formerly occupied regions. Others will say they fight for these things and really fight simply for revenge. Others, simply for looting and killing. Baibakov has found a home with a radical group called the Order of the Red Falcon. They are terrorists."

"What's he doing with this group?"

Markov scowled bitterly over his beer. "Baibakov is enjoying himself, and getting paid to do it."

Bolan ignored the comment. "Who are the Order of the Red Falcon, and what do they want?"

Grohar shifted uncomfortably. "The gray falcon is a very old symbol of the Kingdom of Serbia. This group has changed the color to red, to symbolize the blood of Serbians martyred in this war. They wish the unification and ethnic cleansing of a Greater Serbia."

Bolan looked at Grohar without saying anything. The men shrugged. "They are fanatics. Their leader is a man named Branko Cebej. His wife and three children were killed soon after Bosnia-Herzegovina declared itself a Muslim state. He and his followers wish to kill or drive out all Muslims from Bosnia-Herzegovina. Then, with a reunified Serbia, they wish to resubjugate Croatia. They will accept no negotiated peace that falls short of these goals, and they will commit any act to attain them. They consider the United States and NATO enemy powers on our soil. They consider Serbia to be at war with them.''

Bolan leaned back in his chair. ''They believe this is a war they can win?''

Grohar smiled crookedly. ''Not with tanks and planes, but through attrition, public opinion and terror. Branko believes if they kill enough NATO troops in a guerrilla war, through ambushes, bombings, snipings and the like, that public opinion in the peacekeeping nations will call for the withdrawal of foreign troops. Then their goals can come to fruition.'' He leaned forward. ''This is not outside the realm of possibility, you agree?''

Bolan nodded soberly. For a small faction of determined fanatics, it wasn't an unreasonable gamble. He looked at Grohar hard. ''So why don't you support them?''

''Because I have a family. I do not want war with the United States and NATO. Serbia would pay a terrible price in blood, win or lose. Too many have died already. I will be plain with you. Under the right conditions I and many others in our ranks would settle for a negotiated peace.''

''But this group will do anything to prevent that.''

Grohar nodded. ''This is true.''

''So why don't you put an end to them?''

Grohar's face grew unreadable, and he was silent for a long moment. ''Cebej and his followers are Serbians. They have fought as I have. We are still at war, with the Bosnian Muslims, as well as the Croatians. The Red Falcons have fought bravely, often at impossible odds. Their missions have often succeeded where others have failed. Many among us do not agree with their goals or their tactics, but many respect them as soldiers and as patriots. Many consider the Red Falcons a necessary evil of this war. Others openly support them and their goals. Some consider Cebej a hero. They are a small group at the moment, but their ranks grow. If I ordered my men to attack them, I am not at all sure I would be obeyed. And I will not order Serbians to kill Serbians when we already fight a war on two fronts. Besides, I am but one captain of a militia unit. I am not a general to make such decisions."

Bolan turned to Markov. "What about you? Baibakov is one of your own."

Markov grimaced in distaste. "I am not here as a Russian officer. Technically I am a mercenary adviser with my government's blessing. However, I would gladly kill Baibakov as a matter of honor. But he is difficult to find, and when he surfaces, he is surrounded by these Serbian fanatics. He trains them, teaches them the Spetsnaz way of warfare and then leads them in their butchery. They call him Red Giant and fear him as much as they worship Cebej." Markov shook his head. "Even if I could get close enough, I am not at all sure I could kill him before he killed me." The Russian stared distantly at the wall. "Sometimes I do not believe he is human."

The Executioner folded his arms across his chest. "If you can tell me where I can find Baibakov, I'll kill him."

Grohar snorted. "By yourself? He always has at least a squad around him."

Bolan's smile didn't reach his eyes. "I can find some volunteers."

The Serb sat up in his seat in alarm. "Muslims?"

Bolan nodded.

The captain's face took on a distinctly unhappy look. "You want me to allow you to come behind our lines with Muslim troops to kill fellow Serbs."

"I want you to tell me where to find Baibakov and then stay out of the way."

Grohar's brow furrowed as he contemplated the idea. Markov looked at Bolan in hard speculation. "You will try to kill Baibakov whether you get permission from us or not?"

Bolan nodded. It was simply the truth.

Markov sighed. "Then I will go with you."

Grohar looked back and forth between the two men. "This is insane. I do not like it."

The Russian shrugged. "You do not have to like it. It must be done. You cannot allow Baibakov to start a war with the

United States. As a Spetsnaz officer, I will not suffer him to go on living.'' His voice went cold. ''You will tell me when Baibakov surfaces. Then we will kill him.''

Bolan looked at Markov, trying to read him. He didn't believe the man was telling him everything. The Russian poured himself a drink and stared back. ''This is acceptable to you.''

It was the best deal the Executioner was going to get.

''It's acceptable.''

5

Vlado Sarcev looked up at Constantine Markov with open suspicion. The Russian looked down at the little man with obvious reservations. Both men turned and looked at Bolan as if wondering if he were joking. They were two men on opposite sides of a very unpleasant war. Their only bond was Mack Bolan, and a seven-foot-tall killing machine named Igor Baibakov.

Bolan looked again at the photographs on the folding table Sarcev had set up in his basement. Captain Grohar had been reluctant, but he had come through. As a captain in the Bosnian Serb militia who had distinguished himself in battle, he had connections. Baibakov had surfaced. He and his men occasionally used a small ski chalet up in the hills forty kilometers outside Sarajevo. Grohar's connections had told him that food and supplies had been delivered to the chalet that morning, and the driver had identified Baibakov and Cebej. They had at least twenty men with them.

The Executioner figured they had a twenty-four-hour window of opportunity.

He glanced at the photographs. He had put the full resources of Stony Man Farm on the situation, and Kurtzman had gotten him satellite photos of the chalet and the surrounding area.

Bolan turned to Sarcev. "How many volunteers do we have?"

The militiaman folded his arms. "Fourteen."

He nodded. "How soon can they be ready to move?"

The little Bosnian grinned. "They are ready now."

"I need at least two snipers, and two RPG-7s."

"It is already done."

Bolan turned to the Russian. "And you?"

Markov shrugged. "Five minutes from whenever you say." The Russian reached into the pocket of his coat and pulled out a photograph. "Grohar gave me this."

Bolan glanced at the photograph. Two men in camouflage fatigues stood together outside a tent. Between them stood a short dark-haired woman. Both men were smiling and held AK-47 rifles. The woman grinned and held an Uzi submachine gun above her head as if in victory. The man on the right was Grohar. The other man was only slightly shorter and more powerfully built. His hair was cropped close to his head, and he had a thick handlebar mustache.

Markov jerked his head at the photo in Bolan's hand.

"The man next to Grohar is Branko Cebej. I thought it would be best if you knew what he looked like. The woman's name is Madchen Krstic. She is Branko's woman. She fights beside him." The Russian grinned crookedly. "I believe you will have no trouble recognizing Baibakov when you see him."

Bolan examined Branko Cebej's face. He looked formidable. To lead an extremist group like the Red Falcons, he would have to be. Bolan wouldn't underestimate the woman, either. In civil wars women were often the first victims, and could become the most dedicated fighters. He looked at the smiling face of Grohar. It seemed that at one time Grohar and Cebej had been comrades in arms. Now the captain was going to betray his fellow Serb to their sworn enemies. Bolan looked up from the photo at the grim-faced Russian in front of him. Igor Baibakov was a countryman of his, and a fellow officer of the Spetsnaz elite. Both men were advisers to the Serbs in this conflict. Constantine Markov was here with Bolan this night to kill him.

The Executioner's face tightened. Civil wars were always the ugliest of conflicts, and the lines always twisted and became vague.

Bolan handed the photo back to Markov and glanced at his watch. It would be dawn in two hours. There was no use delaying any longer. "We leave in forty-five minutes." He stabbed a finger at the satellite photo on the table. "This is how I want to do it."

THE EXECUTIONER MOVED through the predawn mist. Light snow covered the ground and frosted the trees in monochromatic greens and grays through Bolan's night-vision goggles. The forest was fairly thin up on the hillside, and the lights shining from inside the chalet seemed as bright as headlights as the goggles amplified them. During their approach Bolan had noticed a number of small objects shifting underneath his boots. On examination he had found that they were spent shell cases. The ground was littered with them. Someone had been firing a lot of weapons on that hillside. They were well behind Serb lines, and Bolan knew the spent cases could only mean one thing. Someone had been doing a great deal of weapons training. The Executioner crouched with an M-4 Ranger carbine–grenade launcher combo across his knee. He peered through the trees at the chalet.

Constantine Markov knelt at his side. The Russian carried an AK-74 rifle with a grenade launcher mounted under its barrel, and a Stechkin machine pistol was thrust through the front of his belt. His Russian-made night-vision goggles made him look like a visitor from space. The two men's weapons and equipment mirrored each other eerily. They were two sides of a coin marked East and West.

Sarcev and the rest of his squad had split into two sections and flanked both sides of the chalet. Bolan had checked their positions and was relatively pleased. The militiamen were nervous about being so far behind Serb lines, but they were also well motivated. Each man was a volunteer. The Red Falcons had been striking at will, and had been elusive as ghosts. Too often Sarcev's men had been left to clean up after the Red Falcons' slaughter. Now the Bosnians finally had a chance to strike back hard. Three of them crouched behind Bolan and the Russian and cradled their rifles as they waited.

Bolan continued to scan the chalet. Sarcev's men had been in place for five minutes now, and they had the chalet in a deadly cross fire. A moment earlier Bolan had seen a silhouette move past the second-story window. Other than smoke curling from the chimney, there had been no movement since. The Executioner calculated. Outwardly nothing was amiss. They had encountered no sentries, but Branko Cebej and his men were well behind their own lines and had little reason to expect any kind of trouble. Igor Baibakov was another matter. He was hunting Bolan, and the giant knew that Bolan was hunting him.

Markov's whisper mirrored the Executioner's thoughts. "I do not like this. It does not feel correct. Something is wrong."

"Would Grohar give us up?"

The Russian's lips skinned back from his teeth in a scowl. "I do not believe so. I have been with Grohar's unit for some time. He is well respected, and he has expressed his concern about the Red Falcons' activities for some time. I believe he speaks the truth when he says that they are a liability to establishing peace. I believe he is a man of honor. If he decided to tell Cebej we were coming, I believe he would tell us he had done so, as well, to avoid conflict entirely."

Bolan considered that. It fit with his estimation of Grohar. "So what do you think?"

The Russian's goggled stare stayed on the chalet for long moments. "I think something is wrong. I do not like it."

Bolan took a long slow breath. He was tempted to scrub the mission; something was wrong, and he could feel it. But this was likely to be the only clear shot they would get.

Sarcev's voice spoke in Bolan's earpiece. "What is happening?"

Bolan spoke quietly into his mike. "Something is wrong."

There was a moment of silence. "Do we attack?"

The Executioner looked at Markov, who shrugged. "Baibakov must die."

If there was something wrong, they would recon it by fire. "We attack, on my signal."

Sarcev echoed him across the receiver. "On your signal."

Bolan raised his M-4 carbine, and Markov raised his AK-74. Both men's fingers rested on the triggers of their grenade launchers. The big American heard the Bosnians behind him shift into readiness. The Executioner spoke into his microphone. "RPGs. Now!"

The woods lit up with yellow fire on either side of the chalet as RPG-7 rockets sizzled out of their launch tubes and hissed toward the second-story windows. The M-203 recoiled as Bolan squeezed the trigger and arced a 40 mm grenade through the chalet's front window. Markov's weapon thumped a split second after, windows shattering as the grenades flew inside. Upstairs the rockets tore through the windows, and the chalet shuddered as the warheads detonated. A second later the two grenades detonated downstairs and lit the shattered windows with the orange flash of high explosive.

Bolan rose and moved toward the chalet at a run. Behind him Markov barked a command in Slovene, and the Bosnians followed, pouring fire into the sides of the chalet. Bolan opened the smoking breech of the M-203 grenade launcher and shoved in a personal defensive round. As he slammed the breech shut, he took the stairs to the porch in three strides and put his boot into the door, which flew open on its shattered hinges.

The doorway opened into a large main room with a fireplace. Crates and boxes littered the floor. Several couches formed a half circle in front of the hearth, and three men had risen from them. One defender looked at Bolan with a snarl as he racked the bolt of his AK-47. The weapon's muzzle rose, and the Executioner drilled a 3-round burst into the man's chest. He then put the carbine's front sight on the second man as a handgun barked in rapid semiautomatic fire. Bolan felt the wind of the bullets' passage and heard their supersonic cracks as they flew over his head high and to the left. The carbine cut loose, and the man fell backward to the floor.

Markov's AK-74 ripped into life, and the third man shuddered as the Russian's burst tore through him. Sarcev's men piled through the door as the Executioner moved deeper into the chalet. Feet thundered on the second floor, and Bolan whirled on the stairs. Two armed men appeared suddenly on the landing, and Bolan fired the M-203 up the staircase. The defensive munition was literally a 40 mm shotgun shell, and as its shot spread, the staircase formed a natural killing zone. Twenty-seven lead buckshot filled the air in a pattern the size of a coffee table. The two men staggered and fell in the withering storm of lead and tumbled down the stairs in a heap.

The Russian moved past Bolan toward an open side door. He tossed a hand grenade around the corner, and the house shuddered as the deadly bomb detonated. He went around the doorjamb with his rifle spraying on full automatic. Bolan headed up the stairs, two of Sarcev's men following him. The Executioner vaulted the corpses and hit the landing in a crouch. Smoke was starting to fill the upstairs; the RPG-7 warheads had set something on fire. Bolan heard more shooting downstairs as he moved down the hallway.

Sarcev's voice spoke in his earpiece. "Three men on front balcony with rifles!"

"Take them out!"

Bolan roared at the two Bosnians behind him as he hit the floor. "Down!"

They didn't speak English, but the meaning was very clear. They hit the ground as Sarcev's light machine gunner poured fire into the second-story balcony from outside. The rapid booming of semiautomatic fire from the sniper rifles thundered over the ripping snarl of the machine gun. Heavy bullets tore through the chalet's walls and flew through the air over Bolan's and the Bosnians' heads.

Sarcev spoke rapidly across the radio link. "Two down! One retreated back into house!"

Bolan took a prone rifle position on his elbows as a door down the hall kicked outward. A man came out, spraying with an automatic rifle on full auto. Bullets flew overhead, then the weapon suddenly fell silent as Bolan cut him down. The Executioner rose and spoke into his mike. "Third man down. Any activity on the sides or rear?"

The militia leader conferred with his flanking teams. "No movement. No one has tried to escape from sides or rear. Smoke is coming out of both windows."

Bolan nodded to himself. The smoke was getting thicker, and he had to crouch to keep his head out of it. He moved down the hallway and kicked open the far door. The room was fully ablaze. One man lay on the floor in a huge pool of blood. Shrapnel from an RPG-7 warhead had torn him apart. Bolan jerked his head at the door down the other side of the hall. Sarcev's men ran down the hall and kicked the door, leaping back as flame swelled out of the burning room. One of the men looked back at Bolan and held up two fingers, then drew his thumb across his neck. Two men were already dead inside. The Executioner squinted against the smoke. The upstairs was getting very hot, and an orange glow suffused the smoke.

"Vlado, anything?"

The little Bosnian spoke rapidly. "No! No movement! Roof is on fire!"

Bolan nodded. "Markov, the second floor is clear. What do you have?"

The Russian's voice was dour. "First floor clear. No Baibakov. No Cebej."

Bolan grimaced and jerked his thumb at the stairway. The militiamen hit the stairs at a run.

On the first floor Markov had smashed open a crate and was rummaging through it. The box appeared to be filled with folding-stock AK-47 rifles. Sarcev's men were stripping the dead Serbs of their weapons, but when they saw what the Russian had found they began to smash open crates, as well.

Bolan glanced around the room. Smoke was beginning to fill the air downstairs. His face hardened. Above the hearth was a banner with a stylized falcon painted in red, its talons and beak dripping blood. Bolan's eyebrows rose as he spotted a row of suitcases along the far wall. He turned to the Russian.

"Markov, check the bodies for any kind of papers or identification."

The man nodded and bent over one of the bodies. Bolan cut open one of the suitcases with his knife. Clothes and personal effects spilled out. He went down the line of cases and discovered they were all the same. Bolan's eyes narrowed. Baibakov and Cebej were already gone. Only a skeleton crew remained at the chalet. Their weapons were crated for travel, and their suitcases were packed.

The Red Falcons were moving out.

Bolan turned to Markov. "Anything?"

The Russian handed Bolan several envelopes, his face grim. "Yes. Each man had one of these."

The Executioner's gaze narrowed as he examined the envelopes—each one contained a plane ticket. The flight left Sarajevo International Airport and had a stopover in Paris. The flight's final destination was New York City and the plane left in two hours.

Bolan spoke into his microphone. "Vlado, have your men ready to leave in one minute. Leave the heavy weapons behind."

The Bosnian's voice sounded confused. "But why? We—"

The Executioner's voice rang out in the unmistakable tone of command. "We move out—now!"

6

The old Mercedes truck tore through the streets of Sarajevo. The gears shrieked and groaned as Bolan downshifted around a corner and headed toward the airport. Beside him Sarcev gripped the dashboard with white knuckles. Constantine Markov and the rest of the militiamen hung on for dear life in the back. They had abandoned their light machine gun and the RPG-7 rocket launchers. Bolan had only allowed them enough time to grab as many magazines for their rifles as they could carry from the burning chalet, then they had raced down the mountainside for the truck.

Bolan's face tightened as he looked at his watch. They had still used up too much time. It was too late to get to his room to try to set up something over the satellite link. Even if there had been time, Cebej would have to be expecting to hear from his men back at the chalet. When he didn't, he would know something was wrong, and he and Baibakov would fade into the sheltering darkness of the hills behind Serb lines. The only chance was to try to intercept them at the airport before they did.

The Executioner stepped on the accelerator, and the old truck vibrated as its engine roared into the redline. A triangle of lights blinked overhead as a plane came into final approach. The road opened, and they were on the approach to the airport. Bolan pushed the accelerator all the way down and held it there. He kept his eyes on the gate and spoke to Sarcev.

"What kind of troops man the perimeter gates to the landing field?"

"British soldiers guard the gates, I believe."

British troops guarding the gate to the Sarajevo airport would be unlikely to admit a truck full of armed Bosnian militiamen led by a Russian mercenary and a heavily armed American with a press pass.

"What kind of security will there be on the field itself?"

Sarcev stared ahead at the gate with mounting alarm. A soldier in a forest-camouflage parka had stepped out of the shack and was staring at the lights rushing toward him. The man wore the red beret of a British paratrooper, and his hand was resting casually on the pistol grip of the SA-80 assault rifle slung across his chest. "On the field, security is the responsibility of the Bosnian military police."

"Do you have any pull with them?"

Sarcev almost smiled. "I am known to them."

Bolan nodded with satisfaction. "Good. Hold on."

The truck's ancient engine was roaring in protest. A second paratrooper stepped out of the gate shack and began yelling into a hand-held radio. The first soldier suddenly whipped his assault rifle around on its sling and brought it up to his shoulder.

Bolan's face remained focused. "Tell your men to hit the floor!"

The militia leader began to shout in Slovene at the top of his lungs.

The paratrooper stood unflinchingly in the truck's headlights. Fire spit out of the muzzle of his rifle as he fired a warning burst into the air. The trooper grimaced into the glare of the oncoming lights and pointed the muzzle straight at the truck. Bolan slid down in the driver's seat with only his eyes showing over the dashboard. Sarcev did a duck and cover into the seat well.

With a loud smacking noise, cracks suddenly spiderwebbed the windshield a foot above Bolan's head. The smacking came in a rapid patter, and the windshield blew apart in a shower of glass shards. Freezing air roared into the cab, and the sound of gunfire was suddenly very clear. Bullets spanged off of the truck's hood, and the hollow barking of a handgun broke out as the second paratrooper started to discharge his pistol at the truck's wheels.

The falling gate came apart like kindling as the truck barreled through it unhindered. Rifle fire chattered behind them as Bolan took the truck out onto the field. "Take a head count, see if anyone was hit!"

Sarcev shouted back into the truck bed, and someone shouted back. He rose up in his seat and looked around the field. "Nicholas was hit in the shoulder but he will live. The Russian is applying a field dressing."

Bolan squinted against the rushing wind in the cab and nodded. The one thing he had feared in this mission was getting into a firefight with NATO peacekeeping troops. He'd just have to let the State Department sort it out. "Which way to the terminal?"

The militia leader grimaced at the ticket he held in his hand. "I have never entered the airport from this position, but I believe you should follow that plane."

The truck turned sluggishly to the right on its punctured tires and followed the plane they had seen coming in as it taxied toward the terminal lights. The Executioner calculated quickly as he passed a series of small plane hangars. Grohar's informant had said Cebej and Baibakov had been with at least twenty men at the chalet. In the attack he and Sarcev's men had taken down eleven of the Red Falcons. That left Cebej, Krstic and Baibakov in the airport with well over half a squad of men. Cebej, Krstic, and the big Russian would be easy enough to recognize, but the rest of their men would be faces in the crowd until they opened fire. If Cebej was even half the leader he was described to be, he would have his men spread out, and if he didn't, Baibakov would make sure of it.

Bolan's gaze narrowed. The possibility of innocent casualties was extremely high. The only option would be to try to take Baibakov and Cebej by surprise, and hope the rest of the Red Falcons would surrender with the death of their leaders. Bolan let out a slow breath. It was not an ideal situation.

Sarcev seemed to be reading the Executioner's mind. "How do you wish to do this?"

The brakes screamed, and the truck nearly went up on two wheels as Bolan brought the ancient Mercedes to a fishtailing halt.

An armored vehicle had pulled out in front of them from one of the small aircraft shelters. Its tracks ground against the tarmac and threw up sparks as it halted in Bolan's path. From the armored vehicle's tanklike chassis rose a turret mounting four quad-mounted 23 mm antiaircraft cannons with a small targeting radar dish behind. All four gaping muzzles of the automatic cannons were locked on the truck and seemed to be staring directly at Bolan and Sarcev. A searchlight blazed into life and flooded the truck's cab with a blinding glare.

Bolan turned to his companion. "They're flying a Bosnian flag from their antenna. Maybe you should go out and talk to them."

Sarcev swallowed. He obviously didn't like the idea of stepping out of the cab, but the little man had no illusions about what four 23 mm automatic cannons would do to the old diesel truck when they opened fire. He cleared his throat. "Yes. Perhaps that would be best."

A jeep with a heavy machine gun mounted on the back was racing up from the terminal to block the truck's retreat. Sarcev pushed open his door and shouted in Slovene. A hatch popped open on the antiaircraft vehicle, and a helmeted head popped up. The man shouted back an angry command. The militia leader left his rifle by his seat and slowly slid out of the cab. He placed his hands over his head and walked forward. He and the vehicle commander began a rapid exchange.

Markov's voice hissed from the back of the truck. "What is happening?"

Bolan didn't turn his head. "The Bosnian military police have a ZSU-23 armored antiaircraft vehicle pointed at us."

"Oh?"

"Yeah. Vlado is talking to them."

The Russian spent a moment mulling that over. "How is he doing?"

Bolan shrugged slightly as he watched the jeep pull up behind them in his side mirror and train its heavy machine gun on the back of the truck. "They haven't started firing yet."

Sarcev turned and walked back to the truck and waved at Bolan. The Executioner glanced at the cannons, then jumped out of the cab. "What's the situation?"

"The lieutenant wishes to know how they can be of assistance."

"Ask him if he can find out exactly which terminal we want and if he can get us to it quietly."

The militia leader walked back to the vehicle and handed up one of the Red Falcons' confiscated tickets. The vehicle commander glanced at it and pointed toward the terminal. A twin-engine jet was parked at the ramp. "He says it is that one, and that he can have it arranged. Is there anything else?"

Bolan nodded. "Yes. Tell him not to let that plane take off under any circumstances."

Sarcev spoke to the lieutenant, and the man grinned as he leaned forward and patted the barrel of one of his 23 mm automatic cannons.

"The lieutenant says that will not be a problem."

THE EXECUTIONER SLID OUT of the baggage drop into the terminal and he tugged a blue cap low over his face. A matching baggage handler's jacket covered his armored vest. He had abandoned the M-4 carbine, and the Beretta was strapped to his chest with the sound suppressor attached. Behind him Sarcev carried an AK-74 rifle with its stock folded in a flight bag, and his Tokarev pistol was under his belt. Bolan glanced across the waiting area.

Markov and two militiamen were dressed in coveralls and manhandling a baggage cart loaded with boxes. Three more men stood by the loading gate with appropriated suitcases. A tone chimed over the intercom, followed by an announcement in three languages that the flight to Paris would be leaving in ten minutes. Bolan looked around the waiting area. At least twenty-five people sat or stood in groups, and more were coming in as departure time drew near. Cebej and his people could hide in the airport until their flight left, but they would have to come through here. Baibakov would be almost impossible to miss. At least one or two of their men would already be at the gate watching, but they would be watching for police or military activity. Not assassins.

Sarcev leaned against a pillar and lit a cigarette. He looked like any other bored laborer on a break as he offered one to Bolan. "They will come soon."

The big American took the cigarette and stuck it behind his ear. He kept the matches in his hand. "Any minute." He looked over at Markov. The Russian's hand slid under his coverall, and he scratched his ribs. His hand stayed in place, and Bolan knew his fingers were resting on the grips of his 9 mm Stechkin machine pistol. His eyes slid left toward the main terminal. Bolan took the cigarette Sarcev had given him and turned to light it.

Branko Cebej was thirty yards away and walking straight at him.

Bolan's gaze went swiftly around the terminal. Everyone had seen his signal. Five men flanked Cebej as he walked toward the gate. All six men wore civilian clothes, and none of them carried any visible weapons. The militiamen began to rest their hands casually on top of their suitcases or flight bags. Bolan surveyed the boarding area again. At least two or three of Cebej's men were unaccounted for, as well as Krstic and Baibakov. The Executioner calculated and he could only come up with one viable option. He couldn't depend on the Bosnian militia to hold the plane for long, and he couldn't depend on Interpol to pick up Cebej in Paris. The French had very tricky extradition laws, and Cebej wasn't currently a wanted man. If it came to a standoff, peacekeeping troops would be called in, and Cebej and his men would most likely be escorted back behind Serb lines to avoid an incident. The Executioner's face hardened.

He couldn't allow Branko Cebej to board that plane.

The Executioner moved forward, and Sarcev put a hand in his flight bag as he moved off to the big American's left. Bolan's fingers slid under his jacket and curled around the grips of his Beretta.

"Branko!"

A voice shouted from behind, and Bolan whirled. One of Sarcev's men knelt over his flight bag and was drawing his rifle. A tall man in a gray sport coat stood a few steps behind him with a pistol in his hand. The sudden roar of the gun was deafening as he shot the Bosnian in the back and shouted again. "Branko!" People began shouting and screaming at the sound of the gunshot.

Bolan ripped the Beretta 93-R from its holster. The plan had just gone to hell. Constantine Markov had his machine pistol out, and the Stechkin chattered as he put a burst into the Red Falcon's chest. "Get Cebej!"

The Red Falcons had thrown themselves in front of their leader and were drawing and firing handguns in all directions. Sarcev had his rifle out and sprayed it into the air on full automatic as he roared at the top of his lungs. Some people dropped to the ground at his order in their language. Others stood and screamed or started to run. Bolan put the Beretta's front sight on the man in front of Cebej and squeezed the trigger.

The Red Falcon dropped as the 3-round burst hammered him to the floor. Two of the men beside Cebej began to fire their pistols at Bolan as fast as they could pull the triggers, and bullets shrieked off the wall behind him as he dropped to one knee. His second burst snapped one of the Red Falcons' head back, and he fell with his face in a red ruin. The other man staggered as Sarcev put a round into him from his rifle, and his second shot put the man down.

The terminal was filled with the sound of screaming. Someone had pulled the fire alarm, and a bell clanged and a siren howled. Cebej and his two men retreated into the running mobs.

Markov moved forward, flanked by two militiamen. Gunfire erupted from behind them, and one of the men went down. Markov and Bolan whirled at the same time. A man stood behind the check-in desk firing a pistol. They both put bursts into him at the same time, and he flew backward into the departure monitor. Two militiamen by the loading gate opened fire, as well, and the Red Falcon and the check-in desk shuddered and came apart as they held down their triggers. The terrorist sagged forward across the battered counter as the Bosnians' rifles ran dry.

Bolan whirled again. Cebej was retreating into the main terminal. More shots rang out as he moved forward, and the Executioner's face tightened. Markov was hit. One of the people who had dropped to the floor at Sarcev's order was a Red Falcon. He shouted his defiance as he fired his pistol from the floor and shot the Russian in the side. Markov staggered and tried to bring his weapon around. The last Bosnian with him was already down.

The Executioner put a burst into the prone terrorist's back, then a second as he twisted under the impact. Sarcev continued forward, jockeying for a shot at Cebej, but the crowd interfered. He continued to scream for people to get down, but his was only one voice in a mob of screaming people and wailing alarms.

Bolan and Sarcev ran low through the crowd. The two remaining militiamen joined them. The Executioner summoned the layout of the airport to his mind and turned to Sarcev. "Tell your men to go right and cut off any escape toward the gates. If Cebej can get onto the field, he could slip through the fence. The only route I want to leave him is through you and me and the military police outside."

The little Bosnian spoke rapidly to his men. They nodded and ran full tilt toward the row of loading gates. Bolan spotted Cebej in the crowd. He and his men were heading toward the passenger gates. They halted as they saw the lights and sirens of the military vehicles and began to move toward the loading gates. Sarcev's men had taken position behind a pair of pillars and fired their rifles overhead as they spotted Cebej moving toward them in the crowd.

Bolan and his companion moved forward, and the three Red Falcons moved back. They suddenly broke and raced backward. They crashed through the door of the duty-free shop and hit the floor behind the counters.

Bolan crouched behind a row of chairs and turned to Sarcev. "Get on the radio and see if there's a back way out of the duty-free shop."

The man reached into his flight bag and pulled out the handheld radio the lieutenant had given him. He spoke for several moments and then looked up from the radio. "The lieutenant wishes to know what is happening."

The Executioner could imagine the lieutenant's situation. The British would be screaming about truckloads of armed troops bursting through their checkpoints. The plan had been to quickly and quietly neutralize the Red Falcons' leaders. From outside it probably sounded as if World War III had just started.

"Tell him we have the remaining Red Falcons trapped in the duty-free shop. Tell him to keep his men in position."

Sarcev spoke into the radio again, then sat listening for a moment. "He says there is a back storeroom, but there is no back entrance. It is a dead end. He says he is sending in his men."

Bolan nodded. "Tell him we have wounded in the loading gate, and to bring in a squad of his men. Tell them to take flanking positions on the duty-free shop."

Much of the screaming had subsided to moans and sobs. Except for those still cowering on the floor, most of the civilians had fled the scene. Remarkably enough, so far there had been no major casualties. Bolan glanced toward the loading gate. There had been casualties, though. Markov and three militiamen lay on the floor. A civilian was bending over Markov. None of Sarcev's men appeared to be moving. Bosnian military-police units were coming in through the loading ramp.

Bolan turned as a chair crashed outward through the duty-free shop's window. A woman's voice screamed pleadingly in French, and a deeper voice shouted in English. "I have hostages! Stay back or I will kill them!"

The Executioner slipped a fresh magazine into the Beretta 93-R as the lieutenant and five of his men came up to his position. They all wore dark blue commando sweaters and fatigues, and all of them carried AK-47 rifles. Five more of his men moved to join Sarcev's men on the flank. Dozens more military policemen guarded the entrance to the main terminal.

Bolan took a flash-stun grenade from his belt. "Vlado, I need to get close. Tell the lieutenant I need a diversion to keep their heads down."

The two Bosnians conferred briefly, and Sarcev nodded. "He says go on three."

The lieutenant spoke a command into his radio, then held up three fingers. He dropped them one at a time. On three he sliced his hand through the air and shouted a command.

The Executioner burst from cover as all of the military police began to fire. More than twenty rifles began to blast fire into the duty-free shop on full automatic. Cabinets of liquor, cigarettes and luxury items blew apart under the massive salvo. Bolan ran under the streaming tracers and dived against the wall under the shop's window. The fusillade stopped suddenly as the rifles clacked open on empty chambers almost simultaneously. There was a cacophony of metal clicking and clacking as twenty MPs changed magazines at the same time.

Bolan pulled the pin on the stun grenade. Inside the shop the woman screamed again, and a voice rang out from the shop in enraged Slovene. Bolan couldn't understand the words, but their meaning was plain.

The Red Falcons were about to prove they weren't bluffing. Bolan released the grenade's safety lever. He counted off the numbers, then hurled the grenade through the shattered window over his head. He clapped his hands over his ears and squeezed his eyes shut. The main terminal echoed with the deafening blast of the grenade, and Bolan could see the glare of the magnesium flare as a bright yellow flash through his closed eyelids. He stood and went through the door.

One of the Red Falcons stood with hands over his ears and tottered blind and deaf on his feet. Bolan shot him down with a burst to the chest. A second man held a collapsed woman by one wrist, and a pistol was in his other hand. He blinked confusedly, slowly moving the muzzle of the gun toward the weeping woman on the floor. Bolan took two quick strides forward and dropped the man with a point-blank head shot. The terrorist toppled backward into the broken glass of a display case.

The Executioner swept the room with the muzzle of the Beretta. An elderly couple clutched each other in the corner, as did a young man and woman in nearly matching blue jeans and leather jackets. Glass crunched underfoot as Bolan took a step forward and looked down a small service hallway. The back storeroom door was ajar.

He hurled himself aside.

Holes began to riddle the door as someone fired a pistol on rapid semiautomatic. Bolan fired a burst back through the door and moved out of the line of fire. He peered quickly around the corner and examined the door. Seven bullet holes formed a neat pattern almost exactly at waist level. Bolan smiled coldly. Cebej was good. In a barricade situation most amateurs crouched in the corners of rooms. This was the first place someone entering looked and fired. The wise lay prone on the floor somewhere toward the middle of the room to present a small target and surprised the entry team.

Bolan slipped a fresh magazine into the Beretta and lay back on the floor. He slid his gun hand around the corner and peered down his sights. He kept his aim six inches from the floor and began to fire the Beretta.

The door shuddered as bullets tore through it from both sides. Cebej's bullets went high down the small hallway. Bolan kept his low, putting the entire clip in a horizontal fan six inches above the floor. He withdrew and rammed a fresh magazine into the spent Beretta. He aimed around the corner and fired a burst.

No shots came back.

Bolan picked up a triangle of broken glass and flung it against the door. The beleaguered panel vibrated, and the glass shattered and fell to the ground. No shots came back. He drew the .44 Magnum Desert Eagle and strode down the hallway with a gun in each hand. The door came half off its hinges under his boot, and Bolan threw himself behind the jamb. He snapped around into the doorway with both pistols leveled.

A man's body lay facedown on the floor slightly to the left of the doorway, a 9 mm pistol held in each hand. A puddle of blood was spreading around his head, and his right arm was torn at the biceps from a bullet wound. Bolan holstered the Desert Eagle and knelt by the body. He raised the head by the hair and peered into the face of Branko Cebej. The leader of the Red Falcons had taken one of the Beretta's 9 mm subsonic hollowpoints through the forehead.

Bolan stood and shouted out through the doorway, "Clear!"

Booted feet thundered on the terminal floor as military police swarmed the shop. The Executioner holstered his pistols and walked back into the terminal as the shouting began all over again. Sarcev walked up to him, still cradling his rifle in his hands as he looked up into Bolan's face. "Cebej?"

Bolan nodded. "Dead. How is Markov?"

"The Russian is dead. He was a brave man."

"Yes. He was." Bolan looked back toward the loading gate. Someone had put a coat over the Russian's face, as well as over one of Sarcev's fallen men. His two wounded were being looked at by a medical officer.

The militiaman cleared his throat. "The Giant is not here, is he?"

The Executioner let out a long slow breath. It was unlikely that Baibakov would take a regular commercial flight. His huge size and scarred face would attract attention anywhere. He would be on a container flight or a transport. Bolan's instincts told him what he didn't want to hear. Igor Baibakov had gone ahead, and Krstic and an untold number of Red Falcons had gone with him.

Their destination was the United States.

7

Igor Baibakov's chair strained under his massive physique as he sprawled in front of the television and watched CNN. His joints were still stiff from his cramped ride in the cargo plane. Hiding among the crates, he had been unable to stretch out his seven-foot frame. The chair creaked dangerously as he extended his massive limbs and then gave the television his attention.

The news was recycling the same report he had seen half an hour earlier. Still, it told him more than enough. There had been a firefight in the Sarajevo airport. Details were unclear as to what exactly had happened, other than that the Bosnian military police had engaged a group of armed terrorists. All of the terrorists were reported dead. The news anchor said that thankfully there had been no civilian casualties. Baibakov almost smiled. He knew the Bosnian military police all too well. He had been playing cat and mouse with them for months. If they had known the leader of the Red Falcons had been in the airport, they would have gone in shooting with an army of soldiers. It would have been a bloodbath. Yet, according to the Western news media, there had been no civilian casualties. All of the terrorists were dead. Baibakov exposed his square, horselike teeth in a delighted smile.

Of course it had been the work of the American commando.

The chair groaned as Baibakov rose out of it and clicked off the television. He stared out the window of the safehouse. It was raining lightly. Out in the darkness he could see the lights of Paris gleaming in the distance. His voice was a rumbling grate.

"Branko is dead. If they knew to strike at the airport, then we must assume the men at the chalet are lost, as well."

Madchen Krstic pushed her dark bangs out of her eyes and looked up from a map of the United States. "Yes."

"We must assume they know that we are coming."

She shrugged and looked at the map again. "It will not help them. They cannot stop us."

Baibakov grinned again. The little Serb woman wasn't the mourning type. She had seen too many people she knew and loved die in the civil war. She and her family had suffered many atrocities at the hands of Muslim fanatics, and she had given the Bosnian Muslims back atrocity full score. It was only natural that she would have been drawn to the cause of the Red Falcons. Baibakov thought back to some of his attacks that she had participated in. Her sadistic butchery had rivaled his own, and it had started to worry Cebej. Baibakov's grin widened. It didn't worry him at all. He liked it. It excited him, and besides, Cebej was dead.

She felt him staring at her and looked up. Her eyelids narrowed slightly, and her right eyebrow rose. It was a calculated look and they both knew it. "You are assuming command."

It was a statement, not a question, and Baibakov simply smiled back at her.

Her lips parted as she looked the giant up and down appraisingly. "I am the commander's woman."

Baibakov crossed the room in two strides and hurled her to the floor. She gasped as he covered her with his massive bulk. Baibakov was glad Cebej was dead, since the Serb leader had started to question some of Baibakov's tactics. Now that he was dead, the Russian could run the mission the way he wanted, and take care of his other objective, as well. The woman was an added bonus. He had barely gotten her skirt up and already she was biting and clawing, and calling him her "warrior." That was all that mattered to her, killing and being in the company of warriors.

But Madchen Krstic had made one small mistake. Igor Baibakov didn't consider himself a warrior. Baibakov was a hunter—he hunted and he killed. Warriors were his favorite prey.

Soon he would return to the United States.

The former Spetsnaz commando considered it the greatest hunting ground in the world.

MACK BOLAN SAT NEXT to Hal Brognola at the conference table and sighed wearily. A two-star Army general and the deputy director of the CIA were present, as well as the State Department deputy chief. The State Department man glanced at Bolan suspiciously. The man didn't know who he was, but he obviously believed Bolan had no business being here. The Executioner had been back in the United States for a week. His mission was considered a great success. He had wiped a major terrorist group that threatened to destabilize the peace process in the former Yugoslavia. The Serbs were making almost no fuss at all about the destruction of the Red Falcons. The combined action with the Bosnian militia was considered a model of cooperation in the region.

Bolan knew better.

The State Department was overjoyed. To them the mission had gone off without a hitch. The mission was also over. The State Department, and other powers that were, knew that "Michael Belasko" was the "on-site operator," but his opinion that there was still a major problem was being frowned upon in all official channels. The President's advisers were telling the Man that stirring up fear of terrorist action in the United States wasn't a wise publicity move. The idea that some giant named Igor Baibakov was in the country and involved in terrorist activity was being dismissed.

But Bolan knew better.

Apparently the Russians knew better, as well.

Russian Military Intelligence had contacted the Pentagon. They were sending over an envoy, and it concerned the matter in Sarajevo. They had asked for the "on-site operator's" attendance. The men around the table rose as the conference room door was opened by a Secret Service agent.

Eyebrows rose around the table.

A tall blond woman in a dark green military dress uniform skirt and blouse marched into the conference room with the rigid poise of a drill sergeant. In her hands she carried a bulky, old-fashioned folding leather briefcase. She stood for a moment and scanned the men in the room critically. Her gaze stopped on Bolan. She stared at the Executioner openly for a long moment. Whatever she was thinking was hidden behind her arctic blue eyes.

The Executioner gazed back in frank appraisal. She was tall and lean, but she filled out her dress uniform well. Bolan had seen many Russian dress uniforms, and this woman had obviously had hers expertly tailored. Her gleaming black shoes had flat heels, and she had excellent calves. Despite her severe expression, she was a very attractive woman.

She removed her cap and turned to the CIA deputy director and saluted smartly. "I am Senior Lieutenant Valentina Svarzkova, of Russian Military Intelligence."

The deputy director saluted back awkwardly and waved toward an empty chair. "Miss Svarzkova, we are—"

The deputy director trailed off as she gave him an icy smile. "You may call me Lieutenant."

The deputy director cleared his throat. "My apologies, Lieutenant. Please, have a seat."

Lieutenant Svarzkova's smile brightened slightly. "Thank you." She ignored the chair the deputy director indicated and took the empty seat next to Bolan. The Executioner examined the twin rows of service ribbons on the left breast of her uniform. He recognized the orange-and-black ribbon of the Medal for Valor. They also told him she was rated as a marksman and a communications expert. Her English was excellent.

The deputy director cleared his throat again.

"Lieutenant Svarzkova, we wish to thank you for your nation's cooperation during our operation in the former Yugoslavia. We appreciate your—"

Svarzkova cut him off. "We have a mutual problem, and his name is Igor Baibakov. If he is not already in the United States, he will be very soon."

The man from the State Department rolled his eyes. "Excuse me, Lieutenant, but according to our information Igor Baibakov is dead."

The lieutenant looked at the diplomat as if he were a small child. "Your information is incorrect. Russian Military Intelligence has known that Igor Baibakov survived and has been selling his services as a mercenary in the former Yugoslavia for some time now."

Bolan's eyebrows shot up. He had been around a number of Russian Intelligence agents in his time, and they were a notoriously closemouthed bunch. Svarzkova was extraordinarily frank. She suddenly turned to Bolan. "Igor Baibakov is alive, is he not?"

"He was the last time I saw him."

Svarzkova nodded and opened her briefcase. She slid out a set of identical files and passed them around the table. Her tone grew somewhat colder. "I will be honest with you. It is no secret that the Russian republic supports the Serbian cause in the former Yugoslavia. We cooperate with your peace initiative there to maintain good relations with the United States. However, we now have a mutual problem." She opened the file in front of her, and the men around the table did the same.

Bolan looked at the photo in front of him. Baibakov stood with the Kremlin behind him dressed in his Spetsnaz parade uniform. A sheet containing his statistics and service record had been translated into English. Svarzkova read them out loud anyway.

"Captain Igor Baibakov, seven feet, 325 pounds. Fluent in English and Spanish. Rated as expert in small arms, explosives, escape and evasion, airborne qualified. Born 1958 in the northern Ural Mountains. His father was a Cossack and a war hero. He became a hunting guide after World War II, specializing in tracking Russian boar and grizzly. His son learned the family trade early, and hunting remains Igor Baibakov's only real passion. Due to his immense size and strength, Baibakov was groomed for the Soviet Olympic team in wrestling and power lifting. However, he had a number of disciplinary problems. These problems were severe enough to have him eliminated from the Soviet sports program. As punishment, he was enlisted in the army and immediately sent to fight in Afghanistan. Disciplinary problems continued. However, he was rated as an expert with small arms, and his ferocity awarded him the Medal of Valor. He was then noticed by a Spetsnaz commander, a Major Pietor Ramzin—I believe you are acquainted with that name.''

Heads nodded around the table. Major Pietor Ramzin had dug a smuggling corridor between the United States and Mexico big enough to drive trucks through. He was the first man in history to have built a covert, hostile military firebase manned by foreign soldiers in the continental United States. He had been convicted of murder, extortion, drug trafficking, possession and smuggling of illegal weapons, transport of illegal aliens into the United States and conspiracy. They had been forced to rewrite the possession-of-destructive-devices statute to convict him of attempting to detonate a nuclear-demolition charge on United States soil.

Ramzin was currently serving four consecutive life sentences in the Leavenworth Federal Maximum Security Prison. Mack Bolan had put him there.

Svarzkova continued. ''Under Ramzin's command, Baibakov excelled. He received numerous commendations for his combat ability, and achieved the rank of captain. His record was shadowed by accusations of atrocities committed against Afghan civilians. However, due to the expediencies of war and Baibakov's obvious talents, such allegations were not deeply scrutinized.''

The lieutenant's eyes narrowed. ''With the recent political changes in Russia, the armed forces were downsized. Ramzin's Spetsnaz unit was decommissioned. We are aware of their actions in the United States. That is history. The fact remains that Baibakov is alive, he is probably already in the

United States and he will carry out the Red Falcons' agenda. Whether you wish to believe it or not.''

The room exploded into argument. Bolan looked at the Russian agent speculatively. ''Why does the Russian government care about what Baibakov does?''

The argument around the table died with Bolan's question, and the woman grimaced. ''Baibakov is an embarrassment to our government. As a former Russian Special-Forces soldier, we cannot have him engaged in terrorist activities in the United States.''

Bolan raised an eyebrow. ''He's done it before.''

The woman's eyes narrowed. ''Yes. But we thought you had killed him.''

''You knew of his activities in Sarajevo and did nothing.''

The woman glared but said nothing. Bolan smiled coldly. ''Due to the expediencies of war, his activities were not deeply scrutinized.''

Svarzkova flushed red.

He continued. ''As long as he was training Serbian militia units and butchering Bosnian civilians, he served your political expediencies. Now that he has killed an American envoy and several United States Marines, he is an embarrassment. Now he is here in the United States because you wouldn't take action.''

Svarzkova's knuckles whitened, but her voice remained calm. ''You are partially correct. Baibakov is here, along with elements of the Red Falcon Brigade. On this we must agree. On this we must take immediate action.'' Lieutenant Valentina Svarzkova looked Bolan in the eye.

''Igor Baibakov must be found and killed.''

AN HOUR LATER Hal Brognola sat across from the President of the United States.

''Hal, what do you think?'' asked the Man.

Brognola sighed. He trusted Mack Bolan with his life, and while he had never trusted the Russians, in this situation he trusted their motives. ''If Striker says he ran into Baibakov in

Sarajevo, I believe him. If he says Baibakov is on his way here on the Red Falcon agenda, I believe that, too. The State Department can complain about snipe hunts all they want. I believe the threat is real."

The President frowned. "What about this Russian woman?"

The big Fed shrugged. "I think she corroborates what Striker has already told us. Baibakov is a major liability to the Russians. They want trade agreements, they want foreign aid and mutual cooperation internationally. Some seven-foot maniac who used to be an operator of theirs running a terrorist network in the United States won't be very helpful once Congress and the Senate find out. In this instance I believe them. They want Baibakov, and they want him terminated."

The President nodded slowly. "I agree." The lines in his face set grimly. "What do you suggest?"

"For starters, the usual. Get Baibakov's description to the FBI and run it through channels. He may be Superman but he's also seven feet tall. He'll be hard to hide."

The President nodded. "And?"

Brognola didn't like the idea of sending a friend of his after one of the worst killing machines to ever walk on two legs, but it had to be done. "Send Striker after him. Baibakov will be using Russian *mafiya* connections to move and get matériel in the United States. He's dealt with them before. Lieutenant Svarzkova can go along as a liaison and an observer. I'm pretty sure she has some cards to play she hasn't shown yet."

The President frowned. "Can we trust her?"

"I believe the Russians want Baibakov dead. She might be useful. If someone is going to watch what she's up to, Striker is the man."

"You think the two of them can hunt down this psychopath?"

"I think it's the best shot we have, and they have an angle no FBI agent has."

The President cocked an eyebrow. "What's that?"

Brognola let out a slow breath. It was a worst-case scenario, and the only real shot they had. "Striker is proposing to use the same tactic he used in Sarajevo. He and Baibakov have a history. Once Baibakov knows that Striker is on his trail, Baibakov will start hunting him."

8

Mack Bolan knocked on the hotel-room door.

"Who is it?" a woman asked.

Bolan considered his answer for a moment. He had fought against, and more recently acted in cooperation with Russian Military Intelligence. He couldn't be sure just what this agent knew. "Me."

There was a short pause. "Who is this, 'me'?"

"Guess."

The woman snorted. "You may come in, Mr. Belasko. The door is open."

Bolan opened the door and found Lieutenant Valentina Svarzkova still in uniform and standing by an open suitcase on the bed. He glanced at the suitcase. "Don't bother to unpack."

The woman stood ramrod straight and stared at Bolan for a long moment. Her hands coiled into fists, and her face was a study in controlled fury. She spoke with steely calm. "I see. Your government is sending me back to Russia?"

Bolan shook his head. "No. But you and I aren't sticking around."

She visibly relaxed. "I see. I am to accompany you in your investigations?"

"As an official observer and Russian liaison."

Her eyes narrowed. "Ah."

"Is there a problem?"

Svarzkova bit her lip in indecision. She shrugged and spoke. "I am a military-intelligence officer. My training is as a field agent. I have received full combat and investigative training. I have been decorated for action in the field. Observer and liaison are—'' she searched for a word ''—constraining.''

Bolan frowned. ''You'll have to be more specific.''

''Your customs men at the airport. They took my gun. Your State Department has informed me I will not require a firearm in my operating capacities as liaison and observer.''

Bolan sighed. ''What kind of gun do you want?''

Svarzkova blinked at him.

He smiled. ''Short of an RPG-7, I can probably get you anything you want.''

''That will not be necessary. I had intended to get weapons at the Russian embassy, regardless of your State Department regulations. However, I did not wish problems when you saw me armed.''

Bolan spread his hands. ''I wouldn't have you any other way.''

Svarzkova's eyebrows rose. Bolan changed the subject. ''Constantine Markov was your man following Baibakov.''

The agent stiffened slightly, and then apparently saw little reason to deny it. ''Yes. He was sent by us to monitor Baibakov once we became aware of his activities with the Red Falcons against the United States. He was to terminate him, but could not get close. We were considering sending in a Spetsnaz strike team when you showed up.''

''So you decided not to get your hands dirty.''

Svarzkova shrugged. ''You and your militia friends were expedient.''

''And expendable.'' Bolan frowned. ''So why did he go along on the attack?''

The Executioner was startled to see the agent smile sadly. ''Constantine was a patriot, and he was Spetsnaz. He considered Baibakov a disgrace. He went along as insurance. Now he has died in vain.''

The Executioner knew all too well what it was like to lose comrades. ''He helped break the Red Falcons in Sarajevo. He saved many lives. He was Spetsnaz, and he died going forward.''

The lieutenant swallowed hard. "Thank you, Mr. Belasko. You are very kind."

Bolan folded his arms across his chest. "You keep calling me that."

The woman folded her arms in return and gave Bolan an amused look. "That was the name used by a man fitting your description in Sarajevo. Another man fitting your description used the name of Brand when he operated in the Russian republic in cooperation with Russian Military Intelligence against the *mafiya*." She grinned. "Do you have a more current name you would prefer?''

"You can just call me Mike."

"Fine." She looked at her watch. "So, tell me. Where are we going?''

"First we go to the Russian embassy and let you get what you need. Then we catch a plane to Kansas."

MACK BOLAN WALKED into the gray-walled security control room of the Leavenworth Maximum Security Prison. Svarzkova walked in step behind him. Two large uniformed guards stood behind a counter, flanking the captain of the guards while two more stood off to the side.

The captain smiled professionally.

"Please place all your weapons on the counter."

The guards had been told they were having important visitors and they were to extend every courtesy. They also knew the visitors' clearances came straight from God. They were intent on projecting steely efficiency. Their eyebrows rose as Bolan placed his 9 mm Beretta on the counter, followed by a snub-nosed revolver and a combat knife. One of the guards quickly ran a metal-detecting baton up and down his body.

"He's clear."

Valentina Svarzkova stepped forward, and the guards stood even straighter. Her demeanor had changed with her clothing, and she was dressed to impress in an entirely different fashion.

She now wore denim jeans and an intriguingly tight blue sweater. A brown leather jacket and running shoes completed her ensemble, and her blond hair spilled loosely over her shoulders. She could easily have been an exercise model. She saluted the captain and drew a CZ-75 9 mm automatic from a behind-the-back holster and placed it on the counter. She then drew a tiny PSM automatic from an ankle holster and put it on the table, as well.

The guard cleared his throat. "Anything else?"

She reached up her jacket sleeve. The six-inch clip-point blade of an AK-47 bayonet rasped out of its sheath. The handle and guard had been removed, and the metal tang was wrapped in black electrician's tape. The guards looked at her with new respect as she placed it on the counter. Even by Leavenworth standards, it was a very professional-looking shank. Svarzkova stood back from the counter and smiled pleasantly. "That is all."

The guard ran the baton up and down her length. "All clear."

The captain nodded at Bolan. "You are clear to enter. The inmate you requested is in holding room 12. Two armed guards will be outside the door during your interview."

Bolan nodded his thanks, and he and Svarzkova went down a narrow hallway and entered room 12. The lieutenant closed the door behind them, and Bolan examined the man sitting at the lone table in the little room. His hair was slightly grayer than Bolan remembered, and his skin was pale from lack of sunshine, but other than that he still looked formidable. He was Bolan's height, and powerful muscles strained the seams of his orange prison uniform. He had been clean-shaved before, but now he had a short Vandyke beard and mustache. His hands were shackled to a chain around his waist, and more chains held his ankles too closely for him to make any sudden movement.

Major Pietor Ramzin's eyes flared wide as he looked into the face of Mack Bolan. "You."

Bolan folded his arms across his chest. "You look well, Ramzin. I see you have recovered from your wounds."

"Yes. I received excellent medical care."

"So, how is prison life treating you?"

Ramzin snorted. "Oh, it is not so bad. Your prisons are much nicer than a Russian gulag, and it is certainly better than the death penalty." The Russian shrugged in his chains. "We have cable television here, and an excellent weight-training facility. The food, too, is much better than we had in the military. The situation could be much worse."

"Making new friends?"

Ramzin smiled shrewdly. "I will admit, your prison is full of uncultured individuals. However, you might be interested to know that most of my surviving men were sent here, as well. So I am among comrades, and have people to speak the mother tongue with." Ramzin's smile went cold. "As for my new friends, even a single Spetsnaz man is equal to four or five of your American Crips or Bloods. We have taught them to respect us. The Aryan Nation trash tried to bring us into their ranks, once. So we broke them like kindling."

Bolan smiled in irony. Ramzin was the kind of man who would be in command in almost any situation you put him, and he suspected half a platoon of former Russian special-forces troops might well shift the balance of power in a prison.

Ramzin smiled at Svarzkova. "And now an old friend brings me a beautiful woman."

Valentina Svarzkova spit in his face. "You are a disgrace to the motherland, Ramzin."

The major's massive arms and shoulders flexed against his chains. With a supreme effort he reined in his anger. He rearranged his face into a smile again. "Ah. How do the Bloods say it? A home girl."

She gazed at him stonily. "I am Senior Lieutenant Valentina Svarzkova, Russian Military Intelligence."

Ramzin regarded her with new interest. Spetsnaz operated directly under the command of Russian Military Intelligence.

Bolan decided to cut to the chase.

"Baibakov is alive."

For a second Ramzin actually looked shocked. Then he grinned from ear to ear. "Excellent."

"We believe he is now in the United States and working with a Serbian terrorist group called the Red Falcons. We believe they intend to strike at American targets."

Ramzin considered this. "You and the lieutenant are here to stop him?"

Bolan nodded. "That's right."

"I will light a candle for you."

Svarzkova lunged forward and struck Ramzin. Her entire body twisted with the blow as her cupped palm cracked against the side of his face with concussive force. It wasn't a slap. It was a martial-arts open-hand strike, and Ramzin was nearly knocked out of his seat.

The Russian shook his head to clear it, then grinned up at the lieutenant. The side of his face was already purpling with swelling, and blood dripped from his nostrils and stained his teeth. "I am pleased the leaders sent a real agent, and not some former KGB weakling."

Svarzkova flexed her hand. "We clean up our own messes."

Bolan stepped forward and looked down into Ramzin's face. "I want your assistance, Major."

Ramzin spit a mouthful of blood onto the floor. "To track down Captain Baibakov."

"He will use *mafiya* connections to get what he needs. Many of those connections will at least start with the contacts you made during your operation in Arizona. You are going to lead me to them."

The major leaned back in his chair. "Why would I wish to betray a comrade to my enemy?"

"You are serving four consecutive life sentences without possibility of parole, Ramzin."

The Russian raised an eyebrow. "And?"

Bolan folded his arms across his chest. "How would you like to see daylight?"

Ramzin was silent for several moments. "Your government would pardon me if I cooperate?"

The Executioner's face was as stone. "No. There will be no pardon, Ramzin. No charges will be dropped. You're a convicted felon and an enemy of the United States. You'll simply be deported."

"To Russia?"

Bolan shrugged. "To anywhere. We don't care. But if you ever come back to the United States, you will be treated as an escaped felon."

Ramzin looked at Svarzkova. "And what of Russia? What would be my status there?"

Svarzkova frowned. "You are not officially accused of any crimes in Russia. When your unit was decommissioned, you were honorably discharged and a decorated hero of the Soviet Union. Your pensions are intact. You would simply be a citizen. But your criminal activities are known, Ramzin. If you are found to be working for the *mafiya*, you will be brought down." She smiled at Ramzin unpleasantly. "And I will personally see to it that you do not live to see trial."

Ramzin looked back up at Bolan. "What of my men?"

Bolan shook his head. "Your men are convicted felons. I don't need them. I only need you. However, if you decline, I'll see what I can do about having you and your men scattered across a number of penitentiaries. I'm sure the Aryan Nation would be interested."

Ramzin scowled. "You leave me little choice."

The Executioner's face remained hard. "You have two choices. You can say yes, or you can say no. You have about five seconds to make up your mind."

Ramzin took a deep breath and then let it out. "Very well. I will assist you."

BOLAN SLID behind the wheel of the black Bronco and started the engine. Svarzkova buckled her seat belt. "When do we take Major Ramzin?"

"In about twenty-four hours. He has to be processed, and

all the papers have to be signed.'' Bolan smiled as he saw her flex her hand again. "Nice right hand."

The Russian agent blinked and then smiled. "There is a correct way to slap someone for maximum effect. As part of the investigative branch of my department, I was required to learn it. One takes turns exchanging slaps with the instructor until the technique is performed to his satisfaction." She tapped her cheek. "One learns very fast this way, or one learns one does not belong in Russian Military Intelligence."

Bolan shook his head. He had learned long ago that the Russian reputation for toughness wasn't an exaggeration.

The agent looked out the window at the massive gray fortress of Leavenworth Prison. "Twenty-four hours. What do we do until then?"

Bolan shrugged. "Get a hotel room, and then you tell me everything you know about Baibakov."

Svarzkova pushed a stray lock of hair out of her face. "Very well."

He pulled the Bronco onto the main road back to the town of Leavenworth. Half a mile from the prison they passed a PG&E truck parked by the side of the road and a man working up on the pole. They didn't see the ten-power binoculars in his tool bag, and after they passed they didn't see him pull out a hand-held radio. The man spoke quickly to the lookout who had made the first sighting in town.

"Confirmed. Targets visited prison. Now returning to town."

A deep, grating voice answered over the receiver. "Acknowledged."

9

Mack Bolan sat and watched with amusement as Valentina Svarzkova ate. She had gone through a salad, an order of loaded potato skins, a chicken-fried steak with french-fried potatoes and coleslaw, three beers and was busy wiping the bottom of her side of chili with the last of the complimentary corn bread. Bolan shook his head.

The shift away from communism to a free-market economy in Russia was still stumbling along a very rocky road, and food shortages were as bad if not worse than they had ever been. Svarzkova was having her first meal in an American restaurant, and the Russian agent was eating as if there would be no tomorrow.

The waitress approached. "So. Would you like dessert?"

Svarzkova nodded her head vigorously. She quickly scanned the menu again, and her eyes lit up decisively. "I would very much like a mud pie, please."

The waitress kept her own thoughts as she went off to fill the order.

Bolan finished his coffee. "So what kind of help can Baibakov expect from the Russian *mafiya* in America?"

"Russian *mafiya* is like any other group of organized criminals. They are organized, yet they are clannish and territorially divided. The more powerful and well-established groups probably would not help him. They would fear the trouble it could stir up. Younger, unestablished men, cowboys, as you Americans say, they might flock to a man like Baibakov for the money and the opportunity for action."

The waitress returned with a slice of mud pie. Bolan waited for the waitress to leave as the Russian agent attacked her dessert. "Your department was tracking the Red Falcons' activities in Bosnia before we became aware of them."

"Yes."

"What kind of targets would they choose in the United States?"

The Russian put down her fork. "As far as our intelligence was able to determine, the Red Falcons' agenda toward the United States is to punish you for your air attacks on Serbian positions outside of Sarajevo, and to drive you out of the conflict through terrorist actions."

The Executioner already knew that. "What kind of targets?"

A line furrowed Svarzkova's brow. "We believe their targets would be mission specific, rather than random."

Bolan frowned. "You mean targets directly linked with United States involvement in the former Yugoslavia."

"We believe so."

The Executioner calculated. He agreed with the findings of Russian Intelligence. The Red Falcons had an agenda, and random violence wasn't Igor Baibakov's style. He was a hunter; difficult targets wouldn't deter him. He would enjoy the challenge. That might be in their favor. The giant might well suffer from target fixation. The key now was to find his *mafiya* pipeline, and figure out his most likely U.S. targets.

Svarzkova pushed her empty dessert dish away. "Delicious."

Bolan put money on the table. "Come on. I have to contact my people."

The Russian looked at him closely. "You have had a thought."

"Yes, but I need to run it through the works and see what they can come up with."

"Do you think...?" She trailed off as she looked at Bolan's face.

"What is it?" He reached into the pocket of his jacket and

pulled out a device approximately the size of a personal pager. It had a small series of lights and a tiny readout display. The device had buzzed in his pocket, and when Bolan looked at it, the top little red light was blinking at him.

Svarzkova peered at the device. "What is it?"

Bolan looked out past the restaurant doors. The motel they were staying at was two blocks away. "Someone is in our room."

Her hand went unconsciously under her jacket. "You locked the door?"

Bolan peered at the blinking light. "I did. And I put the Do Not Disturb sign on the knob."

She glanced toward the street. "What do you wish to do?"

"If someone tracked us here, then they probably watched us go to the prison. If they know that, they probably watched us come in here, as well."

"Who would do this?"

There were only two possibilities. "It might be someone tracking our activities from another government agency."

The Russian's gaze narrowed. "But you do not believe so."

"No. Let's go out the back and take a look."

Svarzkova nodded and followed Bolan through the back of the restaurant. The cooks looked up as they went swiftly through the kitchen and went to the back door. Bolan drew the Beretta 93-R and stepped into the darkness. The day's clouds had passed, and the night was clear and cold. There were few lights in the alley behind the restaurant, but the moon was out and the stars were very bright. Bolan heard the whisper of metal leaving leather as Svarzkova drew her pistol. He moved to the side of the restaurant and examined the parking lot. It was almost nine o'clock, and a few cars were still there. His eyes were drawn to a brown van parked on the street by the lot's one exit. The windows were tinted. The vehicle hadn't been there when he and Svarzkova pulled in.

The Russian whispered at his elbow. "What do we do?"

"Go around to the other side of the restaurant. I'll wait sixty seconds for you to get in place. Then just back me up in whatever I do.''

The Russian agent nodded and moved swiftly back down the alley. Bolan looked closely at his Bronco, and his eyes narrowed. An occasional wisp of mist came from behind the right front wheel well. He and Svarzkova had been in the restaurant for an hour, more than enough time for the engine to cool.

It was someone breathing in the cold night air.

Bolan mentally counted sixty and stepped out with the Beretta extended in both hands. ''Freeze! Police! You're surrounded!''

A man rose from behind a station wagon two spaces from the Bronco and leveled a shotgun. The Beretta chugged as the Executioner squeezed off a 3-round burst. The first bullet shrieked sparks off of the station wagon's hood, and the second two stood the man up and sent him sprawling to the ground.

Bolan tracked the muzzle of the Beretta back to the Bronco as a man rose from behind the wheel well. The brown van's sliding door slammed back on its tracks, and thundering flame lit up the interior from the muzzles of several shotguns. Muted screaming came from inside the restaurant at the sound of the gunfire.

The soldier faded back around the corner as a hail of bullets smashed into the bricks of the restaurant's corner wall. The sound of a handgun firing on rapid semiautomatic suddenly broke out from the far side of the restaurant. In the parking lot a man screamed. Hearing the sound of feet running on pavement between the roaring of the shotguns, the Executioner came around the corner and flung himself prone.

Bits of brick rained down as a pattern of buckshot slammed into the wall overhead. One of the men from the van was running forward firing his shotgun as fast as he could pump the action. Bolan put the front sight of the Beretta on his midriff and fired. The man lurched as the 3-round burst stitched up his body, and he fell on top of his shotgun as he collapsed in a heap.

Bolan rose to one knee and tracked the Beretta for targets. A man with a shotgun crouched behind a large pickup as a handgun barked from the other side of the restaurant. The man flinched as the pickup rocked with the bullet strikes. He popped up when the pistol fell silent and slammed his shotgun across the hood. The soldier aimed low and squeezed the Beretta's trigger. The man jerked and flailed as the burst climbed up his calf and thigh. He collapsed back under cover, clutching a leg full of 9 mm hollowpoints. His shotgun still lay on the pickup's hood.

The Executioner dropped behind the bumper of a sedan and ejected the Beretta's nearly spent magazine. He slid in a fresh clip and slapped it home. A shotgun roared by the van.

A gunman stood between two cars and made the amateur's mistake of lowering his weapon to pump the action. Bolan cut him down with a burst from the Beretta as he raised it again. Svarzkova's weapon barked from the side of the restaurant, and sparks flew from the body of the attackers' van and its side mirror blew apart. A moment later the windshield imploded under the barrage, as well. Inside the van a man in the driver's seat fired back at Svarzkova with a handgun, the engine roaring as he put the vehicle into gear with his free hand.

The sliding door was still open, and from his angle Bolan could see the driver's seat dimly silhouetted through the shattered window. He aimed at the middle of the bucket seat and put two bursts through it. The driver jerked and slumped forward as the engine revved down to an idle.

The parking lot was suddenly quiet except for the screams coming from inside the restaurant and the moans of the fallen. Bolan kept the Beretta leveled. "Svarzkova!"

The Russian agent shouted back. "I am all right!"

Bolan stepped into the parking lot. He had personally accounted for five of the assailants. He scanned the immediate area. The man by the Bronco lay unmoving. Another gunner lay facedown near the entrance to the restaurant, his shotgun a few feet away. Svarzkova came out of cover with her smoking pistol in both hands, and Bolan spoke without taking his eyes off the scene. "I counted six, plus the driver."

Svarzkova looked out at the street. "Yes. I had the same."

The man by the pickup screamed in agony, and the words weren't in English. Svarzkova straightened as she heard her language and marched over to him. The man lay on his side, clutching his bleeding leg. He feebly reached a hand toward the shotgun lying on the hood. Svarzkova kicked his hand away and knelt on his chest. She leaned close to his face. *"Mafiya?"*

The man cursed and clutched at his wounded leg. Svarzkova yanked his head back by his hair and shoved the smoking muzzle of her 9 mm weapon between his eyebrows. *"Mafiya?"*

The man gritted his teeth at the hot metal between his eyes. *"Da! Da! Mafiya!"*

"Lieutenant!"

Svarzkova released the man and rose. "Yes?"

"The police will be here soon, and the FBI will be right behind them. Let them handle the interrogation."

"Give me five minutes, and he will tell me everything we need to know."

Bolan shook his head and glanced around the scene. "No. Think about it. They came for us with shotguns, in a restaurant parking lot. They're amateurs, Lieutenant, like you said, cowboys. They'll know little or nothing, and have been told less. Torturing a suspect will get you deported, and we still have business to attend to."

She heaved a deep breath as his words sunk in. "Yes. You are correct. These are not Red Falcons or Baibakov's men. These men were contracted out." She ejected her magazine and pushed in a full one. "What do we do now?"

"Let's see how many we have left alive, and then let me do all the talking with the police."

The Russian nodded in the affirmative. "Yes. Exactly so. Will there be problem?"

"I doubt it." Bolan looked down the street. "I'm willing to bet whoever was in our room has taken off, but I want to make sure."

The Executioner glanced around again at the carnage as a pair of police cruisers screamed onto the scene. He needed to have a talk with Kurtzman.

AARON KURTZMAN WHISTLED over the satellite link as Bolan recounted what happened. "Baibakov moved faster than anyone anticipated. You're lucky he didn't come for you himself. Our friend wouldn't have botched it up like those *mafiya* yahoos in the parking lot."

The Executioner was all too aware of that. The Russian hit men's amateur status had contributed greatly toward his and Svarzkova's survival.

Kurtzman paused in thought. "Why do you think he didn't do it himself?"

Bolan had considered that. "He and the Red Falcons have an agenda. I don't think he was willing to expose himself this early in the game. Leavenworth is a small town in the middle of Kansas with limited escape routes. Once whatever they're planning is in motion, though, I think all bets are off. He'll come for me if he can."

"We should have foreseen him staking out Ramzin. Logically it was our first step."

"It's easy to forget he's talented, as well as a psychopath, and I didn't see him setting up something that fast, either. Let's both make a note not to underestimate him again."

"So what's your plan now?"

"We pick up Ramzin and see what he can dig up for us from the Russian *mafiya*. Someone has to have heard something if hit men have been hired, and some of the big operators can't be too pleased about Baibakov running a terrorist operation stateside. It could be very bad for business."

"What can I do for you on this end?"

"Russian Intelligence thinks that whatever the Red Falcons and Baibakov are planning will be mission specific rather than a random act. Their mission is to punish us for our involvement in Bosnia, even more importantly, to drive us out. I need you to come up with a list of likely targets they might go for."

Kurtzman paused as he warmed up to the subject. "That's an interesting set of parameters."

Bolan nodded. "I can't guarantee them, but it's what Russian Intelligence believes and I agree with it, particularly with Baibakov involved."

"No. There's no guarantee with fanatics and psychopaths, but it's logical, and it might actually give us a list of targets we can actually defend."

"Great minds think alike."

"You're flattering yourself, Mack."

Bolan grinned. "I'm counting on that, Bear. I need the shortlist, as quick as you can come up with it."

"I'm already on it. Hunt and Akira are here at the Farm, and I'll roust Carmen out of bed. I'll send the idea back to Hal and see what the Feds can come up with from their end. We'll crunch the data, and I'll see if I can have something for you within twenty-four hours."

Bolan nodded. "I'll contact you as soon as I have anything else on my end. Striker out." He closed the link and turned to the motel-room door. When he and Svarzkova had arrived, they had found the door crudely jimmied open. The dresser drawers had been quickly ransacked and the rest of the room roughly searched, but the pair had kept everything except clothes and their personal weapons in the Bronco. Whoever had broken in had vanished. A quick electronic sweep had revealed no bugs.

"You can come in now," Bolan called out.

Svarzkova entered looking vaguely perturbed. She hadn't liked waiting outside while Bolan contacted the Farm. "The FBI is outside. They say they will post guards here at the motel for us for the night." She stared at the com-link. "You are finished."

Bolan stowed the satellite link back in its aluminum case.

"For tonight. By the way, you did very well in the parking lot."

The Russian brightened slightly. "Thank you. You did very well also."

Bolan glanced out the window. The lights atop Leavenworth prison's massive walls were dimly visible in the distance. "You take the bed. I'll sleep on the floor."

Svarzkova followed his gaze out toward the penitentiary, a line furrowed between her eyebrows. "Tomorrow we take Major Ramzin."

Bolan nodded and the agent's voice lowered slightly. "We must be very careful of Ramzin. He is not to be trusted. He is Spetsnaz. They were trained to operate behind enemy lines and infiltrate their targets. He speaks English fluently and has some Spanish he learned cross-training with Cuban troops, as well. He is well versed in escape-and-evasion tactics. I am certain he is entertaining ideas of killing us and escaping."

The Executioner's gaze stayed fixed on Leavenworth prison. He had no illusions about Ramzin's trustworthiness, either. In the hunt for Igor Baibakov, he would be a two-edged sword.

10

The guard presented Bolan with a sixth document. "And this one."

The Executioner signed with another unreadable scrawl. He had well over a dozen of them, and they would challenge even the cleverest handwriting analysis.

The guard nodded as the soldier handed him back the clipboard. All of the forms had been completed. It was no longer his responsibility. "He's all yours, sir."

Major Pietor Ramzin shuffled forward. He looked quite different out of his orange prisoner's uniform. He wore a dark turtleneck and sport coat, and he had shaved his beard and mustache. Bolan waved at his chains. "Unshackle him, but cuff his hands."

The second guard unlocked his waist and ankle chains, then cuffed Ramzin's wrists in front of him. Bolan took the key and motioned toward the door. "Come on."

The two men walked outside and went to the gate. Svarzkova stood by the Bronco, and she gave Ramzin a hard stare as he walked outside the prison. The Russian major paused outside the gate and stared up into the Kansas sky. He took a deep breath.

Bolan glanced up at the clear sky himself. "Smells better out here, doesn't it?"

"Yes. Much better." He peered at Bolan. "I have your word I will not be sent back here if I cooperate, yes?"

The Executioner looked him in the eye. "You have the

promise of the United States government. You cooperate, you go home. You screw up, you grow old and die in there.''

"I understand. But what of you? You do not desire to take vengeance on me?"

Bolan regarded Ramzin without emotion. "You cooperate, you go home."

The major looked into Bolan's stare for clues, but he could read nothing beyond the stony countenance. He nodded slowly. "Very well. Let us get on with it."

Bolan opened the Bronco's passenger door. "You sit in front with me."

Ramzin climbed into the truck and glanced in the back seat. Valentina Svarzkova sat behind him with her CZ-75 9 mm pistol cocked and locked in her hand. Ramzin grunted and turned his glance back to the road. "We must go to the airport."

Bolan started the truck. "Where from there?"

"To New York. There is a man there you need to meet. His name is Ivan Pushkin. There is a chance he may be very helpful to us."

Svarzkova spoke from the back. "And why will this Ivan Pushkin talk to you, much less help us?"

"He knew my father from the great patriotic war against the Nazis. They rode together on top of the same tank in the battle for Moscow. After the war my father stayed in the military, and Pushkin went into the black market. Years later Pushkin's son was sent to fight in Afghanistan. His son was an intellectual and a college student, and he spoke out against the government. Being sent to serve in Afghanistan was a common way of dealing with dissidents in the 1980s. Unfortunately Pushkin's son was somewhat anemic and not much of a soldier. He would not have fared well. Pushkin knew I was Spetsnaz, and he asked my father if I could do something for him. I could not manage a military deferment, but I had him assigned to my unit as a clerical-support officer, which kept him out of the front-line fighting. Pushkin remembers this. It was he who helped me establish my *mafiya* contacts when I first came to the United States. If I ask him, I believe he will help us now.''

Bolan calculated. It jibed with what he knew of the Russian *mafiya*. Unlike the Italian Mafia, Russian organized crime was based more on groups of friends and associates than actual family clans. The Russian *mafiya* was also very young and open to entrepreneurs. Men who had been in the military together or had grown up on the same streets carried these allegiances onward into ventures in organized crime. Ramzin's story was entirely plausible. "How well established is he in the *mafiya?*"

Ramzin grinned wolfishly. "Very well established. He was one of the first to come to the United States. He and his son run much of the *mafiya*'s action in New England. They are very well connected, both here and back home in Russia. If anyone can help us in our endeavor, Pushkin can.''

The Executioner took the cellular phone off of the dashboard and handed it to Ramzin. "We'll be at the airport within half an hour. It's time for you to make a phone call.''

IGOR BAIBAKOV STARED down from his full height at the man standing before him. The man refused to look up and meet the giant's eyes. Boris Izeshkov was a large man, but he was dwarfed by Baibakov's presence. Baibakov stood over him and blocked out the warehouse's overhead light. A woman and several armed Serbs stood behind him and looked at Izeshkov in open disdain. Izeshkov's two disarmed bodyguards stared at their shoes and hoped they wouldn't be killed along with their boss. Baibakov stared unblinkingly at the Russian mobster and considered the man's immediate survival.

Izeshkov had promised him that his men were heavy hitters, who could kill the American commando with no problem. Baibakov shook his head and grinned wonderingly at the man's hubris. A whole platoon of Spetsnaz hadn't been able to kill the American before, and now this gangster had gotten six of his buffoons killed and a seventh in custody. Baibakov hadn't expected miracles, yet he had given these men the priceless advantage of surprise, and still they had failed utterly.

The American commando lived, and the hunt was on.

Baibakov continued to stare down at the man and let him sweat. The man stank of fear, and the giant despised him. Still, the operation in Kansas hadn't been totally without value. Baibakov now knew for certain the American was hunting him, and he knew that the commando had talked to Ramzin. An unknown woman was accompanying the commando in his efforts, and she had engaged in the firefight in the parking lot. She had also apparently given a good account of herself. That was intriguing, and Baibakov wondered who she might be and what she represented.

The giant relented. He still required this man's services for the present time. "You have acquired what I asked for?"

Izeshkov's shoulders sagged with visible relief. The subject was being changed, and in this regard he hadn't failed. "Yes. Everything you asked for is here, in these crates, as you specified." Izeshkov waved an arm at several large, long crates on the floor of the warehouse.

Baibakov nodded. "Open them."

Izeshkov pointed at the crates, and his two bodyguards levered the top crate open. They reached in and lifted out a Barrett .50-caliber semiautomatic sniper rifle. They set the rifle on the crate lid and began to pull out spare magazines and boxes of ammunition. Baibakov grinned with pleasure as he stooped and picked up the weapon and checked the action. The clack of the bolt was smooth and positive. He nodded in satisfaction. "Good. The others?"

The bodyguards opened the other two cases and began to pull out weapons. There was a wide assortment of rifles, pistols and explosives. The Red Falcons began to check the weapons and equipment thoroughly while the *mafiya* men looked on nervously. Madchen Krstic finished checking the action of a Dragunov sniper rifle, and her dark eyes glittered as she nodded.

Everything Baibakov had demanded was scrupulously accounted for. The Russian was satisfied. Boris Izeshkov would make a better supply officer than *mafiya* street soldier, but at least he was good for something.

The *mafiya* man smiled shakily. "It is all there, as you can see. Do you require anything else?"

Baibakov handed the Barrett .50 to one of the Red Falcons and locked his gaze with Izeshkov. The man flinched but was unable to look away from the gray tombstones of Baibakov's eyes. The giant nodded slowly. "Yes. I have another job for you to perform. Listen to me very carefully."

A BEAUTIFUL REDHEADED secretary smiled up at Bolan dazzlingly as she pushed the intercom button. Her accent was barely detectable. "Mr. Pushkin will see you now."

Bolan, Svarzkova and Ramzin, uncuffed, went through a set of magnificent double wooden doors and entered the office of Ivan Pushkin's "legitimate" business headquarters.

Pushkin was squat and bald, but solid looking for a veteran of World War II. He sat behind a huge oak desk in his Manhattan office. His son was tall and thin, with a long emaciated-looking face. He looked almost nothing like his father as he stood beside him. Only the two men's matching steely blue eyes betrayed their kinship. The younger man suddenly grinned and stood at ramrod attention as Ramzin entered the room.

Ramzin shook his head in mock disgust. "Well! If it isn't Private Pushkin." The major returned the salute. "It is good to see you again, Anatoly." He turned to the elder Pushkin. "You look well, Ivan."

Pushkin regarded Ramzin with open speculation. He glanced at Bolan and raised an eyebrow at Svarzkova before returning his gaze to the major. "You look well, Ramzin." His tone fell flat. "I had heard you were in prison."

"Yes, I was."

"And now?"

"Now I am out."

Pushkin nodded, but his eyes looked noncommittal. "Ah."

He looked again at Bolan and Svarzkova and spoke in Russian. "And who is this American?"

Ramzin looked at Bolan for a moment. It was an interesting question. He thought about it for a moment and shrugged. "He represents the interests of the United States government."

Bolan spoke up in Russian. "That is essentially correct."

Pushkin blinked. It wasn't welcome news. "And the woman?"

Ramzin cleared his throat. "She is Lieutenant Valentina Svarzkova, an agent of Russian Military Intelligence."

Pushkin lost his poker face and gaped at Ramzin. "Why have you brought them here?"

The major folded his arms across his chest. "I was compelled."

Pushkin's face began to flush red. "No one ever compelled Pietor Ramzin to do anything. You brought them here in your own self-interest."

Ramzin shrugged. "I do not deny it."

Anatoly Pushkin's hand eased under his jacket as his father grew steadily angrier. Ivan Pushkin shook his head in enraged wonder. "So, Ramzin, you have become a Judas. You would sell me out? I am a comrade of your father's! I have known you since you were old enough to crawl!"

Ramzin shook his head. "No, I did not sell you out. You are not being investigated. These people are here to seek your help."

"My help?"

"Yes."

Bolan stepped forward. "I want Igor Baibakov."

Both of the Pushkins stared at Bolan in surprise. "I gather you know of him."

Anatoly sighed and spoke. "Yes, I know of him. I met him in Afghanistan under Major Ramzin's command."

Bolan nodded. "And now he is here in America."

Ivan Pushkin stared at Ramzin. "What are you getting out of this?"

The major looked him in the eye. "Freedom."

Pushkin nodded and turned back to Bolan. "Assuming I knew anything about Igor Baibakov, what would I get out of helping you?"

The Executioner locked eyes with Pushkin. "Igor Baibakov is in the United States. He is aiding and abetting a Serbian terrorist group known as the Red Falcons. They're going to strike American targets, and I'm not going to allow that to happen. These people are at war with the United States, and I consider anyone helping them, or withholding information about them, to be at war with the United States, as well. If you don't help us, I'll be forced to tell the FBI that Ivan Pushkin was uncooperative in stopping a terrorist campaign on United States soil. You and your organization will then have the full attention of not only the FBI, but the CIA, Interpol and the IRS, as well. Do you understand?"

Pushkin gazed at Bolan stonily, then turned to Ramzin. "You have brought a wolf into my house, Pietor."

Ramzin shrugged. "It was this or grow old and die in jail. Besides, you are indebted to me, Ivan Pushkin."

The old man suppressed a flinch, and Anatoly glared at his former commander. "My father has already been of great help to you, Major. It is not his fault you landed yourself in an American jail."

Ramzin sighed. "That is true, but things are as they are. He will help me again, or all of us will fall."

Ivan Pushkin's shoulders sank. "Very well. I will assist you. It will take me some time to find out these things. I must call in favors from other organizations. Come back tomorrow, and I will give you all that I can."

Bolan nodded. "You have twenty-four hours." The Executioner strode from the office with Ramzin and Svarzkova in tow. Even before the office door had closed, the Pushkin family was speaking in rapid and angry Russian. They left Pushkin's office suite in silence. Bolan did not speak until they were in the elevator.

"They'll help?" Bolan asked when they entered the elevator.

Ramzin watched the floor numbers as the car started to descend and held out his hands for the handcuffs. He answered as Bolan took out the manacles. "I believe they will. You have put us both in a desperate situation, I—"

Ramzin spun on his heel and slammed his elbow into the pit of Svarzkova's stomach. The woman gasped and doubled over. He yanked the CZ-75 9 mm pistol out from the holster behind her back as she sagged to her knees. The click of the safety coming off was very loud.

Bolan thrust his foot into the Russian's solar plexus with all of his weight behind it. Ramzin winced in pain, and the report of the gun in the confines of the elevator was deafening. Sparks shrieked off of the gleaming elevator wall as the bullet ricocheted. Bolan flung the handcuffs into Ramzin's face and grasped the Russian's wrist as he closed with him. The pistol fired into the elevator roof as the Executioner's fist crashed against Ramzin's jaw. The Russian bounced off the elevator wall and brought his knee up at Bolan's groin. The big American raised his own knee to block and lunged forward, his forehead meeting the bridge of Ramzin's nose with the cracking of cartilage.

The Russian's head snapped back, and Bolan followed through with an elbow smash under Ramzin's chin. As the man started to buckle, Bolan drove his fist into the man's biceps, forcing him to drop the gun. Svarzkova's pistol twisted and fell out of Ramzin's suddenly nerveless fingers and clattered to the floor.

Svarzkova sucked in a strangled breath as Bolan helped her to her feet. She took her pistol and leaned heavily against the elevator railing as she fought to draw air into her lungs. The Executioner stared down at Ramzin. His elbow had split the man's chin, and blood leaked out of his broken nose. Bolan knew that Ramzin wouldn't be able to move his right arm the next day. He couldn't blame the man for attacking. The Executioner knew that he, too, would attempt to take out his captors and effect his own escape at the first opportunity. He could understand why Ramzin had turned on him. He just couldn't afford to tolerate it.

Bolan took out his handkerchief and flipped it to the bleeding Russian. "That was your one freebie, Ramzin. Next time I'll just kill you."

The Russian glared and wiped his mouth as the elevator door pinged and opened on the lobby level of the building. Two businessmen in suits carrying briefcases stared in shock at the car's occupants. Bolan grabbed Ramzin by his lapels and yanked him to his feet as Svarzkova holstered her pistol and picked up the manacles.

The businessmen gave them a wide berth as they dragged Ramzin out of the elevator. Once they were in the lobby, Svarzkova snapped the handcuffs around the major's wrists, hissing several sizzling remarks at him in Russian. Ramzin stared dourly into the distance. Bolan halted at the door.

"I still need the information from Pushkin, and I'll need your help in following up on it. As far as I'm concerned, this incident is settled, and you're still going home at the end of this. But I want you and I to understand each other. My government has promised to let you rot in jail if you attempt to escape or hinder our operation. Understand my words, Ramzin. If you make a move like that again, you don't go back to Leavenworth. I kill you. Do we understand each other?"

Ramzin nodded and spit some blood on the floor. "Exactly so. We understand each other perfectly."

Svarzkova spoke icily. "I believe it would be safest if we break his arms."

Bolan almost smiled. Unfortunately, crippling Ramzin would probably not help his ability to deal with the other Russian *mafiya* bosses. "No, just kill him if he makes a move. Let's get him to a hospital so they can fix his face, then I need to see what my people have dug up for me."

It was time to have another talk with Kurtzman.

11

"What have you got for me, Bear?" Mack Bolan asked.

Aaron Kurtzman looked at the pile of computer readouts in front of him. "The shortlist."

The Executioner's voice sounded skeptical. "How short is it?"

Kurtzman shook his head. "It isn't."

There was a pause on the link. "Shorten it."

The computer expert leaned back in his chair. He and the Stony Man cybernetics team had been crunching data nonstop for the past twenty-four hours. "That could be difficult, Mack. Even assuming that the Red Falcons will go for specific targets related to United States intervention in Bosnia, the list is extensive. There are literally hundreds of military targets, from bases involved in sending troops and equipment to individual officers and their families involved. There are hundreds of civilian businesses and organizations involved in supporting and supplying our troops over there. They've all been contacted and put on full alert."

Bolan's tone was wry. "There isn't much I can do to safeguard a military base that it can't do better on its own, and I can't cover hundreds of civilian organizations."

"I know. That brings us down to individuals."

"Like who?"

"The question is where to start."

There was a pause. "Narrow it down to targets on the East Coast."

Kurtzman punched keys on the computer. "Any particular reason?"

"Call it a hunch. It's the staging ground for any troops or military equipment we send, and it's where the seat of our government is located."

"I agree, but most of our targets on the shortlist were on the East Coast already. It narrows things down a little but not much, and it still leaves everyone from the President on down to lobbyists and peace organizations."

"I'm betting they'll do something that will make a real statement, but short of starting an all-out war between the United States and Serbia. I don't think assassinating the President of the United States would help their cause much. It's much more likely to put Americans up in arms. They want to drive us out. Work on that angle."

Kurtzman shifted in his chair. "I need more information, Mack. At this point we're still looking at needles in a dozen haystacks, and that's just targets. Our opponents still have the entire United States to hide in."

"I know." The line was silent for a moment. "I may have some leads for you tomorrow. The Russian *mafiya* is territorial just like other criminal organizations. If I can get a lead on who Baibakov has contacted and where, that may give us clues about his targets."

"That would be extremely helpful."

"I thought it might."

"Be careful around Pushkin. He's dangerous, and you've made him very unhappy."

Bolan's tone lightened. "I'm doing him a favor. If we don't get Baibakov before he strikes, the entire Russian *mafiya* in the United States will be crucified in the media for helping him. People will demand retaliation, and there will be one hell of a witch-hunt to make them pay. Once he gets over being angry, he'll figure that out on his own if he hasn't already."

"I suspect you're right, Mack, but do me a favor and be careful anyway."

IVAN PUSHKIN PEERED at Ramzin's face but decided to keep his thoughts to himself. Ramzin's chin was freshly stitched, and a bandage covered the swollen bridge of his nose. The left side of his jaw had a lump on it, and the Russian major's eyes peered out sourly from raccoonlike bruising.

Anatoly Pushkin was openly appalled. He had naturally heard about the ruckus in the elevator, and the idea that someone could defeat his former commander in close combat was nearly blasphemy. The beaten and bruised proof sitting stiffly at the conference table between the American and the woman intelligence agent was distinctly unsettling. He peered at Bolan with wary respect.

The Executioner decided to skip formalities. "What do you have for me?"

Ivan Pushkin grunted. "You are direct. Very well. I have called in some favors and put my ear to the ground about Baibakov. I can tell you he has received weapons and supplies."

Bolan nodded. The giant's primary instinct would be to arm himself immediately. "What kind?"

Pushkin pulled a pair of reading glasses from his vest pocket and opened a manila folder. "Twelve 9 mm Uzi submachine guns, twelve sound suppressors for same, a pair of Smith & Wesson .44 Magnum revolvers, twelve .22-caliber silenced Beretta pistols, three dozen M-16 rifles, three Dragunov sniper rifles, a pair of Barrett .50-caliber semiautomatic rifles, three dozen Browning Hi-Power 9 mm pistols of Hungarian manufacture, fifty pounds of C-4 plastic explosive, three crates of Russian-manufacture RGD-5 antipersonnel grenades, twenty-four grenades to a crate, four RPG-7 rocket-propelled grenade launchers, with ten rockets per weapon." Pushkin removed his reading glasses and smiled thinly. "At least according to my sources." He passed the list around the table to Bolan. The Executioner scanned it.

"What *mafiya* organizations has Baibakov contacted in the United States?"

Pushkin sighed and flipped a page in his file. "As you are

probably aware, he made contact with one of the minor local *mafiya* heads in Kansas City, a man named Boris Izeshkov." Pushkin paused. "A contract was put out on your life. Your description has been circulated, and that contract is still open. The price on your head is one million dollars. There is also a contract out on you, Lieutenant Svarzkova, though, like the American, they do not know who you are."

Svarzkova looked up from taking notes. "Even if they did, I do not believe that my status as a Russian Military Intelligence agent acting on the behalf of the motherland would stop them from putting a bullet in my brain."

Pushkin snorted and turned an amused eye on Ramzin. "There is also a contract out on you, Major Ramzin, and you are very well known."

Ramzin shrugged indifferently and gazed out of the high-rise window. Bolan had to give the giant grudging admiration. Baibakov was using excellent strategy. Wherever he went, he would tip off the local *mafiya* shooters that there were three very valuable heads for the taking. It complicated things immensely. Wherever the hunt led, armed killers would be waiting. Bolan looked over at Ramzin. The one good thing about it was that it helped ensure the Spetsnaz officer's loyalty. With a million dollars on his head, if Ramzin escaped and tried to disappear into the Russian *mafiya* network, he would disappear permanently. His best insurance was to see the contract nullified by Baibakov's death.

"Where did Baibakov get the weapons?"

Pushkin glanced at his notes. "They were acquired in California and sent to Kansas City, where Baibakov received them. I will save you some trouble. Boris Izeshkov has disappeared along with the inner cadre of his men. I believe Baibakov and his forces have left Kansas, as well. My sources could not discover their next destination."

Bolan grimaced. He had expected that. The trail from Kansas had just gone cold. "Who else has he contacted?"

"According to my sources, he has been making inquiries by proxy in Washington, D.C."

Svarzkova looked up at Bolan. The Executioner wasn't surprised. Baibakov was running a terrorist operation, and Washington was the capital of the country. "I need names."

Pushkin frowned. "That may require time and money. Not all of my colleagues are as aware of their patriotic duty to our host country as I am."

Bolan smiled, but it didn't reach his eyes. "There's no time. Tell them the man who can give me Igor Baibakov can name the dollar amount and the Swiss bank he wants it in." He locked eyes with Pushkin. "That includes you."

Pushkin grunted and shifted in his chair. "I have one other piece of information for you. It is somewhat strange."

"What's that?"

Pushkin's blocky face wrinkled quizzically. "Baibakov inquired about the state of Vermont."

"Why?"

Pushkin spread his hands. "I do not know."

"What kind of organization does the Russian *mafiya* have in Vermont?"

"Little or none that I know of. I have never heard of Russians emigrating there in any numbers."

Bolan mentally filed that away. "What do you...?" Bolan trailed off as he glanced out the window. There was series of long thin shadows, like light shining past ropes.

Pushkin frowned. "What is it?"

Bolan's hand slid under his jacket to the grips of the Beretta 93-R. "What days does your building get its windows cleaned?"

Pushkin shrugged. "Wednesdays, I believe."

The Executioner drew the Beretta and flipped the selector switch to 3-round burst. "We're about to be attacked."

Outside the conference-room doors one of Pushkin's bodyguards shouted. There was a quick series of soft thumps, like a boxer doing a speed drill against a pillow, and the door frame rattled as something slumped against it. There was another shout, and Pushkin's secretary screamed. There was a loud gunshot, then another burst of suppressed gunfire.

Svarzkova and the Pushkins drew their pistols. Bolan kept his eye on the window.

Two hands suddenly reached down from above and slapped two disks the size of hockey pucks against the conference room's floor-length window. Bolan dropped below the level of the conference table and roared, "Down!"

The high-rise window blew inward in a storm of flying glass as the shaped charges detonated. The heavy double doors to the room shuddered as something struck them, but they held. Svarzkova began to fire her pistol through the wooden doors. Bolan kept his eyes on the shattered window that was now open to the sky. Pulleys squealed, and a window washer's scaffold fell in front of the window, occupied by four men in ski masks. They steadied themselves for a moment from the scaffold's sudden drop, then leveled Uzis into the conference room.

Bolan put the front sight of the 93-R onto one of the gunners and fired. The gunman staggered back as he took three rounds in the chest and collapsed to the plank floor of the scaffold. Splinters erupted from the tabletop as a long burst of automatic fire walked across the surface toward the Executioner. He hit his assailant with a burst from the Beretta, but the man kept firing. His second burst stitched upward through the man's neck and head, and the guy fell forward into the conference room.

The Pushkins had been sitting at the wrong side of the table and were without cover. Ivan Pushkin shuddered as a long burst from an Uzi tore into him. His son resolutely fired a small-caliber pistol into his father's assailant, but the gunman didn't go down. Bolan put a burst into the man's chest, and he fell back against the scaffold rail, then toppled over.

The fourth man kept firing, and Anatoly Pushkin spun out of his crouch as a bullet struck him in the shoulder. Bolan fired the Beretta, and sparks shot off the man's Uzi as the bullets struck his weapon. The submachine gun fell from the gunman's bloodied hands. The Executioner's second burst snapped the man's head back, then toppled forward into the scaffold railing and hung there.

Svarzkova shouted, "Mike!"

Bolan whirled. Svarzkova was no longer covering the doors. Her pistol was leveled between Major Ramzin's eyes. The Spetsnaz officer's hand hovered over one of the gunmen's fallen Uzis. Ramzin didn't move a muscle as his eyes flicked sideways to lock with Bolan's.

"Gun! I need a gun! We are in this together now, yes? Without a gun I am simply a target!"

Bolan knew from bitter experience that Pietor Ramzin could more than pull his own weight in a gunfight. The Executioner fired a burst through the double doors and said, "Let him have it!"

Svarzkova hesitated for a split second, then turned her attention back to the doors. Ramzin scooped up the weapon, then pulled several spare magazines from one of the dead gunmen's bodies.

Bolan moved to the far side of the conference table. His burst hadn't gone through the door. The oak panels were thick enough to stop 9 mm hollowpoints. No bullets were coming back from the other side, either, which told Bolan what his assailants had loaded their Uzis with. Svarzkova's weapon was loaded with full-metal-jacket solids, and they were punching through the door with no problem. That alone had kept the men outside the door from attacking.

"How's your father?" Bolan asked Anatoly.

The man's voice shook from the other side of the table. "My father is dead."

Ramzin checked the action of his commandeered Uzi. "They will either retreat or they will blow the door."

Bolan nodded. "Check the bodies. See if the men had any more explosives."

As Svarzkova put four more rounds through the door, Ramzin crept around the table and checked the bodies. "Yes, this man has two more in his bag."

"Bring them."

The Executioner moved quickly toward the door. He could hear voices speaking quietly in Russian on the other side. Ramzin moved to the other side of the door and tossed Bolan one of the explosives. Bolan saw Ramzin had liberated a pistol, as well. He turned his attention to the charge, a small dark, conical cake of high explosive with a simple three-second pull fuse. There was a strip of paper on the bottom, and beneath it the charge was smeared with adhesive. Bolan pulled the paper away and put the explosive at the juncture of the two doors near the top of the frame. Ramzin nodded and placed his near the bottom.

Bolan placed his hand on the fuse and looked at Svarzkova and Anatoly Pushkin. "Follow us after we go through." The agent reloaded her pistol and nodded. Pushkin acknowledged the order, clutching one of the fallen Uzis.

The Executioner put his hand on the fuse and nodded at Ramzin. "Now."

Both men pulled the fuses and took several steps back. The walls shuddered as the charges detonated and the double doors flew off their hinges and back into the lobby. The Executioner came around the door firing. Ramzin's Uzi hissed into life beside him.

Two men had been about to put charges on their side of the door. One man was sprawled in the middle of the lobby, and another lay beneath one of the doors. The explosion had momentarily stunned the other two men, and Bolan put two bursts into the gunner on the left. The man on the right shuddered and fell as Ramzin cut him down. The major shot the man on the floor and crouched as he looked for more targets.

The man pinned under the door groaned as Bolan stepped onto it with both feet. Ramzin moved to the door to Anatoly Pushkin's office, then checked Ivan's while Svarzkova and Anatoly moved out and covered the door that led to the rest of the twenty-third floor. Ramzin continued his sweep and peered carefully out into the hallway. He nodded satisfactorily. "We are clear."

Bolan knelt and ripped the mask from the face of the pinned

man. He was a blond young man in his early twenties, with a face like a hatchet. He swore up at Bolan vehemently in Russian. His eyes flared as Ramzin walked over, and he screamed "Traitor!" at the top of his lungs.

Ramzin shot him between the eyes.

The major stared at Bolan dispassionately as he slung his Uzi. "He was free-lance scum. He could tell us nothing of value."

Svarzkova's pistol was leveled at Ramzin. She spit on the floor, and her voice shook with loathing. "You are a butcher."

Ramzin's eyes glittered. "I will have the *mafiya* filth know, if they come against us they die."

Bolan let it go. Ramzin stooped and picked up a second 9 mm Hi-Power pistol from one of the dead assassins. Svarzkova scowled but said nothing as he began going from body to body and stuffing spare magazines into his pockets.

The Executioner turned and walked back into the conference room. Anatoly Pushkin knelt over his father and cradled his head. Ivan Pushkin had taken six rounds through his torso. His eyes were rolled back in their sockets, and an ocean of blood stained the carpet around his body. Anatoly seemed to be unaware of the wound in his own shoulder as he looked up at Bolan with tears in his eyes. "How has this happened?"

Bolan reloaded the Beretta and holstered it. The answer was simple. Once again Igor Baibakov had acted faster than anyone anticipated.

"Your father's inquiries rebounded on him. Baibakov must have put out the word he would pay big money to anyone with information on people asking about him. Your father did a lot of poking around last night. It must have gotten back to Baibakov. He tipped off the New York hitters that we were here. Between myself, Svarzkova and Ramzin there was three million dollars in this room waiting to be collected. He probably offered money for your head and your father's, as well. That kind of money attracts real hitters, not just street thugs." Bolan waved a hand at the masked bodies. "These men were professionals, probably ex–Russian military or police."

Anatoly looked about the room. "Yes. What you say is sensible."

Bolan's face grew grim. "There is one other thing to consider. They knew we'd all be here in this room, and they knew when. Someone in your organization must have talked."

Anatoly nodded slowly. His tears had dried, and his face was almost expressionless. His voice was very calm. "That person will be found and killed." The younger Pushkin looked up at Bolan steadily. "I hold you partially responsible for my father's death. But he chose to help you, and helping you kill Baibakov is the best vengeance he can have. You have my word I will use my father's resources to help you any way I can to see Baibakov die. After that, there is no friendship between us."

"I understand." Bolan left Anatoly alone with the body of his father. Anatoly wouldn't forget the man who brought Igor Baibakov and Pietor Ramzin back into their lives. Bolan suspected there might well be a price on his head even after Baibakov was captured or killed.

12

Mack Bolan locked the hotel door. He and Lieutenant Svarzkova had checked into a small hotel in Queens as Mr. and
Mrs. Mike Belasko, much to Svarzkova's amusement. Ramzin
was busy in the room next door. The major had politely asked
Bolan for a knife. They had stopped the cab at an Army-
surplus store, and Ramzin had picked out a used Marine Corps
Ka-bar fighting knife. Through the thin walls Bolan could
dimly hear the Russian rhythmically running the blade over a
sharpening stone he had bought.

Svarzkova sat on the bed and looked at him reproachfully.
Bolan sighed. "I know, if you had it your way Ramzin would
be hog-tied and chained to the foot of the bed."

The Russian agent's voice was bitter. "If I had my way, he
would be in the morgue with a bullet in his brain."

"He has a price on his head like we do. He won't be safe
in the United States or Russia until Baibakov is dead, and he
knows it. Besides, we need him, and he won't be much help
in a firefight if we keep him bound and gagged."

Svarzkova frowned and looked away. Russian Military Intelligence was in command of Spetsnaz. As one of its agents,
she considered Ramzin a renegade and a traitor to his country.
She made no effort to hide her feelings about having him
unshackled and armed in the next room. Bolan's eyes narrowed as he looked at her. Her hands were shaking. "How
are you holding up?"

Svarzkova looked down at her hands and smiled ruefully.
"No. I am fine, it is just…"

"Things are happening pretty fast."

"Yes. Things are happening very fast."

Bolan nodded. "This was your first shoot-out."

The Russian agent reddened slightly. "This has been my first two shoot-outs. In Russia I am a field operative. I have been undercover. I have made arrests. I have drawn my gun. But this…"

Bolan understood the feeling. Senior Lieutenant Valentina Svarzkova was in a foreign country and had been ambushed by heavily armed assassins twice in the past three days. They had spent the other half of the past seventy hours in cars and planes tracking down criminals. She was suffering from combat fatigue. Bolan put his hands on his hips. Svarzkova was a lieutenant in the Russian military. In Bolan's experience there was only one thing to be done.

"Call room service. Have them send up a bottle of vodka."

Svarzkova almost clapped her hands with glee. "Excellent!" Bolan's eyebrow rose as the agent flung herself across the bed, grabbed the phone off the nightstand and punched in the number for room service.

"Yes. I would like a bottle of vodka."

Bolan picked up the satellite link. "I'm going to go contact my people."

Svarzkova nodded distractedly without looking up. "Yes. Stolichnaya, please. On ice. With two glasses."

Bolan took the satellite link into the bathroom and opened the case. He pressed several buttons and connected with Kurtzman.

"We heard about your skirmish in Manhattan from Hal. Sounds like Baibakov isn't wasting any time."

"He isn't sparing any expense, either."

"He's put a price on your head?"

"Along with Lieutenant Svarzkova and Ramzin."

"How much?"

"A million each."

Kurtzman grunted. "The Italian Mafia used to have a lot more."

Bolan grinned slightly. "I've been marked down. But these guys were pros. They used a two-pronged attack, shaped charges for entry and they had silenced weapons. The ante has gone up from shotguns in parking lots." He connected a portable fax machine to the link and opened a folder. "Pushkin managed to get us some solid information before he was killed. I'm sending over Baibakov's shopping list now."

Bolan waited while the information was bounced off the satellite and back down to Virginia. A moment later Kurtzman whistled. "Our friend isn't playing around, is he?"

Bolan looked at his own copy of the list. "What does this list tell you?"

There was a moment of silence while the wheels turned in Kurtzman's mind. "It tells me Baibakov has at least half a platoon of hard-core soldiers at his disposal. I'm betting the .44 Magnum revolvers and the Barrett .50s are personal weapons."

Bolan nodded. "What else do you notice?"

"I'm way ahead of you. He acquired only a relatively small quantity of plastic explosive. More than enough to make a couple of car bombs, but nowhere near enough to blow up anything of major significance. I think the plastique is more for tactical use than as their primary weapon. Baibakov has outfitted his people like soldiers going off to a war. I don't think they're planning on blowing up the White House or the United Nations Building. My bet is they intend to pull off some kind of military-style raid, and they're going to do it in strength. That's assuming, of course, that Baibakov hasn't picked up a few tons of ammonia fertilizer and some trucks we haven't heard about. I also don't believe all his men are Red Falcons. I'd bet he's picked up some Russian shooters from the *mafiya* who are looking for action. He'd want only the best, though. I'd expect ex-military men who are fluent in English."

Bolan smiled. Those were his thoughts exactly. "I have more, but it's not good. Baibakov has contacted the Russian *mafiya* in the capital."

Kurtzman sighed. "Well, that was to be expected. It still doesn't help much. D.C. is a big city, and it must have hundreds of legitimate targets for the Red Falcons."

"I have one other piece of information. It's a strange one. Pushkin mentioned that Baibakov had made some sort of cryptic inquiry about Vermont."

For a moment the line was silent. "Vermont?"

"Vermont."

Kurtzman sounded puzzled. "You mean the state."

"That's right. Run that through your shortlist and see if it cross-references with anything."

"Hold on." The Executioner waited while Kurtzman crunched data, and then he heard the magic word. "Bingo."

"What have we got?"

"We have Eudora McCain, United States senator from the Green Mountain State."

A line drew down between Bolan's eyebrows. "She sounds vaguely familiar."

Kurtzman punched more computer keys. "She red-flagged immediately when I cross-referenced Vermont. She's one of the individual targets near the top of our shortlist."

"What makes her a priority?"

"She's always been very cause oriented, and in the past year the fighting in Bosnia has risen to the top of her agenda."

Bolan frowned. "So she joined the peace bandwagon."

"Well, she actually seems more intellectually honest than that. Senator McCain went to Bosnia early in 1995 and toured with a Senate subcommittee investigative team. She saw one of the mass graves being excavated outside of a Croatian village. It had nearly a hundred civilian bodies in it, most of them women and children. Apparently McCain was profoundly affected by it. Ever since her return to the United States, she has been huge in spearheading the effort to send U.S. peacekeeping troops in to stop the fighting. She defends it nearly every day on the floor of the Senate."

The Executioner stared at the bathroom wall without seeing it as the scenes of past atrocities in dozens of conflicts ran unbidden through his mind. He had seen mass graves and the terrible toll civil wars took on the population. He couldn't fault Eudora McCain. Whether or not to intervene in a civil war was a terrible decision to make. You either risked getting your own people killed in a conflict that wasn't theirs, or else you sat on your hands and watched women and children die while you did nothing. Senator McCain had gone with her conscience. Now she was a target.

"In Washington the Secret Service can guard her better than I can. What's her situation in Vermont like?"

Kurtzman searched his file. "Married, with two daughters, both of them away in college. She lives in a big house on Lake Champlain outside of Burlington. Her husband is William McCain, a local entrepreneur, very wealthy, has a lot of clout in the state. He financed his wife's campaign." He paused. "The Senate is scheduled to take a break after their budget session next week. Most of the senators will be going home for a three-day weekend. How do you want to play it?"

Bolan considered the situation. "Have Hal get a Secret Service team on Senator McCain immediately, but keep them low profile while she's in D.C. I don't want to tip off Baibakov."

"You want Vermont to be the trap."

Bolan nodded. "There isn't much in Vermont to stop him. It's a small state and sparsely populated. As I recall, farming and winter tourism are its major industries. Our senator lives in a house by a lake. It's just about as perfect a situation as Baibakov and the Red Falcons could ask for. His only problem will be keeping himself and his men out of sight. I expect most of them may have already been staged."

"Hal will have to clear this with the President."

"Well, get on it."

"So you're off to Vermont in the meantime?"

"I'll need to recon the area. See if you can have Jack and a plane at JFK in the morning, and I'll need my full war load racked and ready to go on the bird."

"Can do. Anything else?"

Bolan rose from the edge of the tub. "No. I'll contact you when I get to Vermont. Keep me abreast of anything new."

"Roger and out."

The line clicked silent, and Bolan stowed the satellite link and the fax. Svarzkova grinned at him as he came out of the bathroom. A bottle of vodka sat on the nightstand, and she held two glasses in her hands. "What is the news?"

"We're going to Vermont."

The agent paused in thought. "It does not sound familiar."

"It's a state to the north of here—it borders on Quebec."

Svarzkova nodded thoughtfully. "Ah."

Bolan glanced at the bottle of vodka by the bed. It sat in a bucket of ice. A good fifth of it was already missing. "You started without me."

The woman didn't seem overwhelmed with guilt about it. "Yes. I have." She stood and handed Bolan a glass. It held a stiff three fingers of straight Russian vodka. The agent held up her glass. "To happiness."

Bolan clinked his glass against hers. *"Tovarisch."*

It was an old Russian toast; the word simply meant "comrades." Svarzkova nodded happily. *"Da, tovarisch."* She rolled the shot back in one smooth swallow. Her cheeks flushed as she smiled.

Bolan tilted back his glass, and the cold vodka blossomed into burning heat in his stomach. He looked Svarzkova in the eye. "I gather you're feeling better."

She met his gaze in a speculative fashion. "I am working on it."

Bolan could see where this was going. He lowered his glass. "This might be considered inappropriate."

The Russian agent shrugged carelessly. "Tonight I wish to be drunk and behave inappropriately. Tomorrow we may die."

The Executioner let out a slow breath as Svarzkova watched his eyes. The grim truth of her words was well-known to both of them. Igor Baibakov was a trained killer, and he was at large with squads of well-armed fanatics behind him. Bolan and Svarzkova both had prices on their heads.

Bolan held up his glass. "Well, you'd better pour me another, then."

13

The dawn sky at JFK was a brilliant orange that tinged the entire airport the color of burned gold. Bolan stood on the tarmac with Ramzin and Svarzkova along with a small pile of bags and cases the Russians had acquired. They had left the hotel just before dawn and gone to the Russian embassy, where Svarzkova picked up two extra suitcases that weighed heavily in her arms. After a heated argument in Russian, Svarzkova had allowed Ramzin inside the embassy. Five minutes later the two of them had come out carrying a similar pair of suitcases and a long flat package that could only be a rifle.

It seemed if the two Russians couldn't do anything about being outnumbered, they had decided not to be outgunned.

A Learjet rolled toward them down the runway. Bolan knew the plane well. It was a Stony Man special. Its engines had been upgraded, and it carried extensive communications and electronic-warfare equipment. The entire airframe had been modified and strengthened, and each wing had two hard points for attaching various weapons stores. At the moment the aircraft was flying clean and looked like any other business jet. The Executioner knew that with the stores inside, the Lear could quickly transform into a bird of prey.

The aircraft taxied to a halt, and the twin jet engines powered down. The door swung open, and the ladder steps popped down into place. A lean figure in a tailored blue flight suit and black leather bomber jacket grinned at Bolan from behind his aviator sunglasses. He ogled Svarzkova for a moment, then turned his infectious grin back on Bolan.

"It's an outstanding morning for flying, Sarge!"

Bolan smiled and shook his head. Short of doomsday, any day was an outstanding day for flying in Jack Grimaldi's flight book. "It's good to see you. Did Aaron give you our flight plan?"

Grimaldi tapped the leather flight book in his hand. "Sure did. It'll be a short hop from here, but we'll have excellent visibility. The Green Mountains should be absolutely beautiful." He turned and grinned again at Bolan's companions and stuck out his hand. "Major Ramzin."

Ramzin looked at the offered hand and then shook it firmly. Grimaldi's grin upped in wattage as he held out his hand to the blond Russian agent. "Senior Lieutenant Svarzkova, it's a pleasure."

Svarzkova smiled and shook his hand. "I am very pleased to meet you, as well, Mr....?"

Grimaldi looked at Bolan. It was a cooperative mission, but giving out the name of Stony Man's number-one pilot to Russian Intelligence was still probably not a good idea.

Bolan jerked his thumb at the pilot. "Just call him Jack."

Grimaldi glanced at his watch. "I'm flying you into the Burlington airport. The powers that be have already okayed your idea, though they want you to have backup when Senator McCain arrives. The word is they're going to send in an FBI fast-reaction team, as well as the usual cadre of Secret Service bullet stoppers. In the meantime I've been cleared to stick around awhile if you want me."

Bolan nodded. Grimaldi was a very useful man to have around. "Why don't you do that."

The pilot smiled and raised his arms up at the vault of the dawn's horizon. "Let's fly!"

IGOR BAIBAKOV LOOKED toward the snow-covered Green Mountains off to the east. He liked them. They reminded him of the Urals. He turned his attention to the long expanse of

Lake Champlain. According to his research, the lake supposedly contained a sea monster. The locals blamed it for all sorts of unexplained events.

Madchen Krstic stood at his side. He knew she was looking up at him, but he ignored her. She was coming along well. With Branko there had been long screaming matches into the night. Baibakov grinned as he raised his binoculars. With him there were no arguments, only his implacable will. She fit herself to his will, in tactical operations and in his bed. She knew he would kill her if she didn't.

Baibakov turned at the sound of footsteps and looked down at Tomas Broz. The man was almost a shorter, stockier, brown-haired clone of Branko Cebej. He was Branko's cousin, and had been the second-in-command of the Red Falcons. Baibakov knew he had entertained thoughts of taking command after Cebej's death. He had thought wrong. Still, Broz had fallen into line quickly. He was a fanatic, like Krstic. He marveled at Baibakov's strategy and was eager to implement his ideas. Broz was also a veteran, and he was well liked and respected by the rest of the Red Falcons. If he wasn't the inspired leader Branko Cebej had been, he was still solid and reliable.

That was all that Baibakov required. The reins of leadership would be kept firmly in his own hands.

Broz glanced at Baibakov and grinned. He was ready for action. "Josef has reported from the airport. A small plane has arrived with four individuals. Two matched the description of the American commando and the woman. The third was positively identified as Major Ramzin. The fourth was the pilot, who stayed at the airport. The other three took a blue sport-utility vehicle and headed west."

Baibakov nodded and then spoke as he looked through his binoculars at the objective. "You are clear on what you must do?"

"Crystal clear. The men are ready."

"Josef knows what he must do?"

"He has already left to take command of the second team. All is in readiness, Commander."

"Good." Baibakov lowered the binoculars and looked down at Krstic, whose eyes glittered with anticipation. "Come. You and I have much to do."

BOLAN CROUCHED in the trees and surveyed the area around Senator Eudora McCain's house. He didn't like what he saw. The house was four miles from the nearest town, and her nearest neighbor was a half a mile away on the other side of a hill. The surrounding area was hills and thick forest. A light layer of snow covered the ground, and the trees grew almost right up to the house. The building itself was a two-story manor made of massive logs, with wide bay windows and large glass doors front and back. There were dozens of places where a man with a sniper rifle could hide and have a good angle to strike from. With a Barrett .50-caliber rifle it could be done from a thousand yards away. The log house faced Lake Champlain, and it had a little dock and a covered ramp for a small boat. There was ice along the shore, but it was thin and broken. It would be no obstacle to frogmen making an attack.

Bolan grimaced. A man in a parka wearing a state-trooper hat was sitting on a deck chair on the porch reading a magazine.

Ramzin blew a breath of steam into the early-afternoon air. The Russian had changed into a dark blue anorak and wool pants. He looked at Bolan and shook his head. "Your senator's home is isolated, and it is nearly indefensible. It would take at least a squad of heavily armed soldiers to hold it against an attack in strength."

Svarzkova chewed her lower lip and nodded. She didn't think much of the location tactically, either.

Bolan took a cellular phone from his jacket and dialed the number. After three rings a man's voice answered. "Hello?"

Bolan looked through the front bay window. The curtains

were open, and Senator McCain's husband was clearly visible. "Mr. McCain, this is Belasko."

Mr. McCain chuckled. "Yes, I've been told to expect you."

"We're outside your house. Tell the troopers we're coming in."

"Right-o."

It seemed that Mr. William McCain wasn't taking the situation very seriously. "All right. Let's go."

The Russians picked up their gear bags and followed Bolan up to the porch. The trooper looked up and smiled. "You're the government agents?"

Bolan nodded. "That's us."

They entered the house, and William McCain waved at them from an overstuffed couch in the living room. He was a tall man with a square jaw and blond hair graying at his temples. He wore a heavy wool sweater with snowflakes on it and khaki pants. He looked like a model for an expensive outdoor catalog. He smiled politely, but he didn't seem all that pleased to see them. He didn't rise from the couch. "Do you really think all this is necessary?"

"How many troopers do you have here?"

McCain held up two fingers. "You met Hanks out on the porch. Tennyson is in the kitchen." On cue a large and **frie**ndly-looking red-haired state trooper came out with a steaming mug in his hand. "Hey, you must be those government people."

Bolan sighed. The only thing two troopers could do in this situation was let the enemy know that they were expected. He suspected they had already done that. "I want to run a sweep through the hills around your house."

McCain looked at Bolan patiently. "Well, if it makes you feel better, sweep away."

Ramzin and Svarzkova began to open their bags. The lieutenant pulled out what looked like a miniature AK-74 rifle with a ten-inch barrel and a folding stock. Instead of a normal clip, a tube the circumference of a beer can and twice as long ran along the bottom of the action to a steel clip behind the muzzle brake. A laser sighting device had been mounted alongside the barrel, as well. Bolan had only heard about the weapon from Kissinger at Stony Man Farm. The 9 mm Bazin submachine gun was the latest weapon in the Russian arsenal. Its helical magazine held more than ninety rounds and was supposed to be almost recoil free. Svarzkova snapped the skeleton folding stock into place and racked the action.

Ramzin had opened his case and pulled out an AKR carbine with a 30 mm grenade launcher attached to it. He loaded a clip into the action and slipped a high-explosive grenade into the breech of the launcher. He put the combination weapon on McCain's coffee table and began to unwrap his long package. He picked up a Dragunov sniper rifle and checked the action.

William McCain and State Trooper Tennyson stared at the advanced weaponry in awe. Bolan began to arm himself, as well. He turned to Tennyson. "I want you and Hanks inside. Draw the drapes. You have a police-band radio with you?"

Tennyson nodded with bugging eyes as he watched Bolan load a fragmentation grenade into his M-4 Ranger carbine's M-203 launcher. The soldier checked the action of the .44 Magnum Desert Eagle. "Good. I'll switch our radios to the police band. I want one of you watching from upstairs, and one of you with Mr. McCain at all times."

Svarzkova and Ramzin both pulled dark tan vests out of their bags. They looked like regular flak jackets, but Bolan recognized the garments as Russian tactical armor. It was crude by American standards. Bolan's own armor was made up of boron-carbide ceramic trauma plates sheathed inside layers of ballistic Kevlar fabric. Russian armorers simply used what was available and had enmeshed titanium plates in woven fiberglass. It was a bulkier, low-tech approach, but proved in battle during the war in Afghanistan.

Tennyson shook his head in bewilderment as the two Russians shrugged into their armor and began to strap on ammunition belts. "Are you guys Feds? You guys can't be Feds."

Svarzkova looked at Tennyson as she strapped her 9 mm CZ-75 pistol over her armor. She saluted and spoke in an official tone. "I am Senior Lieutenant Valentina Svarzkova of Russian Military Intelligence." She glanced at Ramzin, who had strapped one of his commandeered Hi-Power pistols over his armor and was tucking the second one into his waistband. "This is Major Pietor Ramzin, of Russian Spetsnaz. We are pleased to be operating in cooperation with United States civil authorities."

Tennyson gaped.

McCain's condescension was quickly turning to irritation as he rose from the couch. "Listen, I don't know just who the hell you are but—"

Bolan cut him off. "But nothing, Mr. McCain. There is a good chance someone is going to try to kill your wife in the next two days. If you're here, they'll kill you, as well. If our friends are going to go for it, then they are already here, in place, somewhere nearby. Do you understand?"

Tennyson looked back and forth unhappily between the senator's husband and the man armed for the apocalypse. He cleared his throat and called out toward the porch. "Hanks, I think you'd better get in here."

McCain glared at Bolan. "Now, you listen here..."

Bolan regarded McCain impassively. Tennyson's voice cracked. "Hanks!"

For a moment the house was utterly silent.

"They're here."

Bolan grabbed William McCain by the front of his sweater and yanked him to the floor. Ramzin whirled toward the kitchen. There was a stuttering hiss, and the Russian staggered as a burst from a silenced weapon walked up his chest. Ramzin's armor held, and he regained his balance. He fired his 30 mm grenade launcher point-blank into the kitchen. Orange fire thundered out of the kitchen door, and the kitchen windows blew out as the shock wave rolled through the house.

The Executioner rose up from McCain. The living room's bay window shattered as a small olive drab object crashed through the glass. Svarzkova's submachine gun snarled with the sound of ripping canvas as she tracked a dark-clothed figure as it dropped below the windowsill.

Ramzin instinctively yelled in Russian, *"Grenatya!"*

The grenade bounced off of the coffee table with a clack and fell spinning to the floor. Bolan dropped his carbine and flipped the couch on top of the bomb. The couch heaved with a muffled thump, and ripples streaked under its fabric. A few rips opened violently, and plaster fell from the ceiling, but the heavy cotton batting had smothered the detonation and absorbed most of the grenade's lethal fragmentation.

A figure with a silenced Uzi popped up into the shattered bay window a second behind the grenade's detonation, and Svarzkova hammered him down with a long burst from her Bazin submachine gun.

Bolan scooped up his carbine. Tennyson had drawn his service revolver and crouched on one knee. The policeman was looking around frantically.

"Tennyson!" the Executioner roared. "Go with Svarzkova! Get McCain away from the windows!"

Tennyson blinked. "Right!" William McCain looked like a deer caught in a truck's headlights as Svarzkova yanked him to his feet. The trooper grabbed him by an arm and pulled him along as Svarzkova grabbed her gear bag and moved down the hallway deeper into the house.

Bolan took a quick look around the kitchen door. A man lay in a crumpled heap, and broken glass and pans lay everywhere. Two dark figures were moving in from the back porch. He fired the M-203 and whipped back around the doorjamb.

The grenade detonated, and Bolan went around the corner with Ramzin covering his back. One of the men had fallen, and the other had dropped to one knee. Bolan shouldered his carbine and put two quick shots into the assassin's chest. The man jerked with each shot and fell forward.

Ramzin opened fire back in the living room, and Bolan turned. Two men stood on the front porch with their silenced weapons hissing in their hands. Ramzin staggered as he took more hits, but he stood firm and returned fire. Bolan leveled the carbine's sights on the man on the left and put a burst into him. The man tottered but remained on his feet as his companion fell under Ramzin's fire. The Russian tracked his carbine to the remaining man, and he and Bolan cut the assassin down with simultaneous bursts.

The big American grabbed Ramzin's shoulder and shouted above the ringing in his ears. "Are you all right?"

Ramzin nodded and thumped his vest. His armor had held. *"Da!"*

"We have to find a defensible position!"

Ramzin rammed a fresh magazine into his carbine and slipped another grenade into his launcher. *"Da!* Go! Find a room! Radio for reinforcements!"

From back inside the house a gun went off, followed by a long unsilenced burst from an automatic weapon. Glass broke and Svarzkova screamed in rage.

"Cover my back!" Bolan said as he moved down the hallway at a run. The hall opened into a large room dominated by a shattered large-screen television and racks of stereo components. A black-masked figure lay on the floor, and Tennyson was flat on his back next to him with three holes in his chest. William McCain was slumped in the doorway clutching a bloody shoulder. Lieutenant Svarzkova was rolling on the floor, screaming, fighting with a dark-clothed figure in a ski mask. Her submachine gun lay off to one side. The assassin had rolled on top of her and was awkwardly trying to get the muzzle of his Uzi in line with Svarzkova's head.

The woman squirmed as she desperately held the muzzle away from herself and made a yanking motion at her left wrist. Steel rasped and the AK-47 bayonet gleamed in her right hand. The assassin hunched and let out a howl as the agent plunged her knife into his side.

Bolan strode forward and brought his boot up into the gunman's face. The assassin sat up with the force of the blow, and the Executioner shot him in the chest. The killer slumped forward on top of Svarzkova. She snarled and pushed the corpse off her. Bolan grabbed her hand and pulled her to her feet. "You all right?"

Svarzkova wiped her knife on her pants leg and resheathed it. She took a deep breath. "Yes. See to the policeman."

Bolan called down the hall. "Ramzin! What's happening?"

Ramzin called back. "No movement!"

The soldier went over to Tennyson. The state policeman was gulping air and staring wide-eyed at the ceiling. Bolan opened the trooper's shirt. Three bullets were lodged in the trooper's bulletproof vest. It was standard-issue police soft armor, but it had been enough to stop the 9 mm subsonic hollowpoint ammunition in the assassin's submachine guns. Trooper Tennyson would feel as if he had been beaten with a bat tomorrow, but he was otherwise unhurt. The policeman wheezed dazedly as Bolan helped him to his feet and put his service revolver back in his hand.

Svarzkova knelt beside William McCain. He flinched as she examined his shoulder. Bolan glanced down the other hall. He could see the broken window where the two killers had made their entry. He looked over at McCain, who looked pale. "How is he?"

The woman frowned. "Bullet went cleanly through his shoulder." McCain grunted as she probed his upper back. "I do not believe the bullet expanded. I will try to stop the bleeding, but he will require medical attention."

She looked up at Bolan while she applied pressure to McCain's shoulder. "What is happening?"

Bolan slid a fresh magazine into his carbine. "That was the first wave. They tried to come in and do it stealthily. We ruined that plan for them, so now they'll come in force, and they'll do it soon."

Tennyson opened his revolver and replaced the spent rounds from his revolver. "So what do we do now?"

Bolan jacked a fragmentation grenade into his M-203 launcher. "We call in the fast movers."

14

Tomas Broz's eyes narrowed as he trained his binoculars on the house by the lake. He had sent in the first team to take out the commando and his compatriots quickly and silently. The action had been anything but silent, and now it seemed they had failed. Broz could see three of his men lying dead on the porch. He had seen the other men make their entry, and none of them had come out of the house. All was silent. Nothing moved. Baibakov had warned him not to underestimate the American, but Broz simply couldn't fathom how the three of them had been ready for an attack less than five minutes after entering the house.

Broz smothered a vague feeling of dread and picked up his radio. "First team has failed, Commander. I am assuming all of them are dead or incapacitated."

Igor Baibakov's voice came across the radio. "Enemy casualties?"

"One state policeman is a confirmed kill. The American, Ramzin, the woman, one trooper and McCain are still inside. Their status is unknown. What are your orders?"

Baibakov's voice was like granite. "If they live, you must assume they are calling for help. Time is now critical, Broz. Use your superior numbers and firepower, and take the house by storm now, before help can arrive. Confirm the kills yourself, and then extract as planned. I am sending the helicopters for you now. You will contact me when your mission is accomplished. Baibakov out."

Broz's face set with grim resolve. In forty-five minutes he

would be safely in Canada. The Russian *mafiya* was well established in Quebec, and had promised them a safe haven. Once there, the Red Falcons would be free to take their real objective. The act that would break the Americans' will in Bosnia. He grinned savagely at the thought.

But before they could move on to that glorious act, the American commando had to die.

Broz put down his binoculars and rose to his feet. The four heavily armed men behind him got up, as well. His men had been in place for the past fifteen minutes. Now it was time to act. He picked up his radio. "Are all teams ready?"

The other three teams called in. "Ready, Commander."

Broz racked the action on his M-16 rifle. "Fire RPGs! Now!"

BOLAN MOVED down the hall at a crouch. Ramzin knelt in the entryway and peered around the corner and out through the shattered living-room window. He had slung his carbine, and the 7.62 mm Dragunov sniper rifle lay cradled in his arms. Bolan moved past him and grabbed a padded black nylon bag off the floor and crab-walked back into the cover of the hallway. He opened the bag and quickly set up his radio. He punched the Send button and spoke. "Jack, I need you."

Grimaldi's voice was crystal clear across the link. "What's the situation?"

The Executioner looked up as a sizzling hiss split the air outside. He grabbed Razmin's shoulder and yanked him deeper into the hallway as a smoking streak flew into the living room. High explosives thundered, and orange fire lit up the hallway. The Russian rose up off his stomach. "They have rocket grenades."

The frame of the house shuddered as another rocket struck the second floor a moment later.

Grimaldi shouted anxiously over the radio link. "Sarge! Are you there?"

Bolan's voice was steely calm. "We're under heavy attack. I need immediate air support."

"I don't know your exact location from the air. Can you pop smoke?"

Bolan smiled grimly to himself as the smell of smoke began to overcome the odor of burned high explosive. "No, but I'll be in the only house that's on fire."

"Hang tight. I'm on my way."

Bolan slung the radio bag across his back and kept his headset on. He had told Grimaldi to attach the weapons pods while he and the others took a look at the McCain house and the surrounding area. It would still take the pilot at least two minutes to power up the weapons, then at least five more to get airborne and overhead. In the real world it would be ten.

Another rocket grenade detonated against the house and plaster dusted down from overhead.

They would just have to survive for ten minutes.

A storm of automatic-rifle fire opened up outside, and the house rattled as if it were being hit by hail as Bolan and Ramzin moved down the hall and back into the McCain entertainment room. Svarzkova had made McCain an improvised field dressing while Trooper Tennyson watched the other doorway. The bags of assorted gear were piled in the middle of the floor.

Ramzin's face was grim. "The house is on fire—we cannot stay."

Bolan nodded. Being burned out was the least of their worries. He didn't think the Red Falcons were going to wait around for that to happen. The house was surrounded. The entertainment room wasn't defensible against men with heavy weapons, and the Red Falcons would assault any second. Bolan looked at McCain. "There's no door on the northwest side of the house, is there?"

"Um, no. Both doors on the west side of the house face the lake. There's just a chimney and window on the second story facing north."

That would be the least defended area outside. Bolan went to one of his gear bags and pulled out a half-pound block of C-4. He held up the plastic explosive. "We're making a door and breaking out of here."

Bolan led them down the hall to the north side of the house. Wisps of smoke curled near the ceiling as the house began to burn in earnest on the second floor. The hall opened into a large, second living room with a square of couches facing a massive fireplace. The window facing east had been shattered where the first group of attackers had made their entry. Bullets spattered against the wall and tracers streamed in smoking trails through the open window.

Bolan calculated. He had two blocks of C-4. Each of the logs forming the walls of the house was as thick around as a man. They were dovetailed in place, and their immense weight held them in position. The plastique would certainly damage them, but there was no guarantee it would make any kind of convenient door. There would be no second chance, and they wouldn't have the time to try to hack their way out. Speed would be life. Bolan eyed the stone-and-mortar fireplace. Masonry, on the other hand, was brittle. It would shatter rather than flex or splinter.

"Give me some cover."

Ramzin knelt and fired his grenade launcher out the window as Bolan walked on his knees and elbows to the fireplace. The riflemen outside opened up with renewed fury, but their aim was to reach deeper into the house. They didn't see the Executioner or even aim in his direction. Bolan packed the high explosive against a seam of mortar holding the blackened stones at the back of the chimney. When he was satisfied it would stay, he pushed an electrical detonator into one of the blocks, and pulled a small black box the size of a television remote control out of his web gear.

"Get behind the couch. When the charge blows, follow me!"

The Executioner overturned a couch for himself and flipped open the remote detonator's plastic shield. He pressed a button, and a small green light flicked on. The charge was armed. Bolan could hear glass shattering and the sound of men shouting back in the rear of the house as the Red Falcons stormed the house. He pressed his thumb on the red button.

Thunder split the room, and the couch heaved as it was pummeled by flying stone and mortar. Bolan was up even as bits of debris were still falling. The mantel had fallen, and much of the chimney front had sagged away. Trees were visible through a ragged hole three feet in diameter. He pulled a fragmentation grenade from his belt and threw it through the hole. The air outside split with the sharp explosion, then Bolan was at the chimney. He put his boot into the stones surrounding the hole, and they fell away under several quick kicks. The Executioner dived through the hole and came up with his carbine ready to fire.

Bolan smiled tightly. He had gambled and won. The Red Falcons had concentrated their forces on the doorways and windows. As he made his way to the corner of the house, the front door smashed in and the Red Falcons made their assault. He shifted back around the corner as rifles opened up from the woods. The explosion hadn't gone unnoticed. The covering teams knew what had happened. In seconds so would the men inside.

Ramzin came up behind Bolan as Svarzkova and Tennyson pulled William McCain through the blackened hole in the chimney. The Executioner looked at the Dragunov sniper rifle slung on Ramzin's back. "Give me your rifle. Take McCain and the rest up the beach."

The major shook his head. "Wait." He unslung his rifle and handed it to Bolan, who slung his carbine and racked the sniper rifle's action. Ramzin pulled two cylindrical grenades out of his web gear. There was a serial number and three words in Russian Bolan couldn't read on the grenade bodies, but he recognized the chemical symbol emblazoned in large red letters: HCN—hydrogen-cyanide.

Ramzin pulled the pins from both grenades with his thumbs and held down the safety handles. "I had intended to use these against Baibakov if we pinned him down. Now they will buy us time instead. Move out, now."

Bolan nodded grimly. Hydrogen-cyanide was fast and lethal, and it had been banned for use in war by the Geneva

Convention. The streak of tracers drew smoking lines out through the hole in the chimney. Bolan decided not to argue the point. He turned to Svarzkova. "Let's move!"

Ramzin tossed one of his grenades back through the hole in the chimney. As Bolan led the group into the trees, the Russian tossed the other one around the corner of the house. The rifle fire coming from out of the chimney suddenly ceased. Deeper inside the house men yelled in rage and fear.

Bolan heard the hiss of an RPG-7 rocket and dragged McCain to the ground. Svarzkova tackled Tennyson, and the two of them fell in a tangle in the light snow. The RPG-7 warhead exploded behind them. Bolan rose. It hadn't been aimed at them. The corner of the house Ramzin had used for cover smoldered, and large chunks had been blown out the corner logs. The major lay in the snow and didn't move. Bolan turned to Svarzkova. "Get McCain and Tennyson out of here!"

"Leave him! There is no time!"

Bolan ignored her and dodged through the trees back toward the house. Thick smoke churned into the sky from the burning second floor. Behind him he heard Svarzkova swearing in Russian. She suddenly broke into English. "Tennyson! Get McCain out of here!" Bolan heard the snarl of her submachine gun as she began to lay down covering fire for him as he ran.

Bullets struck the trees over the Executioner's head, and suddenly he was clear as he put the burning house between himself and the Red Falcon riflemen. Bolan ran to Ramzin and rolled him over. His face was a mask of blood. His nose had been rebroken, and a large gash split the left side of his face where a flying chunk of wood had struck him. The Russian blinked up at Bolan dazedly. There was no time to check him for a concussion. Ramzin would have to run or die.

Bolan yanked him to his feet and shoved the Russian's weapon back in his hands. Then he slammed Ramzin on the back and roared a command at him in his own language at parade-ground decibels. *"Run, for the trees, Ramzin!"*

Old instincts died hard, and Ramzin's legs obeyed. The

Russian broke into an awkward run for the trees. Ahead Svarzkova's weapon was chattering in long bursts. Streams of tracers ripped through the trees back at her. Bolan moved to the still smoking corner of the house. The pulsing flashes of at least half a dozen rifles firing flickered among the trees facing the front of the house, and a slight, wet shimmer hung in the air between the house and the trees. Bolan whipped the Dragunov to his shoulder, and one of the pulses resolved into a man armed with an M-16 in the telescopic sight. The Executioner put the cross hairs on the man's chest and squeezed the trigger.

The gunner flew backward and fell to the snow.

Rifles trained on Bolan, and armed men broke from the trees in a charge. He could hear the shouts of men on the lake side of the house, as well, and knew he would be caught between them. The Executioner counted in his head. It had been about fifteen seconds since Ramzin had thrown his grenade in front of the house.

The soldier broke for the trees.

The charging men yelled as he burst into view, but Bolan ignored them as he ran. Ramzin's weapon joined Svarzkova's as they tried to draw the fire from the trees. A strangled scream suddenly erupted behind Bolan. He kept running until he passed a large tree, then hurled himself behind it.

Two men lay in the front of the house. One was motionless, but the other twisted about on the ground, then ceased movement. A third clutched his throat and staggered about. The fourth man had pulled up short and was nearly falling over himself as he backed away. He shouted a word over and over as loud as he could in warning. The man clutching his throat fell and lay still in the snow.

Hydrogen-cyanide was colorless and odorless. All the attackers had seen was Ramzin throwing a grenade that hadn't gone off. The leading three men had run straight into the gas cloud without knowing it. Bolan rose and ran through the trees. He spied Svarzkova ahead and Ramzin a few yards away. "Move! Move! Move!"

The Russians broke cover and ran.

Through the trees Bolan could see Tennyson helping McCain. They had broken out of the trees and were trotting over the flat ground of the lakeshore. Bolan dropped behind the bole of a large pine and jerked his head at the Russians. "Keep going!"

The Russians ran past as Bolan sighted through the Dragunov's scope. Armed men in ski masks had moved around from the lake side of the house and were approaching. He swept the scope eastward. More men were giving the front of the house a wide berth and were circling around through the trees. Bolan fired several rounds, and the leading men dropped flat and returned fire. They would quickly have him flanked.

Bolan spoke into his headset. "Jack, where are you?"

Grimaldi's voice broke out across the receiver. "I am inward bound, coming in from the north over the lake." There was a second's pause. "I see smoke, Sarge. A lot of it. I'm assuming that's you."

Bolan raised the Dragunov and fired three more rounds to keep the Red Falcons' heads down. They were leapfrogging from cover to cover, and tracers streaked closer as they walked fire onto his position. "A party of four friendlies is running right toward you on the shore. I'm joining them. Anyone behind us is unfriendly."

"Roger that."

The soldier broke cover and ran through the trees. The Red Falcons saw him almost immediately, and he heard the supersonic crack of a rifle bullet pass close to his head as he wove from tree to tree. Men yelled behind him, and Bolan could hear the crunch of their boots as they charged after him. He raced through a break in the trees, and a hammer blow struck him between the shoulders, the force of it nearly pitching him forward.

The Executioner burst onto the beach and broke into a dead sprint across the stony shore of Lake Champlain. There was a cluster of large rocks a hundred yards ahead. From behind it he could see Svarzkova and Ramzin, and they shouted at him desperately. Bolan ran for all he was worth. He could hear shouting behind him, and more rifles were opening up as the trees thinned. In seconds the Red Falcons would break out of the trees onto the beach.

Bolan looked up at the sound of jet engines.

Low in the sky a gleaming shape seemed to be suspended in the air as it flew directly toward Bolan. In the blink of an eye the shape resolved itself into a plane. Bolan's earpiece crackled. "You're the lone runner, Sarge?"

Bolan grunted out a reply over his burning lungs. "Good guess."

Grimaldi's voice was the essence of calm. "Hit the dirt."

Bolan threw himself down on the rocky beach.

The Learjet screamed in overhead. Yellow flames rippled beneath its wings, and 2.75-inch folding-fin rockets sizzled through the air. Grimaldi pulled his plane into a steep bank as his deadly ordnance flew on. The Red Falcons burst out of the trees into the waiting arms of Armageddon.

The shore erupted in orange fire, and sand and rock fountained into the air as the high-explosive rockets detonated. Bodies flew into the air, and several trees at the forest's edge burst and toppled. Bolan rose and sprinted for the rocks. Grimaldi's voice spoke in Bolan's earpiece. "I'm coming in for another pass. Switching to guns."

The Executioner reached the rocks and knelt beside Svarzkova. Rifle fire came from the trees, but it was ragged and sporadic. The woman's chest heaved, but she grinned at Bolan. "That is our friend, Mr. Jack?"

Bolan nodded as he caught his breath. "He's very resourceful."

The Learjet came in low over the water, and a few tracers streaked up at it from the trees. The aircraft came on implacably. Over the howl of its engines there was a sound like a giant sheet of canvas being torn in two. Tracers streaked down in a steady stream of fire as Grimaldi opened up with his .50-caliber Gatling gun. The tree line shuddered as heavy-machine-gun bullets walked through it at one hundred rounds per second.

The Learjet peeled up into the sky and began another banking turn. "Sarge, I have heavy casualties among the enemy. Survivors are scattering. Most seem to be fleeing back toward the house."

Bolan set down the Dragunov and unslung his carbine. "They must have had an extraction plan, Jack. Go high. See if you spot a boat big enough for at least two squads of men."

The radio crackled. "Roger that."

The Learjet climbed into the sky. Grimaldi spoke almost immediately. "I have three helicopters, coming in low over the lake. Should I go to say hello?"

Bolan put a fresh magazine into his carbine. "Roger that. We're safe for the moment and sitting tight."

The Learjet streaked over the lake. Bolan looked at McCain. He was pale, and the left shoulder of his shirt was stained with blood. "How are you?"

"Thankful," McCain replied, managing a weak smile.

Bolan nodded and looked at Ramzin. The Russian's face was a gruesome mosaic of blood and purple bruising. His left eye was closed, and his nose was mashed flat. The gash in his left cheek was still bleeding. Ramzin's right eye was clear, and it peered back at Bolan. "I am in your debt."

Bolan regarded Ramzin dryly. "I'm not done with you yet."

The major snorted and reloaded his carbine. Off in the distance Bolan heard the snarl of the Gatling gun echo across the lake. Something was happening low over the water. "What's up, Jack?"

Grimaldi's voice was tight. "Hold on, Sarge. I'm busy."

The Gatling snarled again. Grimaldi's voice came across the radio. "All right, Sarge, you're about to have visitors. Look sharp."

Everyone looked up at the thump of rotors. Three helicopters came into view and flew in formation toward their position. A second later the Learjet streaked over them. The helicopters wobbled in Grimaldi's jet wash as he herded them toward shore. It seemed a few shots across their bows had made the chopper pilots see the light of reason. The helicopters slowed as they reached the shore and hovered over the beach. After a moment they descended and landed in the stony sand. They were twin-engine Bell 212 model Hueys with civilian paint jobs.

Bolan squinted against their rotor wash as he rose from the rocks and leveled his weapon. Svarzkova and Ramzin stood behind him as the pilots of the helicopters jumped down from their aircraft and walked forward, hunched over under their rotors, with their hands raised. The lead man was a short black-haired man in a green flight suit and sunglasses. He straightened and looked warily down the twin muzzles of the weapon in Bolan's hand.

The man glanced up into the sky as the Learjet flew overhead, and he shook his head helplessly. "We surrender."

15

Mack Bolan stood on the tarmac at the Burlington airport and watched the Learjet land. He, Ramzin and Svarzkova had each ridden in one of the helicopters to keep the pilots honest. Grimaldi had herded the formation to the airport in the Learjet and flown a holding pattern until all three were landed. The three captured helicopters were being swarmed over by the state police and two local FAA officials. The *mafiya* pilots were being held for flying across the United States border with Canada without permission and failing to file a flight plan.

Cleaning up at Senator McCain's house would be more difficult. There were still armed Red Falcons running around Lake Champlain.

The jet taxied to a halt and powered down its engines. Jack Grimaldi jumped out and grinned at Bolan. "Where're the Russians?"

Bolan pointed to an ambulance parked by the terminal. Another ambulance had already taken William McCain to the hospital, and State Trooper Tennyson had stayed with his bodyguard detail and gone with him. Ramzin had refused to go to the hospital. The remaining ambulance's door was open as a pair of paramedics worked on the man's face. They had stitched up the gash in his cheek and were now resetting his nose with tape. He sat like a stone throughout the whole operation.

Svarzkova stood next to him and winced as she watched the paramedic pull the thread through Ramzin's flesh. The paramedic clipped the thread and gave the man an anxious look. The big Russian looked like death warmed over, and he still held his AKR automatic carbine and grenade launcher across his knees. The medic swallowed nervously. "All finished."

Ramzin rose and nodded at the paramedic. "Thank you very much." He peered at his reflection in the ambulance's rear window and gave himself a noncommittal grunt.

Grimaldi grinned at him sympathetically. "How do you feel, Major?"

The Russian peered at Grimaldi with his open eye. "My face hurts." He turned to Bolan. "What is our situation?"

"I don't think Baibakov was there. I didn't see him, and I didn't hear his .50 caliber. It would have been more professional if he had been running the attack."

Ramzin nodded. "I agree. I know Igor well. He would have led the assault if he had been present."

Bolan looked at Ramzin, and they knew they were both thinking the same thing. "He'll go after Senator McCain in Washington."

Ramzin snorted and spit blood on the ground. "I believe so."

The Executioner turned to Grimaldi. "What's the status on the senator?"

"I contacted Hal in flight. They've tripled her Service protection."

"How many did she have originally?"

Grimaldi rolled his eyes. "Two."

Svarzkova's breath hissed between her teeth. "Six men with handguns against Baibakov." She shook her head disgustedly. "They will be slaughtered."

Bolan had to agree. The agents of the Secret Service were well trained, brave and dedicated, but six agents would be outnumbered and outgunned, and nothing in their training had ever prepared them for Captain Igor Baibakov. "Jack, what kind of stats do we have on Senator McCain in the capital?"

Grimaldi pulled a sheet of paper out of his jacket pocket. "The Bear faxed me in flight. Senator McCain is scheduled to be in the Capitol Building until the Senate concludes business for the day, then she intended to spend several hours in the Senate Office. While she's there, she has her Secret Service protection, and the Capitol police are on full alert.''

Bolan scanned the sheet. ''And after that?''

''She has a house in Arlington, and six agents following her home.''

Bolan handed the sheet back to Grimaldi. ''Contact Hal. Tell him Senator McCain is not to leave the Capitol Building until we arrive.'' The Executioner looked up at the sky. The sun told him it was past one o'clock. There was still time to get to Washington and set up some kind of real defense for Senator McCain. ''Then get the plane refueled. I want to be airborne in ten minutes.''

RAGE SWAM REDLY across Igor Baibakov's vision. The body of his cellular phone began to buckle in his hand as he unconsciously squeezed. With a massive effort of will he reined in his temper. His voice was as cold as the grave.

''How has this happened?''

Baibakov heard a gunshot in the background as Tomas Broz spoke. ''Ramzin and the commando had automatic weapons and grenade launchers.''

The giant felt his rage mounting. ''This was to be expected, Broz. You had them trapped, you had superior numbers and heavy weapons.'' His voice grated as he repeated himself. ''How has this happened?''

Broz's voice shook. ''They used explosives to breach a wall of the house, and then used poison gas to cover their escape. As we pursued, we were attacked by a jet armed with rockets and automatic cannons. Then the plane went after the helicopters.''

Baibakov closed his eyes. The American commando was truly the devil himself. The man had eluded him in Arizona and in Sarajevo; he could expect little better from an unimaginative man like Tomas Broz. Baibakov's teeth ground. He still wished to kill the Serb for his incompetence. "What is your situation now?"

"I and four men are on foot on the west shore of Lake Champlain. I am not sure of our exact location. There are other survivors, but they have become separated. I have heard them engaging police in the hills."

Baibakov reviewed his mental map of Vermont. Broz was approximately eighty kilometers from the Canadian border. Away from the lake the land was hilly and wooded and sparsely populated. Despite his failure, Broz was an experienced guerrilla fighter, and the terrain was remarkably similar to his homeland. He could make it, if he was clever. "Listen to me carefully, Broz. Avoid engaging the authorities at all costs. Get away from the lake and head north. Stay off the roads, and follow the line of the hills. When you get into Canada, head for the town of Frelighsburg. I will have our contact in Montreal send men to meet you. I will have them look for you outside of town five days from now. They will be in a black van. They will take you to Montreal. After I have concluded my business here, I will come for you. You have five days. Do you understand?"

Broz's voice was more confident. "I understand. I have one other thing to report. The woman accompanying the commando, one of my men heard her yelling in Russian."

Baibakov blinked. That was very interesting, but he had more important things to consider at the moment. The giant's voice was steely. "Run, Broz."

He cut the line and put down the phone.

Krstic's dark eyes veiled coolly as she looked up into the giant's face. "Broz has failed."

Baibakov nodded absently as he considered the situation. The commando had skill, luck and unexpected resources. He smiled unpleasantly. It wouldn't be enough. He held in his hand the greatest advantage in the hunt or in war, and that was surprise. "Begin making the phone calls."

Krstic rose and went into the other room, and Baibakov considered his next move. It was time to take care of business himself. He would test the commando's mettle again, and once he was dead, then the real operation would begin.

The giant looked at his watch. The three-man team he had sent west would be reporting soon.

SENATOR EUDORA MCCAIN looked askance at Bolan as he entered her office. She sat at a mahogany desk surrounded by her Secret Service escort. There had been no time to shower or change on the trip from the airport. The Executioner was a big man in a combat black suit and body armor and he stank of powder smoke and burned high explosive. Jaws dropped to the floor as the Russians came in.

Valentina Svarzkova's sweater was torn, her jeans were covered with mud and her long blond hair hung down in disarray. Her lower lip was swollen, and a wide swath of dried blood stained her collar from her roll on the floor with the Red Falcon assassin. Ramzin had wiped the dried blood from his face, and the entire left side of his head was purplish black with bruising and his features were swollen and misshapen.

Eudora McCain didn't rise from her seat. She wore a red power suit, and her dark hair was bobbed in a page-boy haircut. One lock had been artfully allowed to remain gray over her right eye. Other than the fact that she was short, she was a striking woman. Her gray eyes looked Bolan up and down distastefully. "I gather you've returned from Vermont."

Bolan nodded. The senator raised a frosty eyebrow. "I understand you burned down my house."

He looked back at the senator, his gaze unwavering. "The Red Falcons burned down your house. I only blew up the chimney."

McCain stared at Bolan incredulously. Things weren't starting off well. Bolan decided to change tactics. "Senator McCain, I understand you've been to Sarajevo."

The senator blinked at the sudden change of subject. "Yes, I have."

"I also understand you have been witness to some of the atrocities committed there. You've seen the mass graves and the butchery firsthand, and you've talked to the widows and survivors.''

The woman swallowed. It had rocked her view of the world. "Yes, I have.''

Bolan nodded. "The man who tried to kill your husband and intends to kill you is a man named Igor Baibakov. He is a former captain in the Russian special forces and extremely dangerous. He's advising a Serbian terrorist group called the Red Falcons that's responsible for some of the most heinous acts that have been committed in the former Yugoslavia. By speaking out against such acts and spearheading U.S. involvement to stop them, you've become a target. The Red Falcons are here in the United States, Senator, and they intend to kill you. I intend to keep you alive, but I'm afraid I'll have to ask for your cooperation.''

The senator regained her composure. "Well, I thank you for your efforts, but the Secret Service has told me it's very unlikely an attempt would be made on my life here in Washington, particularly after his group was just wiped out up in Vermont.''

Bolan folded his arms across his chest. "It's to Captain Baibakov's advantage if you believe that.''

One of the Secret Service agents took a step forward. He was a short, powerfully built man in a blue suit, with his brown hair cut like a NASA astronaut's. Three of his men stood behind him in formation like clones. "Listen, we don't have any positive proof that this Baibakov is even in the country. As I understand it, you folks took out the Red Falcons up north. He'd have to be insane to go for her here.''

Ramzin cleared his throat. "Madam Senator, I am Major Pietor Ramzin, of Russian special forces. I know Igor Baibakov. I trained him. The Secret Service agent is correct. Baibakov is insane. I believe you are in terrible danger.''

Svarzkova put her hands on her hips. "I concur. You are in terrible danger.''

The Secret Service agent scowled at Svarzkova. "Who are you?''

The woman snapped ramrod straight and saluted sharply. "I am Senior Lieutenant Valentina Svarzkova, Russian Military Intelligence. I am honored to work in cooperation with agents of the United States Secret Service."

The Secret Service agent gaped at Svarzkova while she held the parade-ground salute. Svarzkova's routine was a potent weapon. Most United States federal and civil authorities just didn't know what to do when faced with beautiful Russian spies. Ramzin snapped to attention and saluted, as well. The agent looked back and forth at the Russians and returned the salute awkwardly. "Uh, Gordon Koontz, special agent in charge, United States Secret Service. Pleased to meet you."

Special Agent in Charge Koontz shook his head wonderingly as the Russians snapped down their arms in robotlike synchronization. His jaw worked up and down once as he looked back at Bolan desperately. "Listen, I don't know what kind of operation you're running here, but—"

Bolan smiled in a friendly fashion. "It's above your pay scale, Agent Koontz, but I assure you our goals are the same. Let's work together and keep the senator breathing."

Koontz looked back at Senator McCain helplessly. He had utterly lost control of the situation.

Eudora McCain steepled her fingers, and her jaw set decisively. "All right. Let's keep me breathing." She gave Mack Bolan an experimental smile. "What would you like me to do?"

16

Mack Bolan examined the long black Secret Service Cadillac limousine critically. Its tires were bulletproof and self-sealing. The windows were ballistic glass and would stop shell fragments and small-arms fire. The armored body could withstand direct hits from armor-piercing .30-caliber rifle bullets. Unfortunately Igor Baibakov was known to use .50-caliber rifles and RPG-7 antitank rockets. Still, it was a much safer bet than Senator McCain's Volvo station wagon.

After hearing Bolan's story about the attack in Vermont, Special Agent in Charge Koontz had gotten serious about the senator's safety. He had also broken out heavier weapons for his team to supplement their 9 mm service pistols. Each agent now carried the Secret Service model of the Uzi submachine gun. It was a standard Uzi, except that the tip of the barrel had been cut and crowned to allow the weapon to be short enough to be carried with the stock folded in a standard briefcase.

Valentina Svarzkova kicked one of the Cadillac limousine's tires. "An RPG-7 will stop it."

Bolan nodded. If Baibakov attacked, he expected the limo would be stopped. The Russian wouldn't try a drive-by shooting or want a firefight between moving vehicles. Those kinds of situations were too uncertain. Igor Baibakov was undoubtedly having Senator McCain watched. He would set a trap and keep the odds overwhelmingly in his favor. The key would be to survive the initial attack. Baibakov had been thwarted too many times. He would want the limo stopped, then come in close and confirm the kill.

The Secret Service limo was their best chance. With its bulletproof glass, armored body and sealed passenger compartment it would increase the chance of passenger survival. With luck, they could survive long enough to hit back.

Koontz came out of the Senate Office with his agents in a phalanx around the senator. McCain appeared to have gained ten pounds, and Bolan could tell she was wearing soft body armor. Koontz looked at Bolan squarely. "There have been more threats."

Bolan shrugged. He had been expecting that, and it cemented the likelihood of an immediate attack on the senator. "Oh?"

Koontz sighed. "There's been a bomb threat against the White House, assassination threats against the House majority and minority leaders, and there has been a threat of a nerve-gas release at the airport."

Bolan folded his arms. Senator McCain looked up at the Executioner and cleared her throat. "You think it's a smoke screen. You think I'm still the primary target."

He nodded and turned to Special Agent Koontz. "Are these threats being taken seriously?"

Koontz stared up at the darkening sky. "After what happened in Vermont, they're taking every threat seriously.

He looked unhappily at McCain. "I hate to say this, Senator, but you are no longer the Secret Service's highest-risk target. I've been ordered to release two of my men for other security details. I'm sorry."

The woman blanched, but forced a smile on her face as she waved a hand at Ramzin and Svarzkova. "Well, I still have the Russian army on my side. That's more than the Speaker of the House can say."

Bolan smiled wearily. The senator was making a good showing. He only hoped he could keep her alive.

Koontz looked up at Bolan steadily. "So how do you want to play it?"

"What kind of security do we have at the senator's house in Arlington?"

"There are two uniformed patrolmen in the house, and two more in an unmarked car outside. They're reporting in to me every half hour."

The Executioner considered Baibakov's most likely move. Setting the trap at McCain's house was almost out of the question. It was too obvious, and he would have to kill four police officers before they could raise the alarm. A single gunshot would ruin the ambush and bring the authorities running. Hitting her in the capital was also dangerous. It was a busy city, and a set ambush would be hard to construct and have too many holes to escape through. Bolan frowned.

"Baibakov will hit us once we're out of D.C. It'll be someplace quiet, close to her home in Arlington, someplace that can easily be cut off and has no side door to get out of. Probably some kind of choke point in the road."

Koontz nodded. "I'll buy that. How do you want to play it?"

Bolan calculated. "We have two escort vehicles?"

The agent pointed toward the back of the building. "I've got two sedans parked around back."

A crease furrowed Bolan's brow as a plan came together in his mind. "Valentina, how's your driving?"

The Russian straightened and looked at Bolan seriously. "As a field agent I am trained in both offensive- and defensive-driving tactics."

Bolan nodded as he opened his cellular phone and punched a number. "Did you get what I needed?"

Jack Grimaldi's voice spoke across the line. "Everything you wanted. Andrews Air Force Base was closest, and let me tell you the officer of the day gave me some funny looks. But he got real friendly after he looked up the priority code I gave him. He had his men help me load this stuff, then loaned me a truck to carry it all. I'm in traffic, but my ETA's about ten minutes."

"I'll see you then." Bolan closed the phone and his eyes

narrowed. "It's standard procedure in an ambush to let the scouts on point through before attacking. It gives your main target zero warning. I'm betting Baibakov will let the lead vehicle through before springing the trap on the limousine. This is how I want to play it."

IGOR BAIBAKOV RAN a sharpening stone over the edge of his entrenching tool as he waited. The razor edge gleamed at the dark like silver. A small light flashed at his side, and he picked up the cellular phone. "Yes."

A voice spoke excitedly. "They have left the Senate Office in a three-car caravan, one limousine with two four-door escort vehicles. Senator McCain is confirmed to be in the limousine. They are approaching the Arlington Bridge."

Baibakov nodded. "Have you observed any other kind of covert escort?"

The voice was clear. "None detected. Two of Senator McCain's bodyguards stayed at the Senate Office. The commando, Ramzin, another American, and the woman are still with McCain."

The giant smiled slightly. The American federal authorities were anything if not predictable. The called-in threats had mobilized every Secret Service agent and fast-reaction team available to cover more than a dozen targets in the D.C. area. In the old Soviet Union such threats would have had the army and KGB agents swarming the streets of Moscow in tanks, and the sky filled with gunships. The Americans were too proud of their vaunted freedom to allow such things. Baibakov grinned. It would be their undoing.

Baibakov's smile turned feral. The commando wasn't fooled. He stayed true to his instincts. He knew what was coming, but it wouldn't be enough. He would stay by the senator's side, and it would get him killed. The senator would die, and he couldn't prevent it. The giant regretted there would be no time to do a proper job on her as he examined the edge of the entrenching tool with a critical eye. Still, the beheading of a United States senator ought to be enough to make America sit up and take notice. The commando would die, and the traitor, Ramzin, would die, as well. Baibakov considered the woman. He would prefer to take her alive. It would give him and Krstic the opportunity to break her to their will and find out what she represented.

The giant enjoyed the image of that in his mind for a moment. He replayed it several times in deeper and richer detail before he snapped back to reality. The hunt was what was important. Anything else was secondary, and a distraction. This night America would be dumbstruck, and the next phase would begin.

Then America's will to fight would be broken.

The lookout's voice spoke again. "They are crossing the Arlington Bridge."

"Excellent. Baibakov out." He sheathed the entrenching tool behind his back and hefted the big .50-caliber Barrett semiautomatic rifle.

The trap was set, and the quarry was heading straight into its jaws.

The giant flipped off the safety of the massive weapon and waited with the patience of a tombstone. Krstic crouched beside him in the darkness with her rifle across her knees. Baibakov glanced across the road. In this part of suburban Arlington there could be fifty to a hundred yards between houses as the road wound through the light forest. He keyed his radio. "All positions ready?"

His fire teams reported in one by one. All was in readiness. The voice spoke over the phone excitedly. "They are approaching your position."

"Acknowledged." He spoke into the radio. "Targets approaching."

Baibakov saw headlights lighting up the bend in the road, and he could tell there were more lights behind them. A late-model American sedan came into view, and the long sleek lines of a limousine appeared behind it. The first sedan passed the attack point, and Baibakov grinned in victory as he spoke into his radio.

"Attack! Now!"

THE EXECUTIONER'S EYES flared wide as the trees behind them lit up with orange glare.

"Hard left! Crank it!"

Bolan jumped out of the lead escort car as Svarzkova whipped the wheel around. An RPG-7 rocket flew out of the woods toward the senator's limousine, trailing smoke and fire.

The Secret Service driver accelerated and swerved the big limo in time to avoid taking the rocket head-on in the engine block but not enough to make it miss. The big car rose up on its chassis as the five-pound warhead detonated in the left front wheel well. The stricken limo fishtailed on its remaining three wheels, and sparks shrieked off the road as its left fender scraped against the pavement.

Tires screamed as Svarzkova yanked the sedan into a 180-degree turn. Bolan had already rolled to his feet and yanked the olive drab tube of an M-72 Light Antitank Weapon to the extended position. White smoke from the RPG-7 rocket launcher's back-blast revealed the rocketeer's position in the trees. Thirty yards in, the shape of an open vehicle was a darker outline in the smoke. Bolan sighted and fired.

The 66 mm rocket sizzled out of the launch tube on a streamer of yellow fire. The projectile streaked into the trees and struck the RPG-7 crew's vehicle broadside. The vehicle shuddered as the warhead detonated, and a ball of fire erupted into the air as its gas tank blew. In the fiery glare neither member of the two-man crew was visible as the hulk of the commercial Jeep burned. Bolan dropped the smoking launch tube and threw himself in a rolling dive to the side of the road.

A second RPG rocket streaked out of the trees from the opposite side of the road and struck the limousine head-on as it listed forward. Orange fire lit up the night, and the hood of the limo flew up into the air. The sedan raced past Bolan as Svarzkova and one of the Secret Service agents went off the road and took the car into the trees. The engine roared as Svarzkova headed straight for the rocketeer's position.

Bolan rose and unslung his second LAW rocket from his shoulder and extended it. In the glare of Svarzkova's headlights Bolan could see a second Jeep with a two man rocket crew standing in the roll bars. The loader desperately slid a fresh rocket into the RPG launcher and slapped the ready signal on the gunner's shoulder.

Svarzkova rammed the Jeep dead on. There was a dreadful crash of metal and breaking glass, and the rocket crew bounced inside the Jeep's roll bars with bone-shattering force. The vehicle skewed backward with the force of the blow, then smashed to a stop against a tree. The lieutenant's sedan piled in alongside and slammed to a halt.

Rifles began to open fire among the trees, and Bolan knelt in the ditch by the road. He held his fire. The rear escort vehicle had stopped at the bend in the road, and he knew his second team was deploying. He scanned the trees for his target.

On the other side of the road a massive thump split the night, and a huge muzzle-flash lit up the trees. The limousine's passenger window shattered under the impact of the .50-caliber bullet. Bolan sighted the LAW at the muzzle-flash and fired.

The antitank rocket streaked across the road and detonated. Bolan cursed as a tree burst into flames and fell. The tree cover was too thick to allow the rocket a clear shot. The Red Falcons had picked their fire lanes ahead of time. He had no such luxury. Bolan dropped the spent launcher and unslung his M-4 carbine. He would have to get close.

The Barrett roared and roared again. Two more holes were punched through the passenger compartment of the limousine. Bolan fired a burst at the muzzle-flash, and the weapon fell silent. He threw himself into the ditch as automatic-rifle fire walked over his position, then spoke into his throat mike.

"Ramzin, where are you?"

A hollow thump answered Bolan. The trees suddenly lit up as the warhead detonated, and two of the rifles fell silent.

Ramzin's voice spoke over the radio. "We are deployed and moving into the trees. What is your position?"

"I'm in a ditch on the south side of the road, forty yards from the bend. Baibakov is on the north, twenty yards in."

"Acknowledged."

The Barrett roared again. Baibakov had shifted his position. Other Red Falcons began to spray rifle fire through the limousine's shattered windows, and a grenade arced out of the trees and bounced across the limo's roof. The car shuddered, and a section of the roof crumpled under the blast of high explosive. Bolan rose out of his crouch and moved at a run across the road.

BAIBAKOV SNARLED SAVAGELY as he dumped three more rounds from his .50-caliber Barrett rifle into the limousine. The car shuddered and rocked as the big bullets punched through it. Orange winks lit up across the road and through the trees west of his position as his opponents tracked his muzzle-flashes. Baibakov rolled to a new firing position and tracked the pulsing light of an automatic weapon across the road. The quick patter of its firing signature told him it was a 9 mm submachine gun, and none of his men was so armed for this attack. The giant aimed, and the Barrett .50 recoiled brutally against his shoulder, then he crouched and moved several yards to his right as two more 9 mm submachine guns reached across the street for him with long bursts.

His ambush was going to the devil.

He had lost both of his RPG teams, and the feint in Vermont had left him with few men. Too many of them were already down. The situation was out of control. Krstic crouched a few yards off to his left and fired round after round from her Dragunov sniper rifle through the shattered windows of the limousine. Baibakov's eyes narrowed as he fired another round into the limo himself, then rolled to another firing position.

Something was wrong.

The commando and his allies were making no effort to get to Senator McCain, defend the limousine or cut an escape route. Instead, they were relentlessly attacking. Baibakov fired into the limo again, then carefully peered through his scope. Something was definitely wrong. The interior of the limousine seemed to be lumpy and full of something.

Baibakov looked up at the thump of a grenade launcher. His eyes flared. A man was running across the road, and it came to the Russian with grim certainty that it was the American commando. The giant raised his rifle to his shoulder and aimed.

The world lit up as the grenade detonated against a tree to his right, and the concussion knocked Baibakov to the cold, wet dirt. He rose, shaking his head to clear the ringing in his ears, and picked up his weapon. The Barrett .50's scope was mangled and half-torn from its base. Rage flowed through him. His attack had gone from a perfect ambush to a pitched battle. It galled him, but his priorities were clear. He was no suicidal fanatic, and his mission was far from over.

It was time to break contact.

Baibakov roared at the top of his lungs, "Break contact! Retreat! Now!"

BOLAN HEARD the unmistakable roar of Baibakov's voice over the battlefield and ran toward it through the trees. There was a snarl of an engine ahead, and the soldier jacked an antitank grenade into the smoking breech of his M-203 launcher on the run.

Baibakov was going to break contact.

Bolan spoke into his mike. "I hear engines. Baibakov is going to try and run for it."

Ramzin's voice came across the radio breathlessly. "*Da!* I hear them, as well! Koontz, the pilot and I are moving in."

Bolan ran on toward the sound of the engines. Return fire from the Red Falcons had all but ceased. "Lieutenant! Where are you?"

Svarzkova's voice sounded garbled as she responded. "I am all right. So is the agent with me. We are crossing the road."

"Stay near the forest edge. Shoot any vehicle coming out."

"Understood."

Ahead Bolan could hear the sound of two revving engines. As he sprinted through the trees he could make out their shape, and his line of fire was unobstructed. He crouched and fired his grenade launcher. The stock of the carbine bucked against his shoulder, and the 40 mm grenade sailed in a short arc through the trees. The bomb slammed into a Jeep and detonated. Fire lit up the forest, and the vehicle rocked on its oversize tires. The back of the Jeep was torn up, but the men inside were still alive. An angry storm of tracers streaked through the trees toward Bolan as he went prone.

Off to the left another grenade launcher fired, and the Executioner could see Ramzin momentarily framed in his muzzle-flash. His grenade arced into the Jeep and detonated. The men inside were in the center of its killing radius, and they twisted and fell as the fragmentation round tore them to shreds.

A spotlight came on in the second Jeep and swept the trees. Bolan raised his carbine and fired a burst but not in time. The light transfixed Ramzin as he came forward. Red flame chattered from the vehicle as a light machine gun opened fire, and the major went down hard.

Bolan raced forward, then rolled behind a tree as the spotlight searched for him. He loaded a high-explosive round into his M-203 launcher as the white glare of the light swept over his cover. "Ramzin! Respond!"

Ramzin's voice was weak. "I am hit. I—"

Grimaldi's voice broke across the radio. "Sarge! Get back! Get back!"

Bolan didn't ask questions. He broke cover and ran for all he was worth.

The forest behind him lit up in a lurid red glare, and he felt a surge of heat behind him. Grimaldi's voice yelled in his ear. "Find cover! Anything!"

The Executioner threw himself behind a tree as a fan of fire streamed to his left and a tree three yards away was engulfed in flame. Baibakov was covering his retreat with a flame-thrower. Trees were no cover. The soldier broke into a dead run as the forest around him blazed into an inferno. The fan of fire searched for him, and Bolan felt the heat wash over him as it approached. He hurled himself down as the stream of jellied jet fuel burned by overhead. There was a sudden wet spattering across his back, and the Executioner's stomach clenched as heat pulsed through his armor.

He was on fire.

Grimaldi was roaring in his ear. "Sarge! Sarge!"

Bolan rolled onto his back and squirmed against the cold, muddy ground. Heat seared the back of his neck as he pushed his head back into the mud and snow. Droplets of fuel burned his arm as he flipped the buckles of his web gear and tore open the Velcro tabs of his armor. Pain seared the soldier's hands as he reached behind his head and yanked the burning armor off of his body and threw it away from himself. Then he rolled to his knees and shoved his hands in the snow.

The stream of fire had shifted to Bolan's left, and he could hear gunfire coming from the road. He flexed his hands. They were blistered, but he could use them. The M-4 lay to one side in a small puddle of flame. Bolan took a deep breath, scooped up two handfuls of snow and packed one against his arm and one on the back of his neck. He climbed to his feet and gingerly drew his Beretta.

Over the roar of the fire Bolan could hear the Jeep moving toward the Arlington Bridge, and it was leaving a wall of fire behind it. His neck and hands throbbed. His radio had been ripped away with his armor and web gear, and they lay in a smoldering heap to one side. The Executioner moved toward the road.

Flames soared toward the sky as dozens of trees burned like giant torches, and he gave them a wide berth as he kept to the darkness. He reached the road and saw people firing down the street. The rear sedan was a burning hulk, and the Jeep had disappeared. Ramzin lay on the ground, and Svarzkova knelt over him. Grimaldi whipped around, his .45 MAC-10 submachine gun in hand as he heard Bolan's footsteps.

"Sarge!" Grimaldi ran forward. "We thought you were burned alive."

Bolan shook his head. "I was, but I managed not to be burned dead. How's Ramzin?"

"He took a burst through the legs, and his artery is cut. He needs a hospital, now."

Bolan nodded. "Have you checked on the senator?"

Grimaldi whipped his head back toward the limo. "No, not yet. Baibakov came out of the trees pulling the fire-breathing-dragon routine. We shot at him, but he didn't stop." The pilot jerked a thumb at the burning hulk of the rear escort car. "He burned the other sedan on his way out."

Bolan sighed. "Radio a chopper in for Ramzin and alert the authorities. I'm going to go check on Senator McCain."

He stopped by Svarzkova, who was applying direct pressure to Ramzin's legs. He had taken a rifle bullet through each thigh, and he lay in an expansive pool of blood. She grimaced as she looked up at Bolan. Blood dripped over her mashed lips and chin from a gash across her broken nose. Unless she had plastic surgery, she would be scarred for life. "Grimaldi is calling in a Medevac. How is he?"

Svarzkova snorted and spit blood from her mouth. "I have stopped the bleeding, but Major Ramzin will require a hospital. His left femoral artery is severed. He has lost much blood and gone into shock."

Bolan nodded. "How are you?"

The woman smiled crookedly. "Part of the Jeep came through the window and hit me in my face." She shrugged. "Other than that I am well. Your air bags work wonderfully. Agent Weitz is fine. We killed two Red Falcons, as well as the rocket crew in the Jeep. I believe the forest on the other side of the road is cleared."

"I'm going to dig out the senator and see if there are any blankets in the limo."

Svarzkova nodded and turned her attention back to Ramzin.

SAC Koontz and one of his agents were yanking on the limousine's crumpled passenger door. The Secret Service agent who drove was sitting against the burned fender clutching a broken arm. Koontz and his man heaved again. The door appeared to be jammed tight. Bolan went up to the shattered window and raised his voice. "Senator McCain, are you all right?"

A muffled voice replied.

Bolan grimaced as he gripped the door frame with his blistered hands and braced his foot against the car body. He nodded tiredly at Koontz and his agent. "On three."

The soldier counted, and they heaved their weight against the wedged door. It yanked free, and a small flood of sand and broken window glass poured onto the road. Most of the outer sandbags had ruptured under the withering fire of the ambush. Luckily they had barricaded Senator McCain six bags deep. The improvised field fortification had collapsed on the senator and the agent guarding her under the attack, but it had kept them alive. Bolan began to haul out sandbags and hand them to Koontz.

Senator McCain's face suddenly appeared.

Bolan smiled at her. "Well, hello there. How are we doing?"

McCain tried to shake the sand off of her face. "I have a Secret Service agent pinned on top of me."

"We'll have you out in a second." Bolan pulled more bags off the top of the pile, and it suddenly heaved.

Koontz's man rose up off the woman. "Sorry, Senator."

"Not a problem." She looked past Bolan at the forest fire. "What happened?"

He shrugged. "We were ambushed. We broke it. Baibakov covered his tail with a flamethrower."

McCain blinked as Bolan and the agent helped her out of the limo. "Was anyone hurt?"

Bolan nodded. "Ramzin got shot up pretty bad, though he should live. The driver's arm is broken, and Svarzkova got her face pushed around a bit. How are you?"

The senator shivered and brushed sand off of her sleeves. "Well, the agent dived on top of me when the car was hit, then the car lurched to a halt and the sandbags collapsed on us. After that, all I could hear was gunfire and explosions." The woman shivered again. "I could feel the bullets hitting the sandbags. But I think I'm okay."

Bolan elbowed one of the sandbags. They had lined the floor of the limo with the bags in the parking garage, then picked up the senator outside. Once she was inside and behind tinted windows, she and the Secret Service agent had built a rolling field fortification around themselves. "Three feet of sand is about the best bullet stop in the world. Making a little fort for you inside of the limousine was the best I could come up with on short notice."

"Well, your plan seems to have worked, thank you."

Grimaldi grinned behind Bolan. "Thank the nice boys at Andrew's Air Force Base. When I told the officer of the day I needed thirty sandbags in half an hour, he had two squads of airmen shoveling away within minutes."

Senator McCain smiled wanly. "I'll write them a letter of appreciation." She stared again at the burning trees. Sirens began to wail in the distance. "So what now?"

The Executioner gazed down the road. "A helicopter is coming to Medevac Ramzin out. I want you and Koontz to go with it. There may be a Red Falcon or two running around in the woods, and your house is only a mile or two from here. Baibakov is running. At this point we have to hope the authorities can catch him."

McCain looked at Bolan doubtfully. "Do you think they will?"

He gazed at the forest as it burned. Baibakov had escaped again, and he always left himself a bolt-hole. If he had to bet, the giant would be holed up safe within the hour. Bolan flexed his burned hands and shook his head. "No, Senator. I don't think they will. Baibakov is still at large, and I'm fresh out of leads on how to find him."

17

Valentina Svarzkova looked up as Bolan came into the doctor's office. Her nose had been set and was covered with a bandage and tape. There was a spot of blood on the bandage where the deep gash continued to seep. Her upper lip was magnificently swollen, and it had taken four stitches to close the split on her lower one. She looked as though she had gone a hard ten rounds with someone outside her weight class.

Bolan grinned at her. "Hey, sailor, want a date?"

The lieutenant snorted and touched her lips gingerly. "You would have to be a greatly drunken sailor to wish to kiss this face. How are your hands?"

The soldier held up his gauze-wrapped hands and wiggled his fingers. "Minor to first-degree burns, and I have some blistering on my neck. I'll live."

Svarzkova shivered. "Fire is bad. Sometimes, when my father had been drinking vodka, he would tell my brothers and I stories of the Great War. My father was a soldier, and he fought the Nazis in the streets of Stalingrad. Once my father told us a story of the Germans breaking through his position with flame-throwing tanks." She shivered again at the memory. "You are very lucky."

Bolan nodded soberly. He had seen more than his share of what napalm and white phosphorus could do to the human body. Fire was always bad. He had been very lucky in the woods of Arlington. He had barely escaped one of the most horrible deaths imaginable. "Do you need anything?"

Svarzkova shook her head. "No. The doctor has said I do

not have a concussion, but he wishes to keep me in hospital overnight. I do not wish to stay here. I wish to go where you are going.''

"All right. Let's see about checking you out of here.''

A nurse walked into the office and looked at Bolan. "Mr. Belasko, Major Ramzin has regained consciousness. He is demanding to see you, and he is being very, you might say, adamant about it. Could you please see if you could make him more cooperative? He nearly lost his right leg, and he's lost a great deal of blood. He needs rest, he won't allow anyone to sedate him and he's threatening to kill people if you aren't brought to him immediately.''

The Executioner's eyes narrowed. "I'll see him.''

Bolan followed the nurse into the wards and found Ramzin lying in a private room. The major looked like death warmed over. The only color in his face was from the bruises he had suffered at Bolan's hands and in Vermont. Against the deathly pallor of his skin, they looked horrible. Both of the man's legs were elevated and heavily bandaged. An IV dripped into his arm. His left eye had opened slightly from its swelling, and both bloodshot eyes rolled in their sockets and looked at Bolan as he entered the room.

Ramzin's voice was remarkably lucid.

"You and I need to speak.''

Bolan turned to the nurse. "I need to speak to the major alone.''

The nurse frowned.

He spread his hands. "Give me five minutes with him, and I promise I'll shut him up and make him go to sleep.''

The nurse sighed. "All right. Five minutes. No more.''

Ramzin waited until the nurse had left and closed the door. "First I must ask you for your promise.''

The Executioner stared at Ramzin frankly. "I can't promise you anything, but if it's in my power I'll do what I can.''

Ramzin raised his head with an effort and stared Bolan in the eye. "If the doctor takes my leg, shoot me.'' The Russian sagged back onto his pillow with a sigh. "Then shoot him.''

Bolan almost smiled. "I'll do you one better." He took one of Ramzin's pilfered 9 mm Browning Hi-Power pistols out from under his jacket and tossed it onto the bed next to the Russian. "Keep that under your pillow. I have to go find Baibakov, and I can't sit around here baby-sitting you because you have a contract on your head. If you want to blow out your brains in the meantime, that's up to you. But the nurse told me that you almost lost your leg, not that they were going to saw it off."

The pistol seemed almost too heavy for him to lift, but with an effort Ramzin managed to push the pistol under his pillow. He sagged back onto the bed in exhaustion. "Thank you. You are a good comrade."

"You're welcome." Bolan's tone hardened slightly. "Now tell me why you threatened to kill the nurse unless I saw you tonight. You had more on your mind than making me promise to give you the bullet."

"Exactly so. You are correct." Ramzin sighed. "I have not been completely honest with you, or your government."

Bolan's tone went arctic. "What haven't you told me?"

"You recall the affair in Arizona?"

Bolan's tone didn't change. "I do."

"In my effort to escape I used two nuclear-demolition charges."

"Yes, one was detonated in the tunnels. The other was directly under your base. You prevented that one from going off yourself."

Ramzin nodded his head and closed his eyes. After a long moment he spoke. "There was a third device."

"What happened to it?"

"I buried it in the desert. I kept the third demolition charge in reserve, in case of an emergency. When we evacuated the base, I had no opportunity to recover the device, and when my men and I were captured, I did not reveal its existence to your government." Ramzin met Bolan's hard stare unflinchingly. "I did not intend to spend the rest of my life in Leavenworth. If I escaped, I would need money. There are many people in the world who would like to get their hands on a nuclear device. Failing a conventional escape method, I had entertained thoughts of arranging to have half of the prison demolished with a low-yield detonation, then escaping in the confusion.''

"Why didn't you tell me about it when I sprang you?"

"Even if your government set me free as it had promised, I would return to Russia a penniless former military officer. The streets of Moscow are full of such men, and unlike them, I would be blackballed for my renegade activities in the United States. As you can imagine, my prospects would not be favorable. And as you can imagine, a nuclear device, even a low-yield demolition charge, would bring a high price in hard currency on the black market. I was keeping the device as a nest egg for my return to Russia.''

"Why are you telling me this now?"

The Russian grimaced and looked down at his bandaged legs. "I suspect I will be in Washington, D.C., for the next few weeks. I think perhaps I will not be safe in Washington, D.C. I think perhaps no one in the city of Washington, D.C., will be safe.''

Bolan stared at Ramzin icily. He had no doubt the man was telling the truth. The Russian would have had no qualms about vaporizing half of his fellow inmates to escape. He had once attempted to vaporize Bolan and five hundred innocent Mexican civilians. Now Bolan suspected Ramzin's nuclear nest egg had gone into a worst-case scenario.

"Does Baibakov know where the device is?"

"No. I never told him where I had hidden it. But he knew of the third device's existence, and he ran many of the surveys when we looking for places to hide matériels. I wished quick access to the device if I needed it. I did not bury it too deep or too far away.''

"You think he might be able to find it?"

Ramzin closed his eyes again. "He knows my mind, he knows the area well and he knows what he is looking for. Yes, I believe it is possible.''

Bolan's voice was as cold as the grave. "Give me the coordinates."

Ramzin pointed a finger at the closet. "I wrote them down for you in case I was killed. The piece of paper is among my personal things."

Bolan went to the closet, took out a large wallet and removed a piece of heavy paper. There was a short paragraph of written directions in English and a hand-drawn map with coordinates graphed onto it. Bolan folded the paper and put it in his jacket pocket.

The major's voice rose as Bolan headed out the door. "I wish to be transferred to a hospital outside of the District of Columbia."

Bolan stopped in the doorway and looked at the Russian emotionlessly. "You'll take your chances with the rest of the city."

THE EXECUTIONER RACED the sun across the American Southwest.

The F-15D's airframe vibrated as Jack Grimaldi flew the two-seat fighter on afterburners at two and a half times the speed of sound. Bolan looked off to his left. Valentina Svarzkova sat in the front seat of another two-seat F-15D trainer. An Air Force pilot named Steven J. Anderson was ferrying the Russian agent in the wingman's position. Lieutenant Anderson didn't understand the reason for his mission, but the parameters had been explained to him succinctly by Grimaldi before takeoff at Andrews Air Force Base in Maryland.

"Lieutenant, we're going to Arizona. I'm taking the gentleman. You're taking the lady. Try to keep up."

Bolan doubted Anderson was having any problem with his orders. It wasn't every day that they stuck a woman in his plane, gave him permission to abandon normal flight regulations and told him to break world speed records across the United States.

The twin-engine fighters screamed across the sky.

Grimaldi spoke from the rear seat of the cockpit. "We have an incoming communication from the Farm, Sarge."

Bolan keyed his radio. "This is Striker."

"Striker, this is the Bear."

"Go ahead, Bear. What's the situation?"

Kurtzman's voice was tight. "The White House is trying to keep the situation quiet. They don't want anyone to know there may be terrorists running around the country with nuclear devices. The border patrol has been scrambled into the area along the border to stop anyone going over. They haven't been told what's going on, just to expect an undetermined number of heavily armed fugitives trying to escape into Mexico. The Pentagon is dropping a company from the Tenth Special Forces group into the area. Publicly they're on a training mission, but they've been briefed on the situation. They're flying out of Fort Carson in Colorado and should be jumping within the next hour."

Bolan looked at his watch. "Jack, what's our ETA?"

"We'll be landing in Fort Huachuca in fifteen minutes."

The Executioner nodded. "Bear, we're going to need immediate transportation to get out to Ramzin's coordinates. Preferably a helicopter."

"Way ahead of you, Striker. There is an armed Blackhawk fueled, warmed up and ready for you on the field."

"Thanks. We'll contact you once we're on the ground. Striker out."

Bolan watched the desert grow beneath him as Grimaldi began his descent.

BOLAN LOOKED DOWN as the helicopter swept across the desert. In the distance the Red Star mining outfit loomed up out of the sand. Border-patrol vehicles were visible moving along the road out of the town of Crucible to the east. The soldier glanced ahead. The desert sand was turning from purple to orange as the sun's light spilled over the horizon. The Executioner spied twin columns of rock at the feet of the mountains and pointed. "There!"

Grimaldi nodded and banked the helicopter sharply toward the landmark. Svarzkova rode in the back with six armed Air Force police from Fort Huachuca. The local APs were the closest troops Bolan could lay his hands on. Guarding Air Force bases against terrorists was their primary job, and Bolan had told them it was terrorists they were after. The APs held their M-16 rifles and maintained uniform expressions of grim determination. Two more APs stood behind door-mounted M-60 machine guns on either side of the aircraft. Beneath the black helicopter's stub wings was a pair of twenty-four tube rocket pods, a 20 mm multibarrel cannon, and four wire-guided TOW antitank missiles.

The helicopter's copilot occasionally looked at Grimaldi, then back over his shoulder at Bolan. It was clear to him he was the weapons officer on this mission. What wasn't clear was why he was flying on an armed mission over Arizona. The helicopter descended and stopped twenty yards from where the rock spines suddenly swept into mountains.

Grimaldi shouted over the rotor noise, "That's as close as I can get. Once you and your team are out, I'll orbit with the weapons ready."

Bolan nodded and slapped Grimaldi on the shoulder. The Blackhawk's wheels ground into the sand, and the Executioner moved into the back of the helicopter. Svarzkova stared at him over her bandaged nose. He jerked his head at the desert outside. "Let's go!"

The soldier squinted against the flying sand in the helicopter's rotor wash as he jumped out and moved toward the rocks, Svarzkova and the six APs deploying behind him. The 220-foot spires of rock stood like grim sentinels at a crack in the mountain. The crack was a sandy wash that wound inward. Bolan frowned. A wash wasn't an ideal place to bury a nuclear weapon. Flash floods were a common occurrence in the desert rainy season, and anything buried shallow stood an excellent chance of being exposed and washed away. The crack in the rocks he was in would only channel water and speed up the process.

Bolan followed the cleft in the rock deeper into the mountain, and sheer rock walls rose up cathedral-like around him. The sky above was lightening, but inside the crack it was still dusk. The wash grew steeper and began to wind. Bolan flicked the safety off his M-4 carbine and moved around a bend.

The Executioner stopped short.

The wash ended abruptly. There was a larger crack in the rock ten feet up where water would be channeled and fall into the wash to flood it. Dripping water had slowly sculpted the rock over the centuries and formed an overhang. Beneath it was a ten-foot space that would never flood. Bolan climbed up the incline and stared down as a cold feeling of dread rose up his spine.

A hole had been dug under the overhang. It was four feet deep, and approximately four feet long and two feet wide. Bolan lowered his carbine as he stared into the hole.

They were too late.

18

Mack Bolan sat in a secure communications room at Fort Huachuca and stared at the walls. The Army base was the national test center of the United States Signal Corps, and some of the most sophisticated technology in military electronics was tried and tested there. It had no shortage of secure communications rooms. Valentina Svarzkova sat next to Bolan with her chin in her hands. Her battered face was a study in defeat. The Executioner understood her feelings. The fact was, there was little left he could think of to do. He stared at the soiled bandage on his right hand as he curled his burned fingers into a fist.

Igor Baibakov was at large, and he had a nuclear weapon.

The communications console chirped, and Bolan punched the speaker button. "What's happening, Aaron?"

Kurtzman spoke tiredly across the satellite link. "Baibakov has threatened to blow up Washington."

Bolan unclenched his fist and looked at his hand. "How did he make contact?"

The computer expert saw the line of questioning. "He used a current Russian military code, and he described the make and model of the nuclear demolition charge. It's him, all right. He says he's dialed the yield up to the maximum ten kilotons."

Ten kilotons was about two-thirds the yield of the weapon dropped on Hiroshima. It wouldn't wipe Washington, D.C., off the face of the planet, but millions of people would die, and the seat of American government would be a radioactive hole in the ground.

"What does he want?"

"For starters full withdrawal of all United States forces from the former Yugoslavia."

Bolan's eyes suddenly narrowed. "I don't buy it."

Svarzkova blinked at the Executioner incredulously. Kurtzman paused. "You don't think he has the device?"

"I know he has the device."

"You don't think he intends to use it?"

"Oh, he intends to use it, all right."

Kurtzman suddenly seized the idea. "You think it's a feint."

Bolan nodded. "I do."

"I think you're in the minority there, Mack. Everyone around here is on full alert. They're expecting Armageddon. The President and his immediate staff are already on *Air Force One* and halfway across the country." Kurtzman let out a breath. "You think you have Baibakov's head figured out?"

Bolan smiled slightly. "I think I do. I see a highly trained special-forces officer who knows his enemy well."

Kurtzman was obviously intrigued. "So what are you thinking?"

Bolan stared at the wall. "You tell me, Aaron. Will the administration make a deal? Even if they believe Baibakov will do it?"

"No. If they do, then they've given over United States world policy to anyone who can build a crude nuclear device and smuggle it into the country."

"That's what I'm thinking. Now, what happens if the Red Falcons go ahead and blow up Washington anyway?"

"Armageddon as far as Serbia is concerned. The American people will want blood, and they won't give a damn that it was some splinter group that did it, either. We'd probably level Serbia with conventional weapons and turn them into the fifty-first state."

Bolan nodded. "I don't believe that's what the Red Falcons want, do you?"

"No."

"So the question is, what do they really want?"

"Well, according to everything we've come up with, they want to punish the United States for its involvement in Bosnia."

"And?"

Kurtzman sounded bemused. "They want to break our will to fight and drive us out of Bosnia. Once the United States is out, most of the NATO forces would probably withdraw. Then Bosnia becomes part of Greater Serbia again."

"Exactly. Now, does blowing up the capital of the United States help accomplish that goal?"

"No. It doesn't. But then again, Mack, that's assuming we're dealing with rational human beings. Not a psychopath leading a group of armed fanatics."

The Executioner nodded slowly. "All right, that's a given. But since we don't have any other red-hot ideas at the moment, let's assume that Baibakov and his friends are rational and they have a definite plan."

"All right, I'll bite. What's your idea?"

"I don't have one, Bear—that's your department. I need you to get your team working, and I need an answer fast."

"Go ahead. Shoot."

"I need a target that accomplishes the Red Falcons' goals. Something that would make the President and the American people lose the will to stay in Bosnia, but falls short of dragging all of Serbia into a war with the United States. And it has to be a target you'd use a small nuke on."

"Now, that is an extremely interesting set of target parameters."

"So get on the stick. I don't think we have a whole lot of time on this one."

"I'm on it. Kurtzman out."

Bolan punched the link off. Svarzkova stared at him with a raised eyebrow. "So what do we do now?"

Bolan rose from the table. "How about a bath and food?"
Svarzkova perked up at the mention of food. "Ah!"

BAIBAKOV LOOKED DOWN at the thermonuclear device. It was
roughly the size of a large suitcase and painted in the dull,
nonreflective Russian military shade of green. A small panel
on the top allowed access to the simple controls. It was a
variable-yield device. The twist of a dial altered the efficiency
and timing of the detonation, and that allowed the selection of
an atomic yield between one and ten kilotons. There was a
timer, arming and safety switches and little else to it. Its anti-
tamper measures were simple but effective. Once the weapon
was in place and armed, motion sensors inside the casing
would detonate the weapon if they detected anyone cutting
into the primary casing.

The charge itself was crude by modern standards. It was a
simple gun-type nuclear device. Within the outer casing was
a three-foot steel tube. At either end of the tube was a subcritical mass, which consisted of twenty pounds of uranium
235. On detonation a small charge of high explosive would
fire one of the subcritical masses down the tube like a bullet
to slam into the other one. When the two subcritical masses
collided together, they would instantly go critical, and nuclear
fission would occur.

Baibakov stared at the device speculatively. A nuclear-
demolition charge wasn't the most effective of nuclear weapons for mass destruction. It was essentially a tool, and its military function was to blow huge holes in things. The primary
targets of a charge of this type were large, solid structures
such as hardened underground bunkers and dams.

The giant grinned wolfishly. The designer probably hadn't
envisioned the particular use Baibakov had for the device, but
the giant had little doubt that it would be totally effective. His
grin faded as an unwelcome thought crept from the back of
his mind. He was still disturbed that he had been unable to
kill the senator. He knew that in the larger plan it wouldn't

matter. Killing Senator McCain would have been a symbolic act more than anything else.

However, it wasn't the fact that Eudora McCain still breathed that sat burning in the back of Baibakov's mind. He was a hunter, and he considered himself the best that had ever lived, yet knew from long experience that not all hunts were successful. Sometimes the quarry escaped. Even he would admit that. What truly galled him was that the American commando had beaten him yet again. Senator McCain would have been an easy kill if not for his meddling. The commando had thwarted his every effort in the United States, and in the process killed almost all of the Red Falcons Baibakov had brought with him. The commando had bested him in America.

Something would have to be done about that.

Baibakov glanced over at Krstic. She stood enthralled as she looked down at the device. She stared in awe as if it were the Holy Grail. For her it was. The thermonuclear charge would be God's vengeance upon the Americans, and the first step toward a unified Greater Serbia.

The Russian put the American commando from his mind. The mission would have to come first. He needed to get more men, then he needed to transport the device and plant it at the target site. Baibakov smiled again as he imagined the detonation of the device and its consequences. America would reel with his blow; their will to fight and be "peacekeepers" in Bosnia would be crushed.

Then, while America lay stunned, he would arrange for the American commando to come to him.

19

Bolan sat in the mess hall at Fort Huachuca and watched Valentina Svarzkova shovel down pancakes. If the stitches in her lip were causing her any pain, it wasn't slowing her down for a second. She was working on her third plateful.

Bolan sipped his coffee as he waited for the Russian agent to finish her meal. It had been seven hours since he had talked to Kurtzman. He and Svarzkova had showered, eaten, slept and were working on their second meal. The Executioner knew the computer whiz had done none of the above. He and the cybernetics team at Stony Man Farm would be working at full throttle until they came up with some kind of answer.

Svarzkova pushed her plate away with a happy sigh and looked at Bolan incredulously. "This is military food?"

Bolan nodded. "Yes, but it's Sunday, and you've never had creamed chipped beef on toast."

The woman stared into space for a moment as she mentally ran that through her files. "Ah. Yes. Shit on a shingle. I have heard of it."

Both of Bolan's eyebrows rose as he lowered his coffee. "I'm impressed."

"It is I who am impressed. In the Russian military soldiers do not often get meat, much less complain about it."

The Executioner shrugged. "Soldiers complain in every army."

Svarzkova nodded sagely. "Yes, this is so. However, I do not believe American soldiers have ever been exposed to *kasha* and *selyodka.*"

"And that is?"

"Millet gruel and salted herring," she replied, scowling.

Bolan sipped his coffee. "American military service does have its benefits."

An Air Force sergeant wound his way through the mess hall and approached Bolan and Svarzkova's table. "Good morning. We have a priority communication for you in the message center, Mr. Belasko."

"Thank you, Sergeant." Bolan finished his coffee and rose. "Let's go."

They followed the sergeant out of the mess and down the street to the message center. The sergeant took them to another secure communications room. "I'll be outside if you need anything."

"Thank you, Sergeant." Bolan saw that the message was on standby and punched the intercom. "What have you got for me, Aaron?"

Kurtzman was obviously restraining his excitement. "We may have your target, and we don't think it's even in the United States."

"Tell me about it."

"Given your targeting parameters, we think the USS *Theodore Roosevelt* is our best bet."

Bolan paused. "The *Theodore Roosevelt* is a nuclear aircraft carrier."

"Exactly, and the *Theodore Roosevelt* and the escort ships in her battle group are currently deployed in the Adriatic Sea, approximately fifty miles off of the coast of the former Yugoslavia."

"That's a big target."

"He has a nuke."

Bolan nodded. "You have a point."

"The more I thought about it, the less sense a target in the United States itself meant. Any nuclear attack on anything on United States soil would blow up in the Red Falcons' faces. It kept coming back to your bottom line, Mack—what do the Red Falcons really want?"

Bolan calculated. "You think they want to blow up an aircraft carrier?"

"By the parameters you gave me, it makes perfect sense. It comes down to legitimate targets. D.C. just isn't a legitimate target for the Red Falcons. But an aircraft carrier is one of the great symbols of American military might. Simply parking one off the coast of another country demonstrates our military power and our political will during a crisis. The *Theodore Roosevelt* is stationed off the coast of Yugoslavia. It's already launched numerous air strikes against Serbian positions outside of Sarajevo. Unlike Washington, D.C., the *Theodore Roosevelt* is a genuine combatant over there, and that makes it a legitimate military target."

Bolan nodded. It did make sense.

Kurtzman pressed his point.

"Think about it. At any given time the *Theodore Roosevelt* is crewed by anywhere from six to seven thousand servicemen. Those are guaranteed casualties with a nuke, and that's many times more KIAs than we had in the entire war in the Persian Gulf. The *Roosevelt* carries a standard complement of twenty-four F-14s, twenty-four F/A-18s, fourteen Intruders, ten Vikings, four Hawkeyes and about half a dozen helicopters. That's millions and millions of dollars' worth of military hardware. It takes years to build an aircraft carrier, at a cost of over a billion dollars each. The *Theodore Roosevelt* is one of the Nimitz class, one of our best and the latest carriers, with all of the newest technological upgrades. It would be an irreplaceable loss."

"So would the loss of American prestige if it were blown to bits by terrorists."

"That price would be astronomical, but it goes far beyond the reaction abroad. The reaction at home would be the real killer. There are a lot of Americans who think we have no business being in Bosnia in the first place, and the House and the Senate are still divided about our deployment over there. If we lost an entire carrier and its crew, there would be immense revulsion in the public and Congress. A lot of people would demand we pull out before we suffered any more losses. If I was President, I can't see what I could do about it. When the Red Falcons threatened to blow up Washington last night, the president of Serbia was contacted. He said he had no control over the Red Falcons' activities, and frankly I believe him. I don't believe the administration would declare war on Serbia over an aircraft carrier blown up by a splinter group. Bringing the boys home might well be our President's only real option."

Bolan nodded slowly. He had to give Kurtzman credit. He had given the man a set of target parameters, and he had filled them perfectly. He had to give Baibakov credit, as well; if this was his plan, it was brilliant. The Red Falcons would martyr themselves by the legion to accomplish it. "I think you have our winner, Aaron."

Kurtzman sounded pleased but hesitant. "It's still a guess. A damned good one, in my opinion, but we're still just guessing."

Bolan considered the tactics of it. "Baibakov couldn't use a plane. Even a kamikaze attack would never get through the *Roosevelt*'s air defenses. It would be intercepted miles away by the fighters once it was picked up on radar, or shot down by one of the guided-missile cruiser escorts."

"I agree, and the same would go for fast-attack boats. They'd never get close enough. They'd either be blown out of the water by the escort ships or chopped to pieces miles out by fighters."

"He'd have to go in sneaky."

"He'd have to get in close, too. A nuclear-demolition charge like the one Baibakov has generates a relatively tiny fireball. The *Theodore Roosevelt* is over ninety thousand tons of welded steel and more than a thousand feet long. Outside of five hundred yards she and her crew would stand an excellent chance of survival. Outside of a thousand the blast would probably only shove her sideways through the water. Ideally the Red Falcons would want the charge in direct contact with the hull like a limpet mine. That would guarantee almost ninety percent of the carrier's hull being vaporized.''

"They'd have to go in and do that personally. I'm thinking an underwater assault with divers.''

"That would be the most likely, but the problem with a swimmer assault is they still have to get fifty miles offshore to the carrier.''

Bolan frowned. "They might have a swimmer-delivery vehicle stashed somewhere. They're not that hard to get. The Russians will sell just about any kind of gear on the black market for hard currency. That was how Ramzin got his nuclear devices.'' Bolan's frown deepened. "Even then, something would have to take the delivery vehicle out into deep water. Fifty miles is still way beyond their range.''

Kurtzman cut in suddenly. "Ferries. The Adriatic Sea is only slightly more than a hundred miles across at its widest point. There's literally a web of ferry lines stretching between the major port cities of Italy, former Yugoslavia, Albania and the western tip of Greece. If you paid the right people, a ferry boat could easily slide a swimmer vehicle off its ramp. There's also a large number of small islands off the coast, a lot of them with fishing villages on them. I'm sure some of them might be a viable launch point, as well.'' Kurtzman paused. "What are you thinking, Mack?''

The Executioner grimaced. "I'm thinking if we pull out the carrier and its battle group, Igor Baibakov will still be at large with a thermonuclear device.''

"You think we should let him make a try?''

"Ideally we should try to find him before he goes out. I don't think he'd detonate the weapon on Serbian soil. It doesn't help his cause, and he's not the suicidal type, either. I think we need to hunt him down, and we have to move fast.''

"You think he'll move that soon?''

Bolan nodded. "He's followed standard Russian tactics throughout this whole campaign. Speed, surprise and firepower have been the name of his game. I don't think he's going to wait around while we sort things out. Our only advantage is that last night Baibakov was in Arlington and his device was in Mexico. They have to meet and get to the Adriatic and get set up. If we act now, we can get there before he does.''

''That's assuming we can find him.''

Bolan grimaced. ''Maybe he'll find me.''

''That tactic almost got you killed last time.''

''Give it to Hal and run it by the President. Svarzkova and I will fly back to Washington in the meantime.''

''All right. Kurtzman out.''

Bolan closed the line and rose. Svarzkova stood and stared at Bolan resolutely. ''We go hunting?''

He nodded. ''Yes. We go hunting.''

20

The captain of the *Theodore Roosevelt* stood in his ready room with his arms folded and looked back and forth between Mack Bolan and Valentina Svarzkova. He was a short man with his gray hair in a military crew cut. He had a great deal of command presence, and as he looked at Bolan again a deep line slowly creased between his eyebrows.

He wasn't pleased with the prospect of his ship being blown up in a nuclear frogman attack.

Bolan could understand his irritation. The USS *Theodore Roosevelt* was arguably the largest and most powerful warship in history. He had at his command a tactical air force superior to that of many countries, as well as the weapons on board to fight a limited nuclear war. The major threats the captain had to worry about were enemy attack submarines, missile-armed surface ships and strike aircraft. To combat these potential adversaries he had a fleet of escort ships armed for the anti-ship, antiaircraft and antisubmarines roles, as well as the *Theodore Roosevelt*'s own massive air power.

Frogmen were generally not considered much of a threat to deep-water vessels, much less vessels as powerful as a Nimitz-class carrier surrounded by her escorts of cruisers, destroyers and frigates.

The captain looked at Svarzkova. "So this Baibakov character is one of your boys?"

The lieutenant cleared her throat. "Captain Baibakov is a former officer of the Russian army. His current activities do not reflect the will or policy of the Russian government."

The captain didn't seem very relieved. "Ah." He looked over at Bolan again. "So I'm supposed to just steam along, business as usual, and see if this guy shows up off my bow with a nuclear bomb?"

Bolan smiled slightly. "It's not quite that bad, Captain. The key is we have to let them start the attempt. If you steam away now, they know we're onto them. Then they pick a new target and wait, and we have nothing to go on. If we can catch them in motion, we can shut them down permanently."

The captain sighed heavily. "Yes, I understand the logic. I just don't like the tactic of my battle group being used as bait with a nuclear weapon involved."

Bolan shrugged. "Yes, but it's only a small nuclear weapon."

The captain smiled almost against his will. "Oh, well, what the hell, then. Let's do it."

Bolan spread out a map of the Adriatic that Kurtzman had sent him. "We're presently standing off the Jabuka shoals. This gives an enemy using a swimmer-delivery vehicle three avenues of attack. There are two ferry lines that cross each other west of your carrier group. At our position now, either one could deploy a swim vehicle in range of the *Theodore Roosevelt*. The other opportunity is the offshore islands. A swimmer-delivery vehicle could be launched from the major island of Vis, then leapfrog along the smaller islands to get within range."

The captain nodded. "So what do you propose?"

"You have one Los Angeles–class 688 nuclear submarine with your battle group right now. Three more 688s from the Mediterranean fleet are steaming at full speed to join us now. They should be here in a matter of hours. Two Sturgeon-class boats are coming in, as well. That will give us two passive listening posts that we will deploy along each of the three possible routes the Red Falcons might take. When we detect them coming in, we go in and take them out."

The captain frowned and scratched his chin. "There's only one problem with your plan that I can see. The Adriatic Sea is shallow and muddy by nautical standards. The Jabuka shoal is only two hundred and sixty six meters at its deepest point. Sonar is notoriously inefficient in this kind of water.''

Bolan nodded. ''That's true, but we do have some advantages. They don't know that we're onto them, and they won't know that we'll have a net of submarines looking for them. Also we don't believe that Baibakov could have acquired the latest model of swimmer-delivery vehicles with enhanced stealth features. The United States doesn't sell them, and the Russian military can't spare any. If they did get their hands on a swimmer-delivery vehicle, it should be an older model, and somewhat noisier than the latest equipment Navy SEAL or Russian Spetsnaz are using.''

The captain grunted. ''There's still a hell of a lot we're not very sure about.''

The Executioner had to agree. ''We can't even be sure they're coming at all. You and your ship are just the best educated guess we could come up with. But if they're coming, it'll be soon. They have no way of telling how long you'll stay in position. I'm willing to bet if they move, we're looking at a time frame of the next seventy-two hours.''

''All right. So we wait and go about business as usual.'' The captain steepled his fingers. ''What are you going to do when we detect them?''

''A helicopter will deliver me near their position. Once I'm in the water, I'll use a sonar phone to communicate with the nearest sub. They'll vector me onto the target.''

The captain looked at Bolan narrowly. ''And then?''

Bolan shrugged. ''I'll nullify the threat.''

The captain shifted in his chair. ''I don't mean any insult. You seem very capable. But, I'd be happier if a team of Navy SEALs was taking care of this.''

''So would I. But when Baibakov called in threats all over the East and West coasts of the United States, the SEAL teams *were* deployed. I've been informed that SEAL Team Four is being reassembled and sent here, but I'm what you've got for the next twenty-four hours.''

The captain nodded. "All right. I'll have a helicopter prepped and two crews rotating on standby for you."

BAIBAKOV LOOKED OUT across the Adriatic Sea.

His quarry lay just over the arc of the horizon. At nearly a hundred thousand tons of steel, it was the largest prey he had ever hunted. The Russian frowned slightly. To his mind it wasn't much of a hunt. It was like sneaking up on a mountain. There would be no trophy, either. Anything left over would be so radioactive it would have to be hung in a lead trophy case for the next three or four decades.

Baibakov snorted at an unbidden thought. It was really more like a fishing expedition. He would cast out his line, hook the target and watch its death throes. The idea amused him. The giant looked over at his rod and reel.

The delivery vehicle was little more than a torpedo with a saddle and handlebars. One man steered while up to four other men could hold on to struts sticking out of the sides. There was an equipment rack behind the saddle that accommodated the charge nicely.

Anton, Peter, Michael and Nicolas stood by the swimmer vehicle and examined their new weapons. They were the few Red Falcons that had any scuba experience, though all of them had been training intensively on the Greek resort island of Corfu for the past three weeks to prepare for the mission. In the last week of their training they had successfully "attacked" a Greek naval frigate and an oil tanker. They were amateurs compared to Spetsnaz divers, but they would be competent enough for the job at hand.

Baibakov raised a massive hand at a pile of empty crates ten yards down the beach. "Test fire the weapons."

Anton grinned and stepped forward. He cradled a weapon that looked vaguely like an AK-74 rifle, except that it seemed to have a double magazine and its stock telescoped rather than folded. He snapped out the stock, shouldered the rifle, aimed at the crates and fired.

The gun snarled, and Anton nearly lost control of the

weapon as it recoiled violently on full automatic fire. He lowered the weapon sheepishly. Baibakov looked down at the target. Anton had let out about a 15-round burst, and most of his shots had missed. But one of the crates had gotten hit. Four slender steel darts were impaled in the wooden slats.

The APS underwater assault rifle was one of the latest small arms in Russia's inventory, and the Russian military industries were eager to market it. The weapon had been designed expressly to deal with the problems of underwater combat for special-forces troops. Normal firearms malfunctioned as water entered their actions and filled their barrels. Dedicated underwater weapons were often equally useless on land. They often had limited range and could only fire one harpoon or projectile at a time.

The APS fired a 120 mm steel dart and held twenty-four rounds in the changeable magazine. It could be fired on land or underwater on semi- or full automatic. The only drawback was that the recoil impulse of firing a five inch steel dart on full automatic was horrendous. Baibakov frowned.

"If you must fight above water, fire on semiautomatic. Under the surface the water will help smother the recoil. Fire on full automatic under the water."

The men nodded.

"I cannot imagine you will meet any resistance, but it is best to be prepared. Each of you practice with a magazine full of ammunition to get the feel of the weapons."

The four men nodded again and began to fire single rounds into the stack of crates. Baibakov grunted to himself as steel darts tore through the crates with monotonous efficiency. The Red Falcons were all guerrilla-war veterans, and they adapted quickly.

Peter would drive the swimmer-delivery vehicle, while Nicolas and Michael planted the charge. Anton would provide security. It was a relatively simple operation once they got close. Getting them within range had been the greatest challenge, but the offshore islands had provided the means. A fisherman on the island of Vis had been all too eager to transport them and the swim vehicle to the outermost island near the Jabuka shoal. A motor skiff would return them to Vis, then back to the mainland once the mission was completed.

The Red Falcons fired their magazines dry, then reloaded their weapons. They looked up at Baibakov expectantly.

"Do you have any questions?"

Anton shook his head. "We are ready. Victory is at hand."

Baibakov nodded, then looked at Anton intently. "And if you are discovered?"

The man stood straighter, and his jaw set with grim determination. "It does not matter. If we cannot fight our way out, the weapon will still be detonated. America will pay for its crimes, and we will pay with our lives if necessary."

"Excellent, Comrade." The giant considered the four men standing before him.

Fanatics had their uses.

He looked out across the Adriatic Sea again. "Get some rest. The attack begins in four hours."

21

Mack Bolan sat in the pilots' ready room and waited. He had been waiting for six hours. His air tanks were charged, and his equipment was laid out and ready. Given the word, he could be ready to go into the water in five minutes. The soldier checked his gear again. He was more encumbered with equipment than he would have liked, but until the Navy SEALs arrived, he was solo and every piece was vital.

His swim board contained an illuminated compass, depth gauge and a sighting device to measure angles. In the dark water of the Adriatic it would be his only way of steering himself toward his target. His underwater-surveillance light looked for all the world like a short, fat, bright yellow bazooka. It had been designed to find submerged mines in dark water and could generate a three-thousand-candlepower beam. His sonar phone was perhaps his most important piece of kit. It looked vaguely like a small megaphone, and with it he could talk directly to whichever of the submarines had made a detection. Once in the water, he would navigate with the swim board as they vectored him in to the target. A waterproof radio was clipped to his diving-tank straps to allow him to communicate with the battle group when he surfaced.

The Executioner looked at his weapons. A pair of bizarre-looking pistols lay on the desk beside him. The Heckler & Koch P-11 consisted of a pistol grip with five black tubes mounted in a circle. Each tube contained an individual rocket-assisted dart. Bolan looked at the weapons. He was never happy about using new equipment that he hadn't checked himself out on. However, he had never known a weapon from the German firm to fail. Its lethal range underwater was supposed to be eighteen meters. Bolan knew all too well he would have to get a lot closer than that. Firing anything underwater was an iffy situation at best, and he had his doubts about the stopping power of the thin steel darts. He knew they were lethal, but they would have little hitting power. Shooting an opponent with the rocket-assisted darts would be like stabbing a man with an ice pick. Placement would be everything. He would have to get in close and put the darts into the lethal areas of the body.

Bolan grimaced. He suspected there would be between two and four Red Falcons on the mission, and he didn't believe they would sit by and idly let themselves be massacred.

The soldier looked down at his final piece of kit. A Navy MK III underwater-demolitions knife lay strapped against his calf. The knife had a short, fat, hourglass-shaped handle with a lanyard for maximum retention underwater, and the six-inch black blade terminated abruptly into a wickedly sharp reinforced double-edged clip point. The knife could easily be stabbed into a steel military fuel drum. Bolan checked the elastic straps holding the knife to his leg. In his experience in underwater combat, it always came down to knives in the end. Down in the dark depths, the brutal diving knife strapped to his leg would be his last resort.

The Executioner glanced up as Valentina Svarzkova entered the briefing room with two steaming mugs. "I have brought you some coffee."

Bolan smiled tiredly and took one of the mugs. "Thanks."

The Russian agent clasped her mug in both hands and peered into the bitter brew with a frown. "I would go with you, but I am not scuba qualified."

"I know."

"I do not think Baibakov will be down there. I think this idea of blowing up your aircraft carrier is a suicide mission. If he was still in Spetsnaz, and he had been ordered to do this, he would go. But now he is in command, and I do not think he will go personally.''

Bolan had to agree.

''Almost,'' she went on, ''I think it would be better if he was going. Baibakov is crazy, but he is not suicidal. The Red Falcons, they are fanatics. If they get the opportunity, they will detonate the weapon when you attack them.'' Her blue eyes were greatly troubled as she locked her gaze with Bolan. ''I believe you are in terrible danger.''

The Executioner didn't know what to say. She was right. There was a very real chance he could find himself in the center of a nuclear fireball. ''Don't worry. They'll never see me coming.''

Svarzkova sat up resolutely and pulled up her jacket sleeve. ''Here.'' She unstrapped the elastic bands holding her AK-47 bayonet to her forearm and handed the slender weapon to Bolan. ''Take this. For luck.''

The Executioner smiled. A little extra insurance never hurt, and he'd take luck wherever he could get it. He made a fist and held out his left arm. Svarzkova grinned and strapped the knife onto his forearm over his wet suit. ''There. Now you are ready for anything.''

Bolan slapped the sheath and was satisfied. The knife would stay in place. ''I'll bring this back to you.''

Svarzkova made a show of looking at him coolly. ''You had better. I acquired that weapon from the first suspect I ever arrested. He made an attempt to kill me with it. I took it away from him and put him in hospital. It has been my lucky piece ever since.''

The door to the ready room opened, and the captain of the *Theodore Roosevelt* entered. His face was grim as he looked at Bolan. ''The USS *Baton Rouge* has detected an intermittent noise. It's six miles from the battle group, and they believe it's closing.'' The captain let out a long breath. ''Are you ready?''

The Executioner nodded. ''Tell the helicopter to start its engines. I'll be on the deck in five minutes.''

The captain turned and left the room. Bolan shrugged into the web harness that held his tanks and strapped them down. He pushed the two rocket pistols into their plastic holsters on his dive belt and shouldered his swim board and the underwater surveillance light. "Let's do it."

Bolan strode down the steel passageway and walked out onto the *Theodore Roosevelt*'s flight deck. He narrowed his eyes at the sun and calculated. The sun was beginning to sink low in the sky. If the Red Falcons were six miles out, they would reach the carrier at just about dusk. It was well thought out. They would have just enough daylight to find the carrier easily and attach the charge, then darkness would cover their escape. Given the situation, it was the way he would have done it.

Out on the deck a white-painted Sikorsky Seahawk had its rotors turning. Its doors were open, and two men stood in position behind door-mounted M-60 machine guns. Bolan strode up to the door and nodded at one of the gunners. "You're my ride?"

The man nodded. "Yes, sir."

He clambered into the helicopter. The gunner raised an eyebrow as Svarzkova climbed in after him. She shrugged. "I would go insane waiting on the carrier."

The Executioner handed her a life jacket. A lieutenant shouted to them from the cockpit. "You ready?"

Bolan nodded. "Let's do it!"

The aircraft vibrated as its engines roared up to takeoff speed, then the helicopter lifted off the deck. The Seahawk rose, then dipped its nose as it accelerated over the water. Bolan moved to the cockpit. "Where was the contact the last we knew?"

The pilot shouted over the rotor noise. "Approximately six miles out. The *Baton Rouge* is shadowing the signal on a parallel course about two thousand yards to starboard. I'm going to drop you in on an intercept course one hundred yards to port of the contact. You'll be in a direct line forty-five degrees northeast of the *Baton Rouge*. They'll vector you in."

Bolan nodded and looked out across the water. The Adriatic was gray, and the winter storms had raised up sand and mud from the bottom of the shallow sea. Fifty feet was the visibility he had been quoted on the *Roosevelt,* but looking out across the water the soldier suspected it could be much less. He would probably be right on top of the Red Falcons before he saw them.

The Executioner took a seat in the cabin and waited as the helicopter swept low over the sea. Behind him the aircraft carrier and her escort ships looked like islands of gray steel. To the south he could see small rock islands jutting up out of the sea. Those islands had probably been the launch point. Bolan wondered if Baibakov was there, waiting among the rocks for the fireworks to begin.

The pilot shouted back into the cabin. "Approaching drop point. Get ready!"

Bolan stood and checked his diving rig a final time. It had been checked and rechecked. There was little to do now but get into the water. The helicopter slowed to a hover and began to drop down. Bolan went to the right-side door and pulled his hood over his head and sealed his mask against his face. His air system was a self-contained breathing apparatus, and would let no bubbles escape to betray his presence. His air pressure was fine. He shouldered his equipment and stood in the door frame as he waited for the final signal.

The Seahawk's pilot shouted again. "Ready?"

Svarzkova raised up on her toes and spoke against Bolan's hood. "Luck!"

Bolan slapped the knife against his arm as the pilot shouted, "Diver away! Go!"

The Executioner slid into the cold water of the Adriatic Sea. Visibility was barely thirty-five feet, if that. He looked down at the illuminated compass on his swim board. He kicked his fins and oriented himself forty-five degrees and unclipped his sonar phone. He put the mouthpiece against his mask and aimed himself at the position the USS *Baton Rouge* was supposed to be. Bolan pressed the Send trigger. "*Baton Rouge,* this is Belasko. Do you copy?"

Bolan pressed the receiver against the side of his head. A moment later the tight-beam sonar pulse from the *Baton Rouge* was picked up by the sonar phone's ear. "Belasko, this is *Baton Rouge.* We have your position and are picking you up loud and clear, over."

He pressed the phone to his mask. "Vector me in, *Baton Rouge.*"

"Roger, Belasko. Descend to sixty feet and take a course fifty degrees southeast."

Bolan nosed his swim board down and began to descend. As he hit sixty feet, he shifted around to the southeast and began to kick powerfully toward his intercept point. Bolan turned his head and spoke into the sonar phone. "Completed maneuver, am heading in."

"Roger that. You are on course."

He kicked ahead and kept his eyes on the dull green glow of the compass needle, which pointed him toward his prey like an accusing finger in the gloom. Bolan craned his neck around and squeezed the sonar phone's trigger. "What's my position, *Baton Rouge.*"

"Fifty yards and closing. Swim faster."

Bolan kicked harder through the still depths. "Position, *Baton Rouge?*"

"Twenty-five yards and closing. Maintain speed. You are on a collision course."

The soldier swam through the murk. It was starting to get darker as the sun sank and less and less of its light was filtering into the depths. Bolan scanned ahead. "Where are they, *Baton Rouge?*"

"Ten yards, Belasko."

Bolan grimaced as he shifted his glance through the gloom. "I don't see them."

The voice sounded tense. "You're almost on top of them. Directly southeast."

Bolan looked down at his compass and shifted his position

to coincide with the needle. "Contact, *Baton Rouge*. Belasko out."

The Executioner dropped the sonar phone on its belt leash. Ahead a large dark shape was slowly becoming visible out of the murk. It was a long, dark, humped object that vaguely looked like a tiny whale. Bolan leaned on his swim board and brought the surveillance beam to his shoulder. His right hand drew one of the Heckler & Koch P-11 rocket pistols. Bolan waited. He wanted to get as close as he could before firing.

The Executioner kicked in place as the swimmer-delivery vehicle approached out of the depths. The outline of the vehicle was becoming clear. The torpedo-shaped hull had a rider on top who was steering, and three other men trailed off tow bars like lampreys. Bolan's finger tightened on the trigger of the surveillance light. If he could see them, they could see him.

It was time to take that away from them. Bolan squeezed the surveillance light's trigger.

In the murky water the sudden glare of the three-thousand-candlepower beam was like the spotlight of God. The riders started and looked directly into the light in surprise. Bolan extended the P-11 and put its crude front sight in the middle of the steersman's chest and squeezed the trigger.

A streak of bubbles shot from the muzzle and drew a line directly toward the steersman. Bolan squeezed the trigger twice more, and the sizzling lines converged against the dark backdrop of the steersman. The man jerked as the rocket-propelled darts struck him, and he slowly leaned forward over his steering bar. Bolan shifted his aim and fired at the lead man on the starboard tow bar. A dart shot out and drew a line through the water into his shoulder. The man jerked and raised a dark object in his hand. The soldier fired again, and his last rocket knifed through the water.

Bolan's eyes flared in surprise as red flame burst from the man's weapon and a staccato thumping noise rolled through the water. A formation of hissing lines streaked toward him. He saw his own dart hit, and the man released his weapon and grabbed his thigh. Bolan dropped the spent P-11 and yanked his swim board in front of him. The water was suddenly plunged into darkness as his finger left the surveillance light's trigger. The swim board shuddered in his hands as the swarm of projectiles struck it.

The Executioner released the board and swam off hard to his right. His one advantage was that the Red Falcons had been momentarily blinded. Streams of projectiles streaked through the water where he had been a moment earlier. Bolan swam in closer and drew his second rocket pistol. He extended the surveillance light and lit up the swim vehicle again. The driver was still slumped over the steering bars and not moving. Without his hand on the throttle, the vehicle had slowed to a stop and had begun to slowly sink. The other man Bolan had shot had released his tow bar and was trying to make for the surface, still clutching his wounded leg.

Two Red Falcons were still a threat. One was bent over a rack behind the steersman with a flashlight in his hand. The other man was aiming a weapon into the glare of the light.

Bolan ignored the weapon and aimed at the terrorist working behind the steersman. The Executioner didn't know for sure what he was doing, but a cold feeling told him he couldn't afford to let him finish. He aimed the P-11 and squeezed the trigger four times. The hissing streaks of the rocket projectiles arrowed through the water and drew streaming lines into the neck and shoulders of the man bent over the rack. His flashlight suddenly went out.

A school of streaks streamed back from the man with the weapon. Bolan kicked his body into as straight a horizontal line as possible and held up the bulky surveillance light as a shield. The salvo of projectiles streamed all around him.

The surveillance light shuddered and its beam went out as several darts crashed through its glass lens and shattered the bulb. There was a metallic clank as a dart bounced off the top of Bolan's rebreathing tank, and something tugged at his left swim fin. Sudden fire shot up the soldier's arm as something skewered his left biceps. He released the ruined surveillance light and stuck his right arm straight out as he fired his last rocket at the remaining Red Falcon. The man had bent over beside the swim vehicle. Bolan couldn't see what he was doing in the gloom, but he suspected the man was reloading.

The terrorist suddenly moved, and the rocket hissed over his shoulder and pinged against the hull of the swim vehicle. The Executioner reached down his leg and drew his MK III diver's knife, ignoring the stabbing pain in his left arm, and swam forward as fast as he could.

The Red Falcon raised the weapon and slapped the bottom of his fresh magazine. He shoved the weapon out, and Bolan twisted his body away as the muzzle suddenly spurted flashing fire. The automatic weapon thumped rapidly as it fired over Bolan's shoulder. The Executioner reached out, grabbed the barrel and pushed the weapon away.

Bolan kicked forward and plunged his knife into the man's chest. The terrorist's weapon continued to fire on full auto as the man's finger clenched on the trigger. The soldier punched the knife through the man's wet suit a second and third time before the body went limp.

The Executioner released the corpse and kicked it out of the way. He swam on top of the swim vehicle and pulled the body off the rack. A large square object sat there covered in clear plastic. Bolan frowned. It was too dark to see the control panel. He struck out and grabbed the corpse of the man who had been working on the charge and removed the flashlight from where it hung around his wrist. The soldier swam back to the slowly sinking swim vehicle and played the light onto the charge.

The control panel beneath the plastic wrapping was open. Bolan's skin crawled as he peered closer. The timer had been set to minimum, and the arming light blinked a dull red in the flashlight beam.

The charge was going to detonate.

Bolan knew of no way to defuse the charge, much less defuse it underwater without tools. The only advantage he had were the seconds ticking away. The nuclear-demolition charge was a tool. The designer had never envisioned the need for it to be immediately detonated with the push of a button on the charge itself. The operator would set a timer and then escape. The only way to immediately detonate the charge was with a radio signal, and radio didn't work underwater. When Bolan had surprised the Red Falcon, the man had used the quickest means possible to detonate. He had dialed the timer to the minimum setting and flipped the arming switch. The sequence was locked in. The charge would blow in ten minutes.

The soldier calculated rapidly. The *Theodore Roosevelt* and her escorts were approximately six miles away and relatively safe. The USS *Baton Rouge* was just over a thousand yards off to his left, and the shock wave from the blast would shatter its hull.

Bolan grabbed the lanyard dangling from his dive belt and pulled up the sonar phone. He pressed the transmitter against his mask and got a muffled squawk. Playing the flashlight over the sonar phone, he saw that a steel dart protruded from the transmitter's plastic body.

The soldier cut the lanyard and dropped the useless device into the depths. The *Baton Rouge* was listening passively, and would have heard the underwater gun battle. They would know something had happened. Short of an explosion, a metallic clank was one of the noises that transmitted best underwater. Bolan took his diving knife and hammered it against the hull of the swimmer-delivery vehicle in a rapid rhythm. It was a simple four-word message in Morse code:

"Run, run, run...Belasko."

Two seconds later Bolan's whole body clenched as a wall of sound seemed to slam through his body in a single giant pulse. The *Baton Rouge* had heard his signal and realized the sonar phone was down. They had gone active with their bow sonar and acknowledged his signal with a thunderclap of sound. Bolan shook his head to clear it. Being pinged wasn't a pleasant experience for an exposed diver.

The submarine would be blowing all ballast for the surface, then steaming for their lives. But to get to safety the 688-class submarine would need time and distance. Their escape time was set and fleeting with every instant. Distance-wise, Bolan could still give them an edge.

He could sink the charge to the bottom of the Adriatic Sea.

The swimmer-delivery vehicle was sinking already. It had no ballast tanks, and like a shark, it either moved forward under its own power or it sank. There was no time to let it finish its drifting descent. Bolan pushed the dead steersman out of the saddle and peered at the rudimentary instrument panel. Pushing forward and back controlled the dive planes, and foot pedals controlled its movement from side to side. Bolan revved the throttle and shoved the control bars forward. The swimmer vehicle nosed forward and dived.

Like a motorcycle the swimmer vehicle required someone on the throttle to give the engine power. He would have to rig the throttle. He took the diving knife off his wrist and wrapped the lanyard around the throttle on the control bar. He held the throttle down, then twisted the plastic cord around it tightly to hold the swimmer vehicle on full throttle. It surged forward. Bolan pushed the control bars down into a steep dive, then jammed the diving knife into the rubber-gasketed crotch of the steering column. The swim vehicle began to rapidly descend into the darkness.

The soldier kicked away from the vehicle and began to swim upward. He could see the surface as a dim gray vault above him, and he resisted the urge to swim as fast as he could. The bends would kill him in this situation as surely as the impending nuclear fireball below.

A shape suddenly occluded the surface above, and Bolan yanked himself to a halt as a dim glimmer of steel slashed at him.

One of the Red Falcons was still alive, the terrorist he'd shot in the leg and shoulder.

A hard object slashed against his forearm and rasped off of Svarzkova's knife as Bolan instinctively raised his left arm to block. Bolan balled his knees into his chest and kicked backward to put distance between himself and his attacker as he pulled the bayonet from its sheath.

The injured Red Falcon descended after him but couldn't maneuver very well.

Bolan swam backward as the knife lunged toward his chest. As the blade recoiled, the soldier twisted his hips and lunged forward. The AK-47 blade punched low into the terrorist's stomach. Down in the murky depths there was no room for mercy. Bolan pushed the blade in to the hilt and ripped upward with all his might. It stopped on the Red Falcon's sternum, and the man cringed fetally around Bolan's arm.

The Executioner yanked the blade out and pushed off the dying terrorist. Time was running out. Bolan kicked toward the surface. The sea above him seemed a uniform dark gray as dusk descended, and the vault of the sea seemed endless.

Without warning, Bolan suddenly broke the surface. His hands went to his mask, and he yanked it back over his head and breathed the salt air. The sun was a dim glow on the horizon, and the sea was dark around him. Bolan keyed the radio on his chest strap.

"This is Belasko, calling for immediate extraction. Look for the strobe." On Bolan's other chest strap was a small but powerful strobe the size of a penlight. He pushed the oversize switch, and it began to blink almost as brightly as a camera flash. Almost immediately he heard the sound of rotors beating the air over the Adriatic.

The Executioner trod water as the landing lights of the helicopter swooped toward him out of the sky. A brilliant light lit the dusk, and Bolan was nearly blinded as the Seahawk's spotlight hit him. The aircraft slowed to a hover overhead, and the soldier waved his right arm in a circle as the blast of the rotor wash mashed the sea flat around him. The bright orange hoop of the hoist came down, and he grabbed it and hooked it under his shoulders. After he gave the helicopter the thumbs-up, Bolan was hoisted out of the water.

The hoist seemed to move at a crawl, but finally Svarzkova and one of the airmen grabbed Bolan and pulled him into the helicopter. "We're going to have a detonation in seven minutes. Tell the pilot to radio the battle group and have them move north of this position at full speed."

The airman gaped and moved to the cockpit as Bolan sat on a bench in the cabin. He handed Svarzkova back her knife. "Thanks. It came in handy."

The Russian agent looked at Bolan's arm in alarm. "You are hurt!"

He leaned back against the cabin wall. The aching weariness and cold were worse than the pain. "Yeah. You could pull that out of my arm if you want to."

Bolan tensed as Svarzkova smoothly pulled the dart out of his arm. There was little else to be done until he could strip out of his wet suit. She held up the five-inch arrow of steel and peered at it quizzically. "They had APS underwater assault rifles?"

Bolan shrugged. "Apparently."

Svarzkova put the dart in her pocket. "You killed them all?"

Bolan nodded.

She looked at the Executioner intensely. "Was Baibakov among them?"

"No. You were right. Baibakov didn't go on the mission himself."

Svarzkova nodded. "What has happened to the nuclear charge?"

Bolan glanced at his watch. "It's at the bottom of the Adriatic and should go off in about three minutes."

Bolan rose and looked out over the Adriatic Sea. The *Baton Rouge* had broached and was steaming behind them at full speed. Bolan's face tightened. They were in for a hell of a ride. The seconds crept by as the helicopter headed back to the fleeing battle group. Bolan blinked. For a second there was a barely distinguishable pulse of light. It was more of a momentary lightening of the water than a flash. Seconds later the sea seemed to heave itself up in a massive fountain. The noise was almost a subliminal thunder over the beating of the helicopter rotors. The column of water rose like a mountain of gray water, then collapsed back on itself. The explosion was over almost before it had begun.

Svarzkova frowned in disappointment. "It was not as interesting as I had imagined."

"It's almost dark, and the detonation was over two hundred fifty yards below water. It would have been a lot more interesting if the detonation had occurred on the surface against the hull of the *Roosevelt*. Ask the boys on the *Baton Rouge* tomorrow how exciting it was, and they'll tell you a different story. Surfacing eliminated the danger of crushing pressure, but they're about to get hit by one hell of a shock wave."

Svarzkova nodded. "I hope they will be all right."

Bolan sat back down. "They should be. The 688 is a fine boat."

The woman sat next to Bolan. "So, what do we do now?"

The Executioner leaned his head back against the cabin wall and closed his eyes. He suspected it was a rhetorical question. There was one last piece of unfinished business. It was a seven-foot psychopath named Igor Baibakov.

22

Mack Bolan's lips tightened as he flexed his biceps. The wound twinged when he flexed his arm, but the limb was fully functional. Puncture wounds weren't very debilitating if they didn't go into vital areas. His shoulder actually ached more from the tetanus shot the ship's doctor had given him. The needle had been just about as large as the Russian dart, and its payload was almost guaranteed to cause swelling.

He rolled out of his bunk as a polite knocking sounded against the door. "It's open."

A petty officer opened the door. "You have a priority message, sir."

"Lead the way."

The Executioner followed the petty officer through the maze of passageways and up to the *Theodore Roosevelt*'s communications room. The executive officer nodded as Bolan entered and handed him a phone. The Navy men discreetly left the room.

Hal Brognola's voice came across the phone.

"Well, Striker, the President is relieved."

"Thanks for letting me know. How's the *Baton Rouge?*"

"It took a hell of a beating, but they came through it. Some seamen got tossed around, and a lot of their electronics got knocked out of line. But they steamed under their own power into Rimini for repairs."

"Baibakov is still alive."

"So I gathered."

"He'll go back to Bosnia."

"The President is of two minds about it. He wants Baibakov terminated, but his advisers are still leery about covert action in Bosnia outside of peacekeeping activities. They're saying the Red Falcons have been smashed, and their terror campaign against the United States is a failure."

Bolan's tone grew cold. "He has friends and sympathizers in Bosnia. He'll jump-start the Red Falcons again if he has to do it himself."

Brognola sighed. "That's what the Bear said. What do you want me to tell the President?"

In the Executioner's mind there was only one option. "Tell him to send me to Sarajevo. I'll take Svarzkova and make contact again with the Muslim militia. The drill will be the same as it was from the start. We'll hunt down Baibakov and take him out. I'll make myself his number-one priority. If I fail, we are all deniable by the administration. Have Grimaldi fly in my full battle kit."

"All right. I'll tell him."

BAIBAKOV LOOKED DOWN from the Jahorina mountain range. Sarajevo lay below him nestled in snow. The USS *Theodore Roosevelt* still sailed, along with all of her escort ships. He had seen the detonation from the island of Bisevo. Other than a small tidal wave hitting the island, the effects had been negligible. Anton, Peter, Michael and Nicolas had gone to a watery grave. More likely they had been dissolved into their component atoms. The Red Falcons were almost finished.

Tomas Broz had managed to escape into Canada with two of his men, and the Russian *mafiya* in Montreal had repatriated them to Bosnia. Along with Madchen Krstic, they numbered exactly four. Baibakov's brow furrowed. He had been foiled again. He couldn't prove it, but his gut told him the American commando had been responsible. From long ago in the Sonoran Desert of Arizona to the Adriatic Sea, the American had beaten him. The American had beaten him every time.

Red rage began to suffuse Baibakov's vision as he thought about his string of defeats. His knuckles whitened and cracked, and the remaining three Red Falcons took several cautious steps back away from him. Madchen Krstic stayed at his side and looked up at him, waiting for his command. With an inhuman effort of will Baibakov reined in his fury. As long as the commando lived, he would be a thorn in his side.

It was time to finish him.

Baibakov looked at his remaining troops. It wouldn't be hard to raise more. The former Yugoslavia was full of men who wanted vengeance, or to pursue the old feuds. But first he would have to take care of the American once and for all.

To do that he would have to attract the commando's attention. At that thought, Igor Baibakov smiled horribly. He would vent his fury in the streets of Sarajevo. He would leave calling cards written in blood until the American came for him.

Then he would hunt the American down and remove his head from his shoulders.

BOLAN SAT with Svarzkova in the bar of the Holiday Inn of Sarajevo. He glanced at his watch. They had agreed on eight o'clock, and it was now two minutes after.

Vlado Sarcev came through the entrance to the bar and scanned the interior. The little man's face looked haggard. He didn't smile when he saw Bolan. The Muslim militia leader walked over to the table and looked at Svarzkova warily.

"Who is your girlfriend?"

Svarzkova glared. Bolan spoke before the Russian agent could say something more. "She's Lieutenant Valentina Svarzkova, Russian Military Intelligence. She was a friend of Constantine Markov's." Bolan held the little man's gaze squarely. "She has come to kill Igor Baibakov."

Sarcev looked at Svarzkova with renewed interest. "I am sorry your friend was killed. He died bravely. I regret your loss."

The lieutenant dropped her glare and nodded. "Thank you. Baibakov is here?"

"Yes. The Giant is here."

Svarzkova pressed. "You are positive?"

"Yes. I am positive. You would not ask this if you had seen what I saw this morning." The little man turned and looked at Bolan. "You remember my RPG man, Jup?"

"I remember him."

"He is dead. We found him yesterday. He had been mutilated and hung from a tree outside of his house while his family slept. The Giant came and left like a ghost. Only he could do something like this. There have been three other killings in the past two days. All in the Muslim neighborhoods, all known militia fighters. The Giant is here."

Bolan nodded grimly. Baibakov hadn't run and hidden after his defeat in the Adriatic. The second he had returned to Sarajevo, he had begun a new series of atrocities. The man was daring him to come out and fight. The Executioner finished his ice water and looked at Sarcev. "It is time to put an end to this."

The militia leader's face set. "I can get you fifty men. A hundred if you need them. We are ready."

Bolan shook his head. "With fifty men we will never see Baibakov. He'll just fade away. We need to make him come out."

Sarcev considered this. "I agree. How many do you suggest?"

"Three."

"Three?" Sarcev repeated.

"Three."

The little man looked at Svarzkova. Her blue eyes stared back at him steadily as she held up three fingers. "Three."

Sarcev held up his hands helplessly. "If any other man had said this thing to me, I would say he was insane." He dropped his hands. "Perhaps you are both insane. The Giant is certainly insane. Perhaps this is what is needed to kill him."

Bolan and Svarzkova looked at the little man until he threw up his hands again. "Very well. Let us do this thing."

TOMAS BROZ RAN into the cabin breathlessly. "Commander!"

Baibakov rose from his chair. "What is it?"

Broz took a step back. Even to those who knew him, Baibakov's sheer size was intimidating. "The American! Our contacts in Sarajevo have spotted him! He is at the Holiday Inn, as you said he would be!"

The Russian nodded. He had known the commando would come, and he had known he wouldn't try to hide his presence. "Is anyone with him?"

Broz nodded quickly. "Yes, the woman was with him. She checked into the hotel as Lieutenant Valentina Svarzkova."

Baibakov considered this piece of news. The vast majority of female lieutenants in Russia were medics. However, this Svarzkova had proved herself in combat. That would make her an intelligence agent. Baibakov smiled as the pieces came together. The Russian government had decided he was a liability, and he was to be terminated. Baibakov's grin grew. The Russian services were extremely clannish, and he was Spetsnaz. Spetsnaz was under the direct command of Russian Military Intelligence.

Lieutenant Valentina Svarzkova was an agent of Russian Military Intelligence.

"Who else was with them?"

"They met the Muslim leader, Sarcev, in the bar. They spoke late into the night."

Baibakov cracked his massive knuckles and stretched lazily. "Very well. Get your men together. Tomorrow we go hunting."

His smile turned feral. "Tomorrow we go into sniper alley."

JACK GRIMALDI STOPPED the handcart with a thump and wiped his brow. "They don't pay me enough to carry all of your equipment around."

Bolan closed the door of their hotel room behind him. "Did you get everything on the list?"

Grimaldi grinned. "You tell me."

Bolan opened up a long case and took out his rifle. He couldn't match Baibakov's .50-caliber rifle. The Executioner could carry and use such a weapon, but not with the inhuman ease that the giant waved his around. At thirty pounds, it was just too heavy for a normal human to use in a running firefight. He needed to stay mobile, but he still needed to match the giant's power and range if he could. The .378 Weatherby Magnum was an old friend, and probably as close as he was going to get. The rifle threw a 300-grain bullet at nearly three thousand feet per second. It was a rifle that would stop an elephant.

Unfortunately Igor Baibakov had a rifle that would stop an armored fighting vehicle.

The soldier worked the bolt on the rifle. The action was tuned and as smooth as glass, and the armored variable-power scope was zeroed in precisely to his specifications. The Executioner checked the rest of his equipment. A new .44 Magnum Desert Eagle pistol lay in its box. Bolan knew the weapon had been broken in and tuned at the Farm. Two boxes of conical, steel-core armor-piercing hand loads lay next to the gleaming automatic, and with luck they would pierce Russian titanium body armor if things got down to spitting distance.

The Executioner unpacked his body armor, though no body armor on earth would stop a .50-caliber heavy-machine-gun bullet. Then again, Bolan doubted Baibakov would be alone. The soldier checked the sets of personal radios and headsets, his offensive and defensive grenades and knives. He looked up as Grimaldi began to take out his own weapons and armor.

"What do you think you're doing?"

Grimaldi made a show of looking hurt. "You know, I tried to blow up this Baibakov kook in Arizona, but he refused to stay dead. I'm still kind of irked about that."

"Are you cleared for this?"

The pilot shrugged. "I'm not specifically uncleared, and my orders were to transport your equipment." The pilot held up an M-4 Ranger carbine and glanced pointedly at the .378 Weatherby rifle. "Can you fight with both of these at the same time?"

Bolan knew where this was going. "No, I can't."

Grimaldi smiled victoriously. "Good, then I stay with my mission and transport this for you."

"Get suited up. It'll be dawn in an hour. We go out at first light."

Both men turned at a knock on the door. Bolan cocked the Desert Eagle. "Yeah?"

A heavily accented voice spoke in English. "It is Captain Milan Grohar. May I come in?"

Bolan nodded at Grimaldi, and the pilot flattened himself along the door frame and turned the knob. "It's open."

The tall thin Serb commander came into the room and raised an eyebrow at the carbine Grimaldi covered him with. "I have some news for you."

Bolan uncocked the Desert Eagle. "What is it?"

"Baibakov is here."

"I know that."

Grohar sighed. "He knows you are here, as well. Everyone knows the American is here, and the Russian woman. You have made little attempt to conceal yourselves."

"That's right." Bolan stared at the Serb levelly. "Can you tell me where Baibakov is, Captain?"

"Yes. He is in a cabin in the foothills north of here. He has three men and the woman, Madchen Krstic, with him. I believe they will begin to recruit more men into the Red Falcons soon." He met Bolan's gaze pointedly. "But I believe he intends to kill you first. It will give him more status, and I believe it is a personal thing between the two of you now."

"That sounds about right."

Grohar took a map out of his pocket. "I have marked the coordinates of the cabin on this map. I believe you must act quickly. He will be coming for you soon."

As Bolan took the map, Grohar sighed heavily. "There are few Serbian troops in the area. I will see what I can do to keep it so." The captain's face hardened. "Constantine Markov was a friend of mine, and a good comrade. Igor Baibakov is a psychopath, and he is not needed in this war. I hope that you kill him. I hope you survive."

The Serb turned and walked out the door. Grimaldi looked at Bolan quizzically. "You think it's a trap?"

Bolan shook his head. "No. He gave us good information on the Red Falcons before. But it really doesn't matter if it is. Baibakov will be there one way or the other. He won't be able to resist the chance to kill me with his own hands."

23

Dawn began to creep through the gray clouds over Sarajevo as Bolan climbed into a small green panel van outside of the Holiday Inn. They left out the back and placed Do Not Disturb signs on their doors, and with luck no one would know they had left for several hours. Valentina Svarzkova sat in the vehicle wearing dark tan fatigues under a Russian titanium armor vest. Her blond hair was pulled back into a single braid. A dark tan beret with no branch or unit insignia covered her head. A Dragunov sniper rifle stood up between her knees, and her 9 mm CZ-75 pistol was strapped over her armor. Bolan knew the AK-47 bayonet and a tiny PSM assassination pistol were concealed somewhere on her person, as well.

Vlado Sarcev sat next to her in plain khaki field pants and a dark green sweater. He carried his AKM rifle, and his 9 mm Egyptian Tokarev pistol and a hunting knife were attached to his belt. The range-finding binoculars Bolan had given him were in a leather case on his belt.

Jack Grimaldi climbed in behind Bolan toting the M-4 carbine and a pair of binoculars, as well. He grinned at everyone in the van. "Morning!"

Svarzkova looked up in mild surprise. "Jack."

Sarcev looked at Bolan. "I thought you said three."

Bolan shrugged. "Officially he's just my spear carrier."

The militiaman chose not to pursue the matter. "Ah. I am pleased to meet you, Mr. Jack."

The Executioner glanced at the contents of the van. Seven crates of AK-47 rifles and ammunition sat stacked against the side of the van, as well as four crates of RPG-7 rockets. Bolan nodded in satisfaction. "Good. That should be enough."

Sarcev frowned. "It was like pulling teeth to get these. The Muslim militia cannot afford to waste weapons like this."

"I'll see to it that you get double back." He looked up front. "Who's our driver?"

"He's my cousin Lazlo. He drives like an insane person."

A young man with impossibly curly brown hair and wire-rim glasses grinned enthusiastically and held up an Uzi. "Hello!"

"He knows what he has to do?"

The little man nodded. "Oh, yes. He volunteered."

The Russian's gaze narrowed. "You have changed the plan?"

Bolan unfolded the map and put a finger on the mark Grohar had made. "Baibakov is supposed to be here. We're going to drive up into the hills in this van. When we get close, we're jumping out. Lazlo is going to keep going. Baibakov has to have sentries posted. When they shoot at the van, Lazlo is going to abandon ship and run for it. The Red Falcons will find a van full of weapons. While they investigate it, we hit them."

Svarzkova frowned. "This is not a good plan for Lazlo."

Bolan nodded. It wasn't. But the Muslims in Sarajevo would sacrifice much to see the big Russian dead. "He volunteered for this job, just like we did." Bolan took out a radio and a headset for each member of the team. "Everyone ready?"

The woman nodded. "Let us do this thing."

THE VAN WOUND through the hills outside Sarajevo and climbed steadily toward the mountains. They were about one and a half miles from Baibakov's lair. Once they rounded the hill they were climbing, the cabin would have a view of the road. As they passed through a thick patch of forest, Bolan spoke to Sarcev. "Tell Lazlo to slow it down."

The milita leader spoke rapidly in Slovene, and the van slowed to a momentary crawl.

Bolan stood. "Tell Lazlo to get out at the first sign of contact."

He nodded as Bolan opened the back door. "Let's go."

The Executioner jumped out of the van, and Svarzkova and Grimaldi followed him. A second later Sarcev leaped out, and Lazlo gunned the engine and pulled away up the hill. The Stony Man pilot blew out a breath of steam in the cold air. "I don't envy the boy's chances."

Bolan glanced at his watch. "We've got about a mile or so to cover, and it's all uphill. Let's move."

Bolan and Grimaldi walked to one side of the road while Svarzkova and Sarcev took the other. They climbed steadily upward into the forested hills. The snow wasn't deep, but it was mushy and slick and made for slippery going.

The team froze as a thunderclap split the mountain air. The report of the .50-caliber rifle was unmistakable. Tires screamed, and there was a sudden breaking of glass and rending of metal. The van had crashed. Bolan spoke quietly into his radio mike. "All right, double time, let's move it."

More shots from smaller-caliber weapons rang out as Bolan led his team to the edge of the hillside. The soldier raised the Weatherby rifle and sighted up the road with his scope.

One thousand yards up the road the van was piled into a tree. Steam hissed up out of the smashed radiator, and the back door was open. Bolan scanned the area with his scope, but Lazlo was nowhere to be seen. Sarcev knelt by the side of the road with the lieutenant and peered at Bolan. The Executioner held up a fist and whispered into his mike. "Hang back and cover me. I'm moving forward."

Bolan crept closer through the underbrush with Grimaldi behind him. He reached an outcropping on the side of the hill and waited. The mountain thundered again with the report of the big .50, and the Executioner whipped the Weatherby to his shoulder and swung the scope in the direction of the muzzle-flash. He traversed his view and suddenly saw the yellow blast of the Barrett as it fired again, downslope past the van.

It appeared Lazlo was still among the living.

Through his scope Bolan saw the long heavy barrel of a Barrett .50 sliding back into a camouflaged hide. The Executioner put his cross hairs in the middle of the camouflaged screen and fired.

The Weatherby bucked against his shoulder as he worked the bolt rapidly for a second shot. A rifle cracked up on the hillside above, and Bolan crouched behind the rocks as a bullet whipped through the branches overhead.

Svarzkova's Dragunov answered with three quick rounds. Bolan glanced at Grimaldi. "Did we get a hit?"

The pilot shrugged. "I couldn't tell. The blind moved—you hit it. But I don't know if you hit the man behind it."

Bolan moved higher along the outcropping. "I'm going to fire a shot. Why don't you lob a grenade on whatever fires back."

Grimaldi flicked up the ladder sight on the M-203 and nodded his readiness. Bolan popped over the outcropping and fired at the blind again. Rifles cracked up on the hillside as he ducked down and Grimaldi popped up a few yards below him. The M-203 thumped, and a moment later a 40 mm grenade detonated on the hillside.

The Executioner broke cover and ran through the trees, Grimaldi's carbine snarling in a long burst of covering fire.

The soldier threw himself into a fold in the hillside. "Svarzkova! You and Vlado move forward. We'll cover you."

The Russian agent's voice came back across the radio. "Exactly so!"

Bolan moved to the top of the fold as Grimaldi's weapon opened up again. Higher on the hill a weapon returned fire. The Executioner searched through his scope and found a man in fatigues crouched behind a stump. His head and shoulders were exposed, and the soldier put his cross hairs in the middle of the man's head.

The Weatherby rifle roared, and the man toppled away from the stump with his head in red ruin. Bolan slid back down into the fold and moved into a thicket. A moment later the

Barrett boomed again, and rocks and dirt exploded from the lip of the fold. Bolan's eyes narrowed.

The shot wasn't even close.

The big .50 roared again, and Bolan raised his rifle and peered through the scope. The Barrett was still firing from the same position. The soldier sighted carefully and saw the barrel of the weapon sag as he was about to fire.

Baibakov hadn't moved from his position, and his firing was erratic. The Russian was wounded or he was playing possum.

Bolan moved toward the position and suddenly froze. A figure was moving through the trees ahead. The Executioner raised his scope and sighted. It was a man, armed with an AK-74 rifle, a 30 mm grenade launcher mounted beneath the barrel. Svarzkova's weapon barked at a target higher up on the hill, and the Red Falcon raised his grenade launcher high to arc in a grenade.

Bolan put the Weatherby's cross hairs on his chest and pulled the trigger.

The 300-grain bullet smashed the man backward like a sledgehammer and hurled him to the ground. Bolan crouched and waited for an answering shot, but nothing came. He spoke into his radio. "Svarzkova, did you hit anything?"

"I have one man down on the hill."

Bolan calculated. He had two down, both Red Falcons. If Grohar's intelligence was still current, that left Baibakov and the woman. Bolan aimed up at the .50's hide. The barrel still stuck out of the screen.

"I have two down, and a possible wounded up on the other side of the hill. Hold your positions and keep a look out for the woman. I'm moving in to take a look."

Bolan moved from cover to cover up the hill.

Grimaldi spoke. "No movement, Mack. We have you covered."

"Acknowledged." At one hundred yards Bolan slung the Weatherby and drew his Desert Eagle. He flicked off the safety and began to swing wide to flank the hide as he crept in. The hide was a screen of camouflage fabric and brush between two large rocks. Bolan froze at a small movement at twenty-five yards. The barrel of the .50 had moved slightly. He swung around wider and he heard a noise.

It was a wheeze of pain.

Bolan moved behind the hide, the muzzle of the .44 Magnum pistol preceding him. He came around the rock and leveled the huge pistol. The Executioner's eyes flared.

A dark-haired woman lay on her back with her left shoulder hunched away from her at an ugly angle. The Weatherby Magnum round had shattered Madchen Krstic's shoulder, and she was bleeding profusely. She looked up at Bolan through dazed eyes, and the Executioner's blood froze with instinctive certainty.

Baibakov had flanked them.

Bolan spoke rapidly into his mike. "Krstic is down, Baibakov is still at large, repeat Baibakov is still—"

The Barrett .50 boomed down by the road, and Bolan could hear it through his earpiece, as well. A man cried out, and Svarzkova swore in Russian. The soldier broke into a headlong sprint down the hill as the confrontation came across his earpiece.

There was a clattering noise, and Svarzkova called Baibakov a coward in Russian. A smaller clatter followed, and Bolan could hear Baibakov's booming laugh. Svarzkova spoke in a voice tight with rage, and the Executioner knew enough Russian to understand what was happening.

Baibakov had gotten the drop on Sarcev and Svarzkova, and the militia leader was either down or dead. The giant had made the woman drop her rifle and pistol, and she had drawn her knife. Her voice was a hiss over the radio link. She was daring Baibakov to kill her in close combat.

Bolan flew down the hillside with the Desert Eagle in his hand. "Jack, where are you?"

The pilot spoke breathlessly across the mike. "In-bound, Sarge!"

A small pistol barked rapidly down by the road, and the

giant's roar of rage echoed across the hills. Svarzkova cried out across the radio.

Bolan's feet crunched onto the gravel of the road as he ran to the Russian agent's position. "Svarzkova! Report!"

The woman's strained voice came across the radio. "I am injured."

Grimaldi burst out across the road and ran to the rocks where Svarzkova and Sarcev had positioned themselves. The pilot's voice was tense on the radio. "Sarge, we have trouble."

Bolan rounded the rocks and skidded to a halt. Grimaldi knelt beside Sarcev. The little Bosnian writhed on the ground while the pilot applied a tourniquet. A .50-caliber bullet had taken his left arm off at the elbow. Grimaldi jerked his head while he tied off Sarcev's arm with a field dressing. "Look after the woman!"

Bolan turned. Svarzkova sat with her back against the boulders. In one hand she still held the little PSM assassination pistol. Her other hand rested on her right leg.

Baibakov's entrenching tool was sunk halfway through her thigh.

The Executioner knelt beside Svarzkova and holstered his pistol. Her face was as white as a sheet as she looked up at Bolan. "I hit him. I hit him several times. I think I hurt him."

Bolan nodded. The little PSM fired a tiny .22-caliber bullet with a sliding steel jacket. It had almost no stopping power. It had been designed to do one thing, and that was penetrate body armor. Bolan smiled at her while he broke out a field dressing. "How did you manage to get him to go for his shovel?"

"I dropped my rifle and pistol like he ordered. I think he wanted to use me as a hostage." Svarzkova smiled up at him tremblingly. "So I drew my knife and appealed to his insanity. He liked that. He drew the entrenching tool, and when he did so, I drew my PSM and shot him. I tried to shoot him as many times as I could, but I was sitting down. Then he was gone."

Bolan looked at her leg. The entrenching tool would have to come out. "This is going to hurt like hell."

Svarzkova gasped and cried out as Bolan pulled the blade out of her thigh. He clamped his hand over the wound and ripped the field dressing open with his teeth. "Good girl. Lift your leg up."

He wrapped the bandage around her leg and tightened it over the dressing, nodding in satisfaction as he reapplied pressure. "The femoral artery is still intact. I think you're going to live."

Svarzkova grabbed Bolan's arm with a palsied hand. "Then get him."

The soldier looked over at Grimaldi and Sarcev. The pilot had gotten the tourniquet on and was elevating the limb. "How is he?"

"There's no way they'll ever sew his arm back on, but the veins have collapsed and the bleeding is under control. He's in shock, but I think he'll live. Go get the son of a bitch before he disappears. I'll keep these two breathing."

Bolan rose. Baibakov's Barrett rifle lay by the edge of the rocks where he had dropped it. He scanned the weapon quickly and saw blood on the action. Baibakov had been hit. The Executioner unslung the Weatherby and moved into the trees. The giant's trail wasn't hard to follow. He left huge boot prints in the thin snow, and he was making no effort to hide his movement. He was headed for the Serb positions deeper in the hills.

The Executioner broke into a run.

Occasional drops of blood left red stains in the snow as Bolan trailed the giant. Unless his injuries slowed him down, Baibakov would outdistance him. He had the lead, and the stride of a giant. The soldier decided to take a cue from Svarzkova and appeal to the man's insanity. The Executioner roared at the top of his lungs.

"Baibakov!"

The giant's name echoed across the hillside. Bolan moved slowly through the silent forest, pausing when he saw a long flat patch of rock ahead. The rock table rose out of the snow a few inches and was roughly fifteen yards long and five yards wide. The trail broke at the rock. Bolan peered through the trees. Baibakov had either gone on, or he was flanking him.

Bolan set down the Weatherby and drew his Desert Eagle. Thin morning mist moved slowly through the trees. All else was still. He took the .44 Magnum pistol in a two-handed grip. It was too still. The Executioner scanned his surroundings. Fifteen yards to his left there was a dense thicket. Bolan let his gaze swing over and past it.

The Executioner suddenly shifted to put a tree between himself and the thicket.

"Baibakov!"

The Russian exploded out of the thicket. A scalp wound had turned his face into a mask of blood, and he roared like an animal as he charged forward. A 9 mm Stechkin machine pistol snarled and spit fire in his hand. Bolan put the Desert Eagle's front sight onto the giant's chest and fired.

Bark splintered and flew as Baibakov's extended burst tore up the tree trunk Bolan was using for cover. The Executioner ignored the bullets streaming at him and continued to fire. The Desert Eagle bucked and recoiled in his hands, and he could see the bullets striking Baibakov, but the giant continued to charge toward him.

The Executioner raised his aim for a head shot.

Baibakov flung his spent pistol, and the Executioner had to dodge to one side to keep from being brained. His head shot was spoiled, and the Russian was on him.

Bolan fired his last round, and a pair of huge hands slammed into his chest, driving him backward into the snow. As he came up, he threw the pistol at his adversary, but the giant let the gun bounce off his armored chest and drove his boot into Bolan's chest. The blow bounced off the Executioner's ceramic armor, but the force of it sent him sprawling, and the half-drawn Beretta 93-R pistol spun out of his hand. Bolan rolled again with the force of the blow, and his hand went to his belt. His fighting knife rasped out of its sheath with a steely ring.

Baibakov stood wide legged in the snow like a figure out of a nightmare. His huge teeth grinned through the blood covering his face, and steam rose off his massive form. He reached behind his back and drew a long double-edged fighting knife as Bolan came up out of his crouch.

His voice grated happily. "Come."

Bolan flung his knife at the giant's face.

Baibakov instinctively raised his hand to block, and the Executioner moved. He took three strides and dived for the Weatherby rifle where it lay in the snow. The Russian was almost on top of the soldier as he whipped the rifle up between them and squeezed the trigger.

The Weatherby roared as Bolan shot Baibakov point-blank in the stomach. The man's knife sank through the Kevlar fabric of Bolan's body armor and crunched to a halt on the ceramic trauma plate. The two fighters looked into each other's eyes as the barrel of the Weatherby held them apart. The giant's mouth worked, but no sound came out. No body armor on earth would stop a .378 Magnum round at point-blank range, and even the inhuman strength of Igor Baibakov couldn't withstand nearly three tons of muzzle energy tearing through his vitals.

As the Russian shakingly tried to pull his knife out of Bolan's armor, the soldier flicked the Weatherby's bolt and shot Baibakov a second time.

The giant shuddered and collapsed on top of the muzzle like a tent pole. Bolan dragged his knees up and shoved the man off him with both feet. The Executioner stood and stared down at Baibakov's blood-covered face.

The Russian was dead.

The Executioner whirled at the crunch of a boot and worked the Weatherby's bolt as he brought the rifle to his shoulder.

Lazlo stood five yards away with a length of tree branch in both hands. The left lens of his glasses was cracked, and his left eyebrow was split and bleeding down his face. He stared at the muzzle of the rifle nervously and spoke in broken English.

"You fought on ground. I was to be hitting him. But he is dead now. You kill him first."

Bolan lowered the rifle. "Well, thanks anyway."

Lazlo nodded earnestly. "You are welcome."

"Are you all right?"

Lazlo grinned. "Big rifle shoot van engine. Van crash into tree. Van kaput. My face—" the young man slapped his hands together forcefully "—meet windshield. I get out. I run."

Bolan nodded and smiled. "You have done well."

"Thank you." Lazlo looked at Baibakov's body. "Giant is surely dead?"

"Yes. The giant is dead."

Lazlo nodded. "Good."

EPILOGUE

Valentina Svarzkova looked up from her hospital bed as Bolan walked in. Her leg was elevated, and her thigh was bandaged to her knee. She was pale, but she beamed as he handed her a bouquet of flowers.

"How are you?"

"The food here in this hospital is worse than Russia."

Bolan nodded in satisfaction. As long as Lieutenant Valentina Svarzkova's number-one priority was still her stomach, she was all right.

"I can have them fly you in some millet gruel and salted herring if you like."

The Russian agent scowled. "That is not amusing."

"You're right. There's nothing amusing about millet gruel and salted herring." Bolan grinned. "How's your leg?"

Svarzkova looked down at her bandaged thigh ruefully. "I am to retain full use of my leg. I am also to retain an immensely large scar."

Bolan shrugged. "Scars are sexy."

Svarzkova blushed to the roots of her hair. She looked down at her flowers rather than meet Bolan's gaze. "You are very nice." She suddenly looked up and grinned at Bolan. "Did you know, when I was in training as a field agent, the political officers told us America Special Forces troops were all drug addicts and killers of babies?"

Bolan nodded. "Yeah, well, we're not perfect."

Svarzkova giggled and looked down at her flowers again. Her face slowly sombered. "How is Vlado?"

"He's two doors down from you. Once his wound has healed over, we're going to have him flown to Germany to be fitted for a mechanical prosthesis. The U.S. government will foot the bill. It's the least we can do to repay him."

Svarzkova nodded. "Yes. He is a very brave man." She frowned. "What about the woman, Madchen?"

"She's going to live. She's in the hands of United Nations troops now. When she's recovered, I believe they intend to try her for war crimes."

"What will become of Ramzin?"

Bolan sighed. "We keep our bargains. When his wounds are healed, he will be returned to Russia. Then he's your problem."

Svarzkova leaned back into her pillows. "Well, at least Baibakov is dead."

"I couldn't have done it without you."

The Russian agent sat up again. "Then you owe me."

Bolan folded his arms across his chest. "I suppose I do."

Svarzkova's eyes went cunning. "Then get me some real food."

The Executioner grinned. "That I can do."

**Don't miss out on the action in these titles featuring
THE EXECUTIONER®, STONY MAN™ and SUPERBOLAN®!**

The Red Dragon Trilogy

#64210	FIRE LASH	$3.75 U.S.	☐
		$4.25 CAN.	☐
#64211	STEEL CLAWS	$3.75 U.S.	☐
		$4.25 CAN.	☐
#64212	RIDE THE BEAST	$3.75 U.S.	☐
		$4.25 CAN.	☐

Stony Man™

#61910	FLASHBACK	$5.50 U.S.	☐
		$6.50 CAN.	☐
#61911	ASIAN STORM	$5.50 U.S.	☐
		$6.50 CAN.	☐
#61912	BLOOD STAR	$5.50 U.S.	☐
		$6.50 CAN.	☐

SuperBolan®

#61452	DAY OF THE VULTURE	$5.50 U.S.	☐
		$6.50 CAN.	☐
#61453	FLAMES OF WRATH	$5.50 U.S.	☐
		$6.50 CAN.	☐
#61454	HIGH AGGRESSION	$5.50 U.S.	☐
		$6.50 CAN.	☐

(limited quantities available on certain titles)

TOTAL AMOUNT	$
POSTAGE & HANDLING	$
($1.00 for one book, 50¢ for each additional)	
APPLICABLE TAXES*	$_____
TOTAL PAYABLE	$_____
(check or money order—please do not send cash)	

To order, complete this form and send it, along with a check or money order for the total above, payable to Gold Eagle Books, to: **In the U.S.:** 3010 Walden Avenue, P.O. Box 9077, Buffalo, NY 14269-9077; **In Canada:** P.O. Box 636, Fort Erie, Ontario, L2A 5X3.

Name:_____

Address:_____ City:_____

State/Prov.:_____ Zip/Postal Code: _____

*New York residents remit applicable sales taxes.
 Canadian residents remit applicable GST and provincial taxes.

GEBACK18

**A violent struggle for survival
in a post-holocaust world**

JAMES AXLER

DEATH LANDS.

Watersleep

In the altered reality of the Deathlands, America's coastal waters haven't escaped the ravages of the nukecaust, but the awesome power of the oceans still rules there. It's a power that will let Ryan Cawdor, first among post-holocaust survivors, ride the crest of victory—or consign his woman to the raging depths.

Don't miss out on the action in these titles!